The Wheel of God

The Wheel of God

BY GEORGE EGERTON

Edited with an introduction by
Elizabeth Dangelantonio

Whitlock Publishing
Alfred, NY

The Wheel of God by George Egerton first published 1898

First Whitlock Publishing edition 2015

Whitlock Publishing
P.O. Box 472
Alfred, NY 14802

ISBN 13: 978-1-943115-09-9

The book was set in Adobe Garamond Pro on 55# acid-free paper that meets ANSI standards in archival quality

Table of Contents

Acknowledgments

I'd like to thank Dr. Allen Grove for all his valuable insight, assistance, and patience throughout this entire process.

I'd also like to thank Dr. Donna Decker, who recommended this book to me and for keeping the interest in George Egerton alive.

Who Was George Egerton?

> "She was in love with the idea of herself — a proud and lonely being in whom sexual allure and moral earnestness were most curiously blended..."
>
> — Terence de Vere White

When you think of the traditional Victorian woman, rarely do you imagine her with the sexual confidence to engage in multiple affairs, two marriages and a divorce, various younger lovers, and the boldness to stare unashamedly with hazel eyes from behind *pince-nez* glasses.

She was born Mary Chavelita Dunne in 1849 in Melbourne, Australia to Irishman Captain John J. Dunne and Welshwoman Isabel George. She was one of six siblings, the others being Nancy, Jessie, Jack, Milla, Bun, and Kitty, and a deceased infant sister, Tony. She identified most strongly with her Irish heritage, describing herself as "intensely Irish" in a letter to her aunt. Capt. Dunne, having served in the Māori Wars in New Zealand, was not well reputed for his ability to earn or save money. He did not provide for his children, either financially or with emotional support, and after their mother's death in 1875, the Dunne children were left primarily in Chavelita's care. Chavelita, "Chav" to most, was sent to boarding school in Germany on the dollar of a relative who saw potential in her. When she returned to Australia, she found her brothers' educations entirely fallen to the wayside, and her sisters not much better off.

She worked as a nurse in London for a while and dreamed of an artistic future, but she never found success in either nursing or art. Around this time, Chav left for America, presumably to work, though her search for a steady job was unsuccessful and she soon returned to Europe. There is little information available about her adolescence, and existing letters lack detail from this period in her life.

In 1886, her father's successful fly fishing guide, *How and Where to Fish in Ireland: A Hand-Guide for Anglers*, published under the pseudonym "Hi-Regan," turned a steady profit; the book remains an authoritative guide even today. Capt. Dunne didn't share the proceeds with his children, however, so Chav was still largely responsible for their needs. Some of her siblings were sent to South Africa to stay with family, and some remained in Australia, but there is little to no mention of them past Chav's early letters.

In 1886 Chav departed to tour Norway with Herman Melville's widow, Charlotte Whyte Melville, and her chaplain-turned-lover, the tall, bearded, and alcoholic Henry Higginson. Higginson was an American who had left his wife in the States to usurp the Mrs. Melville's previous chaplain and obtain the position himself, and later Higginson and Melville married. It wasn't long before Charlotte was writing to Capt. Dunne complaining that her husband and Chav were "carrying on" together. A private detective was ordered to follow the pair; he tracked them down and sent word to Capt. Dunne. Following news of their elopement, Capt. Dunne was hit by a wave of paternal protectiveness that had escaped him until this point. He pursued Higginson with a gun and was consequently arrested and detained for having an unlicensed firearm. Chav and Higginson never married, for Higginson technically had two living wives when he eloped with Chav. Higginson even took on Mrs. Whyte Melville's name in order to flee the country. Mrs. Whyte Melville was never heard from again to anyone's knowledge.

Chav and Higginson purchased an estate, Slotnaes Park at Langesgund, in Norway in 1887. They lived there until Higginson's death in 1889, likely from alcohol abuse. Chav sold the estate, but could not leave Norway behind. She engaged in a brief romance with Nobel Prize winning author Knut Hamsun. Having learned Norwegian fluently, Chav translated his works into English, although they wouldn't be published in England until 1899. Translating Hamsun's works must have sparked the literary bug in Chav because within the next few years she would become a writer professionally.

In 1891 Chav married a penniless Newfoundlander, Egerton "Egie" Tertius Clairemont. Egie and her father shared similar interests such as fishing and sport, and the two wrote each other often. They also shared the same fondness for spending money but not working to earn it. This meant that Chav and Egie were regularly on the verge of bankruptcy, and their only viable option would have been to move to South Africa to live with Chav's family there. Chav decided to try her hand at writing and getting published before leaving Europe. She first sent a small collection of stories to T.P. Gill, literary columnist for *The Weekly Sun*. He wrote her enthusiastically about the quality of her work and recommended she send them to publishers Mathew Elkin and John Lane. When they received her manuscript, they sent them on to be reviewed by poet Richard Le Gallienne, who returned them with glowing praise.

In 1893, using the pseudonym George Egerton, Chav's first collection of short stories, *Keynotes*, was published through Mathew Elkin and John Lane of The Bodley Head. Aubrey Beardsley designed the cover. The book sold 6,000 copies and put the author's name in the spotlight. She also published *Now Spring Has Come,* a collection of short stories inspired by her affair with Hamsun. The pseudonym, "George" to honor her mother's maiden name and "Egerton" to honor her husband, allowed Chav to write more freely under a man's name. Many were shocked to discover that a woman had written the book, especially considering the openly sexual nature of some of the stories, but John Lane was fascinated by Egerton and easily swayed by feminine charm. Less than a year later, the sequel collection of short stories, *Discords,* was published. Though the content was largely the same, her prose still enchanted readers. By now Egerton's success was catching the attention of more than just readers; *Punch* magazine caricatured her as "Donna Quixote" and published a mock short story called "She-Notes" by the fictional "Borgia Smudgiton." She must have taken the critique in stride, for she never wrote to anyone to complain about the parodies. As her literary career began to blossom, so did her personal life: in 1895, her son, George Clairmonte, was born. In her letters she often refers to her son as "Boy" or other unaffectionate terms, and the quality of her writing and her popularity declined after his birth.

In 1898, Chav published *The Wheel of God,* a largely autobiographical novel, the main character sharing a name with the author. Dedicated to Captain Dunne, the story follows Mary Desmond through the death of her mother, her father's all but total abandonment, and her decision to travel to the United States to get a job so she can continue to support her siblings financially. She finds a small rental apartment in New York City and gets a job doing secretarial work. She makes a few friends and sparks a few men's interest, but a tragedy causes her to reconsider her stay. A proposal gives her the incentive to leave America and travel with her husband. Mary returns to England a widow, and she finds herself caught up in locating a new job, marrying, and finding herself again in a world that discourages the single woman. She remarries, though she ends up regretting this decision because her second husband is a spendthrift and a flirt, and Mary continues to struggle with her own identity.

Higginson and Clairmonte were both written into the story, though Higginson's section is a far more complimentary piece of writing:

> "You are the first woman I have ever asked to marry me. I am not sure I know why I am doing so, either. You are at a turning-point. You are erotic, even if you don't know it… You have a great capacity for love going to waste in you; why not turn a little of it over to me?"

Though Higginson's character is unnamed, and Higginson never formally proposed, this quote shows clearly how differently Chav saw the men in her life. Clairmonte is portrayed as Mary's husband, Cecil Mariott, a spendthrift, flirtatious, immature man:

> Cecil was bound to drift, bound to sink, bound to be a wastrel of life and its chances through physique, temperament, and inclination. To be true to himself, even, meant inevitable misery. She had tried every way: tenderness bored him; appeals to his honor or principles were fruitless, — his conception of either was elementary.

Clairmonte was not pleased to be portrayed in such a manner by his wife. Even after the success of her first works, Chav and Clairmonte continually found themselves in financial straits, and Clairmonte's less than frugal habits and failure to hold a job meant Chav's writing was their only source of income. Following *The Wheel of God,* their marriage began to disintegrate. Despite her own financial woes, she gave him adequate funds, and he left to stay in South Africa, much to the chagrin of her family with whom he was staying. He returned upon her request after his health began to fail, but soon afterwards he impregnated their housemaid. After this he was sent to America whence he never returned. She divorced him in 1901, and he died later that year.

Chav suffered from no lack of male admirers and was quoted as saying, "I have found no man love me *long* platonically." Even her publisher, John Lane, was fond of her in more than a friendly publisher-author way. While Clairmonte was away, Chav returned to Norway where she fell in love with a young Norwegian man known only as Ole. There is little information about him other than what was contained in their correspondence which she published in a collection called *Rosa Amorosa: The Love-Letters of a Woman* in 1901. The letters are passionate in a way her writing about her husbands never was, and it is clear that her affections for Ole were unrivaled by any of the men she actually married. She wrote to her second husband, "You will find it and all else I think of love in *Rosa Amorosa,*" when she was asked to explain her feelings about sex and marriage.

Beginning in 1894, Chav's attentions turned to a new admirer, the poet Richard le Gallienne (RLG). He had had some responsibility in helping her get published since his praise of her manuscripts gave them more credibility. After the death of RLG's wife, he began writing Chav regularly. His letters are at first very formal, signed "Sincerely" and including many mentions of their deceased spouses. In between letters they visit one another, attend plays, and have dinner. Soon the letters' valedictions became "Love." He began to refer to her as mythical beasts such as "witch" and "sphinx," and even goes so far as to refer to her as "Sybil" and himself as "Narcissus." These names refer to Oscar Wilde's *The Picture of Dorian Gray* and the comparisons involving the actress Sybil Vane and Echo and Dorian Gray and Narcissus. In *The Picture of Dorian Gray,* Sybil Vane is a beautiful and talented actress who falls in love with Dorian Gray, and he loves her because she is innocent and everything he is not. They soon are engaged, but when Sybil experiences love in her life, her acting suffers and Dorian leaves her; she poisons herself and dies. This comparison is relevant because it suggests that, like Sybil and Echo, Chav had been unrestrained in her openness about her feelings for RLG, and as in the case of Sybil, that eventually his love would be revoked. The connection is severed with the arrival of her son, George Clairmonte, in 1895. It became obvious that RLG's infatuation with Chav had been nothing more than that. His final letters are far more reserved, show less interest and no pet names, and are signed, "Dick."

With Clairmonte dead, Le Gallienne out of the picture, and Ole remembered only in letters, Chav began a relationship with the drama critic Reginald Golding Bright, fifteen years her junior. Their correspondence takes on an almost Oedipal turn, with her addressing him as "boy" and "good little son" and herself as his "little Mother." Bright was enchanted by Chav, and the disparity in ages only made the attraction greater; he was eager to impress her. When she returned to Norway in 1901 to visit Ole, she wrote to Bright lamenting the distance between them. Urged by her letters, he sailed to Norway where they married in 1901. It seemed like Chav was trying to get into the theatre world more than she was truly in love with Bright, and many of their friends disapproved of the marriage.

With the turn of the century, having left short stories and novels behind, Chav began writing plays. Bright's connections with renowned playwrights such as Oscar Wilde and George Bernard Shaw made it easier for Chav to pitch her scripts. Shaw rejected her first manuscript, a play titled *His Wife's Family,* but Arnold Daly produced it in New York City, to no success; the play required modifications to make it appeal to an American audience but was still a flop. In a letter, Shaw commented that Egerton had "not got the property of dramatic dialogue." Chav never spoke well of Shaw later in life; he had hit a sore spot in suggesting she change anything she wrote. The rest of her theatrical attempts were wholly and disastrously unsuccessful. Her plays all had strong female leads, which attracted actresses, but the wordiness of the plays and Chav's unwillingness to make any cuts meant that there was little interest generated in playing those leads. During her attempts to write for the theatre, she became friends with actress Ellen Terry, the most renowned Shakespearean actress in England. Terry sent Chav tickets to her performances, and the two communicated via letters and postcards in the early years of 1900. Chav's final theatrical attempt, *Camilla States Her Case*, was produced in 1925 and performed at the Globe Theatre. Following its failure, Chav withdrew herself from the theatrical scene and by now had given up writing professionally altogether.

World War I began in 1914, and her son was drafted into the army. In 1915 he was killed in action, shot by a German sniper while protecting a trench. His body was never recovered. This experience hit Chav hard, but his adopted son's death hit Bright even harder. As Chav and Bright had no children together, Bright lavished young George with fatherly attention. Van Der White wrote, "The dry, pessimistic, skeptical, argumentative man I met in 1927 had been shot through the heart by a German sniper in 1915." Chav's friendships had dwindled by this point, and with the death of her son she became even more reserved, even from her husband. She did, however, maintain connections with various family members. In 1926, Chav began a correspondence with her younger cousin, Terence de Vere White, with whom she wrote and visited until her death.

1939 marked the beginning of World War II for Europe. Food rationing was introduced in January, a few days after two million 19-27 year old men were drafted. 1940 was a heavy year for Britain in terms of the war: the first London air raid took place in August, and German blitzes led to events such as the

Battle of Britain, and Chav and Bright's London apartment complex was bombed in one of these air raids. The two survived, but Bright died the next year, presumably from undiagnosed diabetes complications. By now, Chav was old, broke, and three times widowed. She moved around England in her last years as her health deteriorated: she suffered a minor stroke in 1945 and was forced to move into a nursing home. She was found dead at the bottom of the stairs, likely from another stroke, on August 12. She was 85. In 1957, Terence de Vere White collected and published a selection of her letters and diary entries, titled *A Leaf from the Yellow Book*.

On Literature's New Woman

While the New Woman character in literature has transcended generations because of her confidence, self-awareness, openness towards sexuality, and subversion of gender roles as well as her important place in feminist history, some of the earliest New Woman writers have been largely forgotten — George Egerton being one. Described as a proto-modernist, Thomas Hardy credits her with the inspiration for his character Sue Brideshead in *Jude the Obscure*, and *The Wheel of God* reads as template for Joyce's *The Portrait of the Artist as a Young Man*. Mary Desmond, the heroine of *The Wheel of God*, much like Egerton herself, found herself as the breadwinner early in life and devoted much of her time to working and earning money. She marries once, and upon her husband's death returns to England. When she marries Cecil Mariott, her strong-willed nature disappears, yet even then she still tends to him and provides him with funds to supply his frivolous spending and traveling. Mary Desmond is self-aware, unashamed to call her husband out when she catches him with a mistress, and is never deluded enough by love or romance to lose sight of who she is: she knows her marriage is doomed and that getting married at all was the wrong decision for her.

In addition to Mary Desmond, Egerton portrays herself as another character in The Wheel of God, the author "John Morton." John Morton's purpose is to express verbally the emotions

Mary has been feeling throughout the novel, and introducing her in the last few chapters serves to illustrate the struggle Mary has faced in finding her own person and how it takes the influence of another woman to help her do so.

The New Woman, a term coined by Henry James, described the educated, independent, working woman who possessed a more open sense of self. She was a predecessor to the feminists of the 20th century. Defined by historian Ruth Bordin, "the term New Woman always referred to women who exercised control over their own lives be it personal, social, or economic."

At the end of the 19th century and beginning of the 20th, the lower and middle class women were presented with a new range of options: they could attend institutions of higher learning, own property, and live financially independent of a husband. Women could now divorce their husbands without financial ruin, and though society still looked down on sexually active women, more sexual freedom was a key point. Women could now choose a husband based on more than social standing because women now had education, jobs, and money of their own. Egerton herself embodied many of the characteristics of the New Woman: she was financially responsible for herself and her family, was married more than once without scandal, had engaged in an affair with a married man, had obtained some education, and had many professions over the course of her life. The New Woman was most often employed in typing, shorthand, collating, and other secretarial work. New Women had to live lives of economy due to low pay, but the ability to be gainfully employed in any capacity was a big step for women's rights.

George Egerton was among the many New Woman writers. Henry James, Henrik Ibsen, Thomas Hardy, George Bernard Shaw, Kate Chopin, and George Gissing are just a few of the prominent authors of New Woman Fiction. Bram Stoker's Dracula features two New Woman characters, one who seems to embody the stereotyped ideal of the overtly sexual New Woman, Lucy Westernra, and Mina Harker, who embodies the New Woman as a working woman, one who is employed in secretarial work while remaining a doting wife. This contrasting idea of who the New Woman was shows the differences between what authors were writing and how those characters were being received. Often the results were a satirized, caricatured portrayal. At the turn of the century, the New Woman ideal was starting to fade out, as it no longer became uncommon for women to be working and to have more freedom in marriage. George Egerton was an avid believer in women's sexual rights, but she worked hard to separate herself from women's civil rights activists of her time. The Roaring Twenties and the emergence of the flapper mark the end of the New Woman era.

Save for a few lone scholars, George Egerton is astonishingly unread. She is remembered most in Ireland and in Norway, the two places where she felt most at home, having otherwise fallen from memory almost entirely. A woman before her time, her being forgotten is a shame, but also understandable: her career was short-lived and produced just a handful of critically approved works. However, the revival of this text will allow a new generation of readers interested in New Woman fiction and the work of marginalized woman writers to enter the fascinating personal and professional world of George Egerton.

ELIZABETH DANGELANTONIO
ALFRED UNIVERSITY

Buzwell, Greg. "Daughters of Decadence: The New Woman in the Victorian Fin De Siècle." *Discovering Literature: Romantics and Victorians.* British Library, n.d. Web. Feb. 2015.

Diniejko, Andrzej. "The New Woman Fiction." *The New Woman Fiction.* The Victorian Web, 2011. Web. Feb. 2015.

Egerton, George. *George Egerton: The Wheel of God (1898).* Ed. Paul March-Russell and Carolyn Winifred De La Lowe Oulton. London: Pickering & Chatto, 2011. Print.

Egerton, George. *A Leaf from the Yellow Book: The Correspondence of George Egerton.* Comp. Terence De Vere. White. London: Richards, 1958. Print.

Graff, Ann-Barbara. "George Egerton." *George Egerton.* Nipissing University, 2004. Web. Feb. 2015.

Knechtel, Ruth. "George Egerton [Mary Chavelita Dunne Bright] (1859-1945)." *The Yellow Nineties Online* (n.d.): n. pag. *1890s.ca.* 2010. Web. Feb. 2015.

Mendes, Clare. "The New Woman." *Victorian Literature.* Oxford Bibliographies, n.d. Web. Feb. 2015.

"The New Woman." *The Norton Anthology of English Literature: The Victorian Age: Topic 2: The Woman Question: Texts and Contexts.* W.W. Norton and Co., n.d. Web. Feb. 2015.

"Short Stories by New Woman Writers." *A New Woman Reader: Fiction, Articles and Drama of the 1890s.* Ed. Carolyn Christensen Nelson. Ontario: Broadview, 2000. N. pag. Print.

A Brief History of George Egerton (Mary Chavelita Dunne Bright)

1845 The Māori Wars, now known as the New Zealand Wars, a series of conflicts between the indigenous Māori and the New Zealand government, begin; Captain Dunne is a volunteer soldier in some of the wars

1859 Mary Chavelita (Chav) Dunne is born in Melbourne, Australia to Irishman Capt. John J. Dunne and Isabel George of Wales.

1872 The Māori Wars end

1875 Isabel George dies on March 26th; Chav is sent to Germany to attend boarding school; later she begins training in London as a nurse

1886 Chav travels to Norway with Henry Higginson and Mrs. Charlotte Whyte Melville; Capt. Dunne's *How and Where to Fish in Ireland: A Hand-Guide for Anglers* is published

1887 Higginson and Chav run off together; Capt. Dunne is arrested for assault; Chav and Higginson settle down in Norway

1889 Higginson dies

1890 Chav engages in brief romance with Knut Hamsun; Chav translates Hamsun's *Hunger*

1891 Marries Egerton Tertius Clairmonte in November

1893 *Now Spring Has Come* is written and published; *Keynotes* is published; Chav adopts the name George Egerton (GE)

1894 *Discords* is published. GE is ridiculed by *Punch* as "Borgia Smudgiton"; GE begins correspondence with English author and poet, Richard Le Gallienne

1895 Son George Clairmonte is born

1899 GE's translation of Hamsun's *Hunger* is published

1898 *The Wheel of God* and *Fantasias* are published

1900 GE visits Norway where she falls in love with a young man known as Ole

1901 Divorces Clairmonte; he dies later that year; She marries Reginald Golding Bright; *Rosa Amorosa* is published

1905 *Flies In Amber,* her final collection of short stories, is published

1907 After being rejected and mocked by George Bernard Shaw, GE's first play, "His Wife's Family," is produced in New York but flops

1910 "The Backsliders", another play, is published but rejected for production by Shaw

1914 World War I begins

1915 A German sniper kills George Clairmonte at age 20 during WWI

1925 "Camilla States Her Case," GE's final theatrical attempt, is performed unsuccessfully at the Globe Theatre

1926 GE begins correspondence with her cousin Terence de Vere White

1939 World War II begins

1940 GE and Bright survive an air-raid bombing on their London home

1941 Reginald Golding Bright dies on April 14 from undiagnosed diabetes complications

1945 GE suffers a minor stroke. GE dies on August 12 from a suspected further stroke

1957 Terence de Vere White publishes *A Leaf From the Yellow Book*

A Note on the Text

This text of this edition is based on the 1898 novel published by G.P. Putnam's Sons, the Knickerbocker Press. I have corrected obvious typographical errors and removed some of the idiosyncrasies of the original text, such as quotation marks around place and character names.

The Wheel of God

Contents

The Seed in the Sheath

CHAPTER I

A LITTLE CHILD WAS LYING bathed in the moonlight. The eyes looked strangely deep and dark in the expressive face, sharpened by the white light. Her long locks had been braided for the night, and stuck out like a pigtail at the side of her head. The comer of a book was visible under the pillow. There was a smell of burnt candle-fat in the room, for she had only closed the book when the light had guttered over, carrying the last bit of wick with it.

She had been reading *Jane Eyre*, and was still a-quiver with the strangeness of it. What was this love of which all the poets sang; that made men set out on ventures bold; and women sit and weep at lonely casements; that ran like a magic golden thread through every tale of romance and chivalry?

Her cot-bed was in an alcove, formed by a stairway to lofts above, in the old nursery of her father's home. Great iron bars lined the high, narrow windows; they made her think of grim tales of dungeons, of the Inquisition, of Lewis' Monk. Two four-poster beds, with thick white cotton fringe round the testers, and dimity curtains, with lines of rose garlands, and faded blue love-knots, stood in two corners. The curtains used to flutter into menacing, ghostly shapes in the gloom, and the furniture creaked, and the mice scuttled and squeaked, in play or anger, behind the worm-eaten wainscoting. Nevertheless, she loved the old nursery — it was a world of her own. There was a wonderful fourfold screen, covered with aqua tints, woodcuts, and many cuttings — O'Connell was there, in a curly wig and green velvet cap, Emmet saying good-bye to Sarah Curran, the Colleen Bán (Gerald Grifs, not Boucicault's), Grattan addressing the House, Sir Robert Peel, "Bony" Queen Caroline, Count D'Orsay, Fanny Essler, Tom Sayers, and Frederick the Great, with beauties out of Lady Blessington's Journal, and fashion-plates previous to. Watercolor prints of old London cries, election squibs, illustrations, and verses of secular and profane wording. Some of them she disliked greatly. One in particular, of a nervous-looking gentleman in a full-bottomed wig, sitting on the edge of a chair, with a fat dame perched on his knee. She was embracing him vigorously, and a scroll issuing out of the reluctant swain's mouth said —

"Oh, spare your kisses, lovely dear,
  I beg you will not persevere.
You'll spoil my wig; you'll stop my breath,
  Oh, dearest life, you'll be my death"

There were books too (in after years how she regretted the books, that she learned were almost unpurchasable!). First editions of all the coming classics, quaintly colored almanacs and primers. Some she liked merely for the pictures, such as a Sandford and Merton, in pantalettes and tasseled caps, flying kites in a blue meadow, with quaint, long SS in the letter-press. She reveled in the books in the old nursery. There were books in the drawing-room, too, in the tulip-wood cabinet, with the red silk curtains; gift-books, with gold scrollwork on their bindings, and dedications in delicate Italian writing on the title-pages.

Books with "morals" at the end of each tale; how she detested "moral!" what was moral? It spoiled a story anyway, and she always skipped it. She used to say. Thank you, for them, and steal away to the shelves and chests in the old nursery.

There was a *Herodotus' History of Greece*, many volumes of the *Romance of the Peerage*, with portraits of Leicester and Amy Robsart, and other characters of that wonder age. A collection of the mistresses of the kings, with curious reading (she could never find them in later years). Volumes of the *Penny Magazine*, with splendid rough woodcuts. *The Nettle* (it only reached three numbers), *Boccaccio, Peregrine Pickle, Humphry Clinker, Tom Jones*, an illustrated *Don Quixote, the Castle of Otranto*, and The Astonishing Adventures of a Lady of Quality, a big *Shakspeare* with illustrations — the Moor doing Desdemona to death, with a rolling eye and a fair-sized feather-bed, fascinated her; Otway and Aphra Behn, and many others. She devoured them indiscriminately, strutting on the boards of the old nursery in the role of a hundred heroines. Yet the old room held other marvels that appealed no less to the very child in her.

There was a square shade made of six panes of glass, joined by faded rose ribbons; it sheltered a wonderful thatched cottage, fashioned of cardboard, had tiny windows with lace curtains, and a porch made of pillars of ingeniously rolled paper. Sprigs of moss and the most fairy-like roses climbed up the walls. It was in some way associated with her docile moments; when she sat and purled a seam in the dining-room, the big room where the firelight danced on the massive silver; the fire was fed out of the great green wooden tub, with shining brass bands, that held black, brick-like rods of turf, hard as ironwood.

Another shade protected what seemed to her a wondrous work of art — a waxen Circassian lady, sitting cross-legged on a cushion; wide Turkish trousers fell in folds to her slim, fair ankles; her little bare feet reposed in turned-up silver slippers. She had dark, aquiline features, and sparkling black china eyes; a bird-of-paradise tail, of gorgeous spun glass, waved proudly from her crimson turban; her zouave jacket, of royal blue, was gold-broidered, and clasped by a sparkling crescent over her chemisette of delicate lace. Her short skirt was rose-worked; she held a red and green bird on one taper finger, and a rose in the other lily hand. How the child admired her! She was the keynote to the East, the open sesame to realms of imagination — visions such as a good Mohammedan might have welcomed in Paradise. She appealed to the other half of her nature — the half that made her hold up the end of her nightgown and dance wild steps to strange tunes singing in herself. In lonely years later on it all came back; she used to regret the old rosewood worktable that held so many forgotten treasures of dead aunts — there was a little inch-measure coiled inside an exquisitely wrought silver pineapple; one twirled the tuft of prickly leaves on top, and the red silk measure ran out with a silver whisper. A reticule, too, of velvet, embroidered with bunches of grapes in seed pearls, and golden leaves and straying tendrils. Nothing was inanimate; everything had a subtle psychometry of its own that it gave forth to the eager, seeking soul of the child, sensitive to the hidden influences. A sampler hung on the wall, worked in gold and silver beads: "Lost, a golden hour, set with silver minutes," — she never read more; that was enough to make pangs of conscience in her breast, when she lifted glowing eyes to it from tales of adventures and gallantry, certainly unfitted to her tender years. It recalled catechism unconned, and hopeless unsolved problems in the "rule of three." She enjoyed Uncle Toby, and yet she lay awake and peered through the curtains of her tiny alcove bed, and watched (not always in vain) for the flower elves to creep out of the hyacinth bells, or peer over the edge of the trumpet daffodils, and glide down to dance *Elfenreigen* in the silver bars of the moonlight.

There was an altar, too, with cheap vases, multicolored tapers, and a Virgin of Sorrows in the center, before which she used to kneel, and tell her white beads, and beat her breast in *mea culpa* for the daring, skeptical fancies that had a trick of darting through her perfunctory prayers. She believed in her guardian angel; she used to leave him the nicest bit of tart, and the most tempting blob of cream, untasted on her plate as offerings; and she always made room for him in bed on frosty nights.

She loved Jesus at Christmas-time, when He was little, and pink, and dimpled in the crib; but it seemed stupid to be just a carpenter's son, when He might have been a glorious king, and made the whole world happy. Of course Sister Aloysius explained that, by saying He wanted to understand and be with the poor and lowly. They explained everything, but the explanations reminded her of her grandmother, when she used to look over her spectacles, with a smile lurking in her deep Irish eyes, and say, "When you get big you will understand!" She had a vague presentiment that there were some things one never grew big enough to understand. A thousand speculations chased one another through her busy child-brain; creation with its enigmatical beginning; and eternity, that was the most dreadful of all — for ever and ever — just think! if one were squashed flat into a horrid, squelchy pulp, like the fat spider cook killed with the heel of her shoe, one would not be dead; one's soul would have to go on and on, and never end, never — Hell, Purgatory, and Heaven! Someway, heaven interested her least of all.

A ray of intenser moonlight streamed in through the bars. The child rose on her elbow, puckering her brows anxiously. Each object spoke to her as a little human being might. It was never quiet in her head. Sometimes things talked and suggested things to her; then she got frightened, and prayed Jesus, Mary, and Joseph to take the thoughts away. Sometimes, when she held the kitten in her arms, she felt such gushing waves of love and tenderness for it, that she wanted to squeeze and squeeze it, until she grew frightened at the desire in herself, and dropped it for fear of killing it. And when at home she nursed her little brother, she was tempted to bite a bit out of his soft little neck, just in the hollow, below where the hair springs. Something whispered to her to do it, jogged her inner elbow, laughed at her, urged her to do wicked things, to say coarse words that the stableman used when he was angry with the dairymaid. It puzzled her sorely to know why God let her have these thoughts when He had the entire arrangement in His own hands. The big dark chambers in her inner self troubled her, and made life less nice to live; sometimes, too, she got tired and sorely afraid. She looked out again, puckering her brows — looked at a little shoe over near the big bed. She must get out of bed; she did not want to, it was chilly; she always fancied, too, that something was ready to spring at her out of the lurking shadows. She wished she were home with the little brown mother. The granny was very good to her, but it was not like home; it did not even smell like home. It was funny how different people smelt; there was a smell that belonged to her own mother and father and brothers and sisters that stirred her to the very heart depths. The "home smell" she called it once to her Aunt Frances, but was told that she was a nasty little thing to say so. She had held the tears back until she got out into the meadow, and lay down with her face in the sweet vernal grass, amongst the stems of the red sorrel seed that her playmates used to strip for coffee when they played at shop. She could not help noticing things, if God made her so, and they *did* smell different; the mother smelt of the woods wild and sweet; and when she laid her face to the dear breast it always made her want to cry. It was strange, all the things one could not talk about without being railed at. She peered out again. Yes, poor little shoe, it did look so lonely; she must get out and find the other, and put them side by side; it always bothered her to see things that belonged to one another separated. She slid out of bed and grabbed the shoe, looking fearsomely round for the other; it was over near the big four-poster, with the patchwork quilt made of thousands of octagon-shaped bits of print and chintz — such funny patterns! Tiresome little shoe! a spring, a clutch; both little shoes nestle side by side in the white light. A shadow wavered up the wall; the child darted back to bed, drawing up the clothes, and crossing herself as she nestled down. She always had to face the door, for she never could sleep unless she could see the whole of the room. She smiled as she snuggled down; it was such a comfort to think the shoes were settled together for the night; she felt as if she had done a good deed, an act of charity — and so fell asleep happily.

CHAPTER II

ONE EARLY, CLEAR OCTOBER forenoon a little girl was walking with a springing step through grimy Meath Street in Dublin. Her boots were daintily cut, little flat-heeled French boots; the very fashion of her clothing, unconventional and simple in cut, but of exquisitely chosen material, would have individualized her, even if the resolute little face, poise of head, always thrown a little back, and fearless, easy carriage had not done so. Meath Street was at its worst this soft, gray, Irish forenoon; squalor and sordid poverty; slatternly, bedrabbled women; neglected, filthy children; yelping curs; yelling draymen, driving wagons of "Guinness" thronged it; whilst itinerant fishwomen bartered or "barged" in choicest Dublin-billingsgate. It is a singular fact, that this people, so uniquely clean in morals and so nice of the virginity of their bodies, are so — one might say inventively — disgusting in their language. No word of it escaped the child, but no word of it rested with her. The power of selecting, of wiping out absolutely what she did not wish to retain, was becoming second nature to her. She walked as in a dream of her own; every street had its history, gleaned out of odd numbers of the *Dublin Penny Magazine* or old books skimmed at the bookstalls in Drury Court, next the Four Law Courts, whilst waiting for a never punctual father. She knew the houses and courts where the Huguenots had lived — silk weavers and carvers in ivory and wood; knew the names of the long vanished tenants of mansions rich with superb paneling and ornate carving, now given over to humanity and vermin. She knew every turn of the "Liberty"; great and little Elbow Lane, Cross Stick Alley; every bit of stone carving, quaint gargoyle, or fountainhead, to be found between Harold's Cross Bridge and Thomas Street.

She looked up: a slant of sunlight made a golden shield of a third-story window. An amused, appreciative look crept into the dreamy eyes; she stepped quickly from the pavement into the roadway; a tattered red flannel petticoat was hanging over the window-ledge, a black-browed woman was holding the head of a fair-haired child down upon it, as she combed it, scattering largesse on the wayfarers beneath. It reminded the child of a little Murillo of the same subject an artist had shown her some days before — only the mother there was a Spanish gypsy. There was no disgust in her look; she accepted life as she found it; she was forming her character unconsciously for after life, and paving the way to error on the part of her friends. Too often they misdoubted her refinement, because in some way she seemed to miss seeing any coarseness in the natural facts of life. They failed to realize that she regarded them as entirely outside things, not touching in any way the crystal case of her soul.

She turned up Thomas Street, crossing over and going down a narrow passage at the side of a public-house. On the right, as it widened, were a distillery and a tan-yard; farther to the left an extraordinarily high wall. She entered a door opening into a kind of box office — the official entrance of the Marshalsea, H.M. prison for debt, known otherwise to "jarvies," the district postmen, and all concerned, as Caulfield's Hotel (Sir Thomas Caulfield was the Governor). A man in a uniform resembling that of a prison warder greeted her with a smiling, "Good day. Missy!" calling, "Mrs. Mac!" as he passed her through to another small room. A low-sized, red-faced woman, with a smell of porter that seemed to ooze from her clothes, answered his call, and passed her hands in a perfunctory manner down the child's clothes in search of the prohibited liquor. Then she went through another door into a square graveled courtyard, with a flagged pathway all round it; it was flanked by high buildings studded with numbered doors at regular intervals, — the quarters of the pauper inmates, and such as paid half a crown a week for their room. She returned the ceremonious curtsey of a faded-looking woman who was walking mincingly round the block, and, crossing to an arched gateway on the right, came into a second square.

The Governor's quarters, bright with gay window-boxes and curtained windows, occupied the western block. Peals of laughter echoed from some of the inmates' rooms, and the piercing notes of many canaries, confined in a long cage on a window-ledge in the northern block, above the doorway marked, towards which she directed her steps. A strong smell of beefsteak and onions came through the doorway. A big man in a beflowered dressing-gown and Turkish fez, which he lifted airily in exaggerated greeting, calling her, "fair floweret from the outer world," was sitting near it on a camp-stool, reading the morning paper. She avoided his hand and entered. There was something prison-like about the stone stairs and whitewashed walls, with the black doors numbered in white; but there the resemblance ended. The first door on the left showed an enormous kitchen with a glowing grill. A fat, cheerful-faced woman in a fresh print gown, with two girls, younger and fresher editions of herself, and a kitchen-maid were bustling to and fro. A quarter of venison, game, fowl, and vegetables covered the long table. Mrs. Flanigan catered and cooked for the gentlemen who paid eight shillings a week per room, and lived like fighting cocks. The child saluted her gravely and mounted the stairs, passed the landing where the canaries chirped and chattered and trilled in shrill harmony, to the next floor. The bass notes of men's laughter, the crash of chords on a tinkley piano floated down to her. She knocked on a door to the right and went in. Her father, Major Patrick Desmond, had a very cozy room. A gay rug covered the camp-bed in the comer, an Indian screen hid the bath, for each inmate furnished or added to the regulation supply at pleasure. A big easel stood near the window, the wall was covered with caricatures, and half a dozen men sat and smoked and drank whiskies and sodas in spite of the regulations. The very good dinner parties, given by the inmates to one another and to friends outside, never lacked good wines — some official must have netted a fortune and possessed the wisdom of a serpent and a genius for smuggling.

Every one was searched on entering, yet every one inside had a *garde de vin*.

"Hello, little woman, my eldest daughter unmarried!" (How she hated that formula!) A lean, brown man, with a handsome, devil-may-care face, who was sitting near the fire (the Major liked a fire in July) smoking a colossal cigar, turned round.

"Never knew you had given any hostages to fortune, Paddy. How do you do, little lady? charmed to make your acquaintance!" A big, burly man, with an unruly spade beard, inquired for her mother; the others were deep in a discussion as to the chances of a pending racket match. Bets were exchanged freely, three of the men being visitors. The big man had let himself be served with a long-standing writ in order to get arrested, as the Major, his best of pals, was likely to stay in for some time.

"Moll," cried the latter, "you must get us a couple of dozen of balls."

The child drew her brows sharply together, saying: "I want to speak to you."

"Go to my room, old man, no one there."

The speaker was a little man, buried in a big chair, a dove-eyed man, with his hair parted in the middle, and a caressing voice, and the worst reputation in Europe as a husband.

His room was luxuriously furnished, the walls covered with hangings and pictures.

"We must have some money — mother isn't well; she cried all night —"

"Well, what the divil can I do? I thought I'd have some by this morning's post —" he considered.

"Go and live in the other block on bread and cheese," came to the child's tongue, but she kept it down and slid aside from his hand. He went out, came back shortly with some sketches and a note, saying, as he tied them up:

"You can take them when you go back. You know Sackville Street — well, it's a turn some way down; you'll see Hewitt, Wine Merchant, on the window-screen. Tell your mother to come to-morrow; I'll have some money without fail."

"I won't," the child replied simply. "She isn't fit to drag about, and it's just as likely to no purpose as the last time."

The Major gave his mustache a fierce twirl, held open the door, and bowed her out with ironical deference. Those two had tried issues of will before. The noise of falling chairs and rattling glass echoed from the other room. The big man and another, coats off, were wrestling, testing the merit of a famous Lancashire grip.

"Hurry back with the balls, two dozen, and tell Walters if he doesn't keep up to the mark we'll skin him alive."

"Yes, Walters," in reply to the man at the fire, "best racket balls in the world. John's Lane, Patrick's Close, Moll, you can't miss it, next the cathedral," and he went on humming —

> "St. Pathrick was a gintleman —
> he came of dacint people,
> In Dublin town he built a church
> and on it clapped a —"

"Shall I drop the little lady there?" asked the lean man with the handsome head; "my cab is waiting, and I don't think it's safe for me here much longer. I believe Malloy is kicking his heels outside "Spad's" (Spadaccine's), and there are three other beggars knocking round somewhere."

"They won't be likely to look for you here, but you are an infernally cool hand, L'Estrange, always were. I'd give a fiver to see Malloy's face when he hears of your visit. Have another peg?"

They all trooped downstairs together. The Major slipped into Mrs. Flanigan's domain, paid her a flowery compliment on her curry of the night before, and launched into a dissertation on the necessity of clean white blotting-paper as a factor in the cooking of red mullet.

Jack L'Estrange pulled down the blinds of his cab and leant in the comer in silence. The child's eyes read his face, studying each feature, noting with an artist's eye the curve of nostrils, setting of eyes, curl of ear, with an unconscious intentness. Suddenly he looked at her.

"Well, made up your mind?"

Something in his look disturbed her in an odd, new way. She flushed painfully. The quick contrast of color transformed her. The man lapsed into silence again with closed eyes, but his lips twitched; he muttered irritably, "Damn it!" adding, "I beg your pardon, little lady — got thinking — the money's a confounded nuisance."

"Not having it is," she said, with quaint conviction.

"So you have bitten into the apple already. What would you do if you had it?"

"A lot, you mean. Oh, I'd buy mother a place in England in the warmest part, and have horses, and cows, and poultry, and fruit-trees, and flowers—"

"You don't like Paddyland, then?"

"No, I dislike it for mother's sake. She isn't of it. When I go past Lamb's in Grafton Street I always want to go in and buy her lots of flowers and fruit — not gooseberries and apples, and just common flowers, but pineapples and pomegranates and fat, yellow peaches. Sometimes I get her one or two; they are awfully dear; she loves them. I am" — with a burst of confidence that made her seem the little child she really ought to have been — "saving up for a pair of slippers — such pretty ones, fine, fine gray kid with fur. I went into Pierrot's and asked the price; they are very dear, but someway mother can't wear cheap things; they never fit her. She doesn't look cheap, you know; some people do."

"By Jove, no!"

"Do you know mother?"

"I have not that honor; I have seen her—"

The child nodded understandingly; the driver slackened the pace and tapped the glass with his whip. "A-ah, that means ware hawk! Well, good-bye, little lady; stick to the mother, they're bad to beat. Jump out quickly when I open the door." The child sprang out, the door slammed to; the wizen-faced driver in sober livery turned his head and winked at the jarvy of an outside-car behind them; the latter responded by running his vehicle deliberately into a barrel of eels at the curb. The child fled before the torrent of abuse of the irate eel-vender and the oaths of the red-faced man who had been the occupier of the outside-car before the upset. Captain L'Estrange's cab, with his coachman, "the weasel," was known to every jarvy in Dublin; and a tip was always forthcoming when they failed to let a bum-bailiff overtake that reckless and deeply involved soldier.

It was a good walk back. She went direct to the fine racket court and joined the crowd of spectators in the wooden boxes at the end of it. The Major was a crack player, and her eyes followed him with a resentful admiration of his quickness of eye, deftness of wrist, and response of face to the sympathetic applause that is such a spur to the Celt. The faded lady of the morning said:

"I always come to see your dear papa play. It's quite like the old tourneys. He is such a fascinating man, so clever, so chivalrous, so courteous, quite of the old school; and his friends, so devoted. It is a long time since we have had such charming inmates; we are quite, quite gay. They send me game and flowers; I've had quite a little feast. And your dear, precious mamma — a-ah, one sees few women walk like that in these plebeian days. Poor lady, the separation, so cruel! Come and visit me when you spend a day here; I have a beautiful harp."

Miss le Touche had been an inmate for twelve years and ultimately died there. A salvo of applause rounded as the Major brought the game to a victorious issue for his backers by some brilliant volleys. He came down the court radiant, shook hands with Miss le Touche, took the balls from the child, and hurried her off. She was hungry; the door of the canary-owner's room opened as she came down with the sketches, and a little, rotund man, with a flat, pale face (he always reminded her of a white slug), came out. He was dressed with exquisite neatness.

"I told your papa I would give you some lunch, my dear," he said.

The room was well furnished, lined with books; another large cage and aquarium stood in the windows. The child sat on the extreme edge of a chair near the door, with the sketches in one hand, her eyes alert for his every movement. She disliked his way of placing his hand on her shoulder, or of pinching her cheek; she always wet a comer of her handkerchief and wiped the place as she went downstairs. She drank a glass of milk and ate a piece of seed-cake, edging away from him, and stretching out her hand at arm's length when she insisted on leaving. She could feel his little red eyes on her neck as she went downstairs. She turned to the left from the entrance, downhill towards the quays, through narrow alleys and cobble-stoned streets, flanked by distilleries and tan-yards. The men stopped rolling the barrels and slackened the rope to let her pass. She had a long walk before her. How well she knew all the landmarks — to the left, the dome roof of the Four Courts, the dirty, bare, disused quays, with their melancholy air of saying, "We were built in a day of greatness, when trade was good." The tide was out; the malodorous Liffey ran in a sluggish stream in the middle, with stretches of slime on each side. The sun had paled. She walked quickly, for the dusk seemed to gather early. There was something bird-like in her movements; nothing escaped her; the light on the gilding of a spire, the silver fringe of a doud, a drunken soldier lolling happily on an outside car. She noted every quaint alley, or archway, or carved entrance to some moss-grown court all along the quay, wove tragic stories about them, crossed herself as she passed a church, though at heart religion was more a matter of speculation with her than a sentiment; an honest distaste for forms, perhaps inherent in her blood from maternal Protestant forbears, worked in her always.

Aston quay had an odd fascination for her. Quaint prints of people, of whom she had read and dreamed, stared out of many of the curio shops, in company with odd bits of ivory carving and cruel-looking daggers. There, too, Italian modelers worked in clay and plaster, making images of the Virgin and saints for a profit, with a satyr or dryad or a joyous Bacchus for art's sake. There was a romantic atmosphere that appealed to her in the foreign names over many of the shop doors.

The lamps were lit as she reached Carlisle Bridge, and the oil lamps of the stallkeeper, who sold apples and nuts and treacle billies, flared against the black background, in which the custom-house loomed in the distance. She turned up Sackville Street and looked at the address again. She would have to turn up near Graham Lemon's, the monster sweet-shop. She knew him well; he was the owner of a fairyland of sugar plums, a kingdom of lollypops, and he invariably called her nice little maid, and gave her a stick of bath-pipe. She always gave him a kindly thought, because he meant well; but in after years, when life got a grimness in its humor, he symbolized a certain type of humanity for her. She used to call them Graham Lemony-people who, with a wealth of good things at their disposal, conscientiously withhold them, from a Puritan belief that sweets must be bad because they are nice; and who seek to stay hedonistic longings with some particular sort of bath-pipe.

She turned to the left and hesitated, seeking the numbers — Hewitt, Wine Merchant, met her eye, printed in gold letters on a perforated screen in a broad, low window. She entered the hall and knocked on a glass door to the right; no reply, only the sound of men's voices, and the smart slithering kiss of steel on steel. She opened the door and went in, closing it gently in obedience to a signal from a man sitting on an office stool, and stood quietly in the corner near the door. The scene often came back in later years with the precision of a Dutch picture. A low room, another darker room visible through a door at the end; a warm Turkey carpet on the floor, a clear fire in the grate, the flames flickering and dancing and throwing into brilliant relief bottles, glasses, quaint jars, and measures on the shelves. Some polished barrels stood against the wall and in the farther comer. A man sat on one of them; he wore a high silk hat, with a curious narrow, flat brim, on the back of his head, and very large plaid trousers; he was sipping green stuff out of a glass. Another man — his face, as well as his astrakhan-collared coat, struck her as familiar — sat straddle-legged across a chair, resting his chin on the back of it, as he watched the two men fencing in the middle of the room.

The slighter, shorter man had the advantage, and the man on the stool kept up a running comment on the merits and demerits of French and Italian methods in the noble art of fencing. The bout ended, the bigger man unmasked; she knew his dean-shaven, heavy face by sight; his handsome massive throat was somewhat ostentatiously displayed by a Byronic collar and artistic bow tie.

"Are you Mr. Hewitt?" she asked the man on the stool. He nodded, took the note and sketches, read it and handed it to the big man; he looked from it to her.

"How is your father? Haven't seen him about—"

"Why, he's in Caulfield's," interrupted the other.

"Oh, the deuce he is! not a half-bad place either. My friend Du Bedat lives there permanently, to escape his wife and her family. Estimable female, daughter of a dean, looks upon Du B- as a firebrand to be snatched from the burning."

"Old B's idea of paradise is rather that of a good Mussulman; only he likes to anticipate it a bit. Do you know who is there?" to her.

"Big Captain Blake, his cousin Major Hackett, Mr. L'Estrange goes to see them."

"Phew! we must look them up. Wonderful man, your father — genius, simply a genius;" they had been looking at the sketches. He said something in French to the man with the odd hat, of which she only caught *mon cher* Paul. She was a woman grown when she recognized him in a print as Paul de Koch. Something in the tone hurt her sensitiveness, as air to a suddenly unbandaged wound. The tears sprang to her eyes, and she sucked in her nether lip as she forced them back. The man with the fur collar gave her a sympathetic look out of a pair of very keen and humorous eyes, and proposed to make a cocktail. It drew off their attention, but the look came back, and she always had a warm, grateful thought whenever she saw the same eyes and the identical coat on the cover of some cheap edition of *The Luck of Roaring Camp, and Other Tales*. She stood at the desk.

"And your mamma — is she well?"

"No, thank you, she is not at all well."

"Are you going back to your father to-night?"

"No, I am going home now!"

He tore up the note he had written, put some one-pound notes in an envelope, and said:

"I need not write, then; give these to your mamma."

The child was tired, over-acutely strung; she used to feel as if she had eyes and ears everywhere; although she was heeding him, she could hear the big man say —

> "Little Nancy Etticoat
> Had a white petticoat
> And a blue gown, —"

Beating rhythm with his left hand. "It's difficult, *mon cher* Paul; it's confounded simplicity…

> "Petite Marie Flandres
> Assise dans les cendres—"

He paused as she opened the door; she gave them a grave little bend of head as she went out, stopped in the hall, took out one note, and buttoned the rest inside the breast of her gown. The dusk had gathered, fleeting rifts of dark cloud came scudding across the murky blue overhead. The pavement glistened with damp. She paused at the crossing — Sackville Street looked so wide, and the two lines of light ran up to a point at the top, with Nelson's Column like a smoky pillar in between. She crossed, feeling very small, yet the only real thing in all that immensity of street — the only real thing — all the rest were shadows — just shadows.

She climbed into a bus on the other side; it was fortunate she had kept the two pennies meant for her lunch; it was nearly six; the mother would be anxious, for she hated her to come through those dreadful streets alone. She had never told her, though, that a horrid man had followed her the week before. She closed her eyes; her knees pained, and her back ached a little; a pleasant feeling of drowsiness stole over her; as at *Benedictus* when the long vespers have been chanted through, and the thrill of the *Magnificat* has subsided with the rustling back to a kneeling position of the standing figures, and the soothing low strains of the Sanctus soar out as the outward whisper of an inward soul-hush. She roused at St. Stephen's Green, and the events of the day, not in itself an unusual one for this child of varied experiences, repeated themselves in detail. She was endowed with a pictorial memory, so that each word she heard flashed in printed type before her inner eye, and each event as recalled came as a tiny picture, with all its details perfect to her inner vision. The features, the gestures of all these men she had seen came back; she did not know many women; few visited her mother; her father's women-folk were bigoted, with shrines for little conventional gods erected in their souls (and in no place are the little gods of baser metal than in snobbish Ireland). The mother, with her wild grace and charm for men, big, passionate child-heart, and alien faith, was caviar to them.

Curious things men, like children, she mused. She had seen so many of them in her short child-life; they seemed to have no real sense — that is, when they were nice; they made such a fuss about small things, and yet they let important things go by. She could not imagine grownup women playing the fool, as she had seen men do. Once she had heard a lot of them, barristers and Queen's councilors, steeple-chasing round an hotel room, each riding a chair. Lots of the chairs got smashed, and they laughed, as Miley did when he cut the bellows and found the tongue would not dap any more — and yet the bailiffs were in big Councilor Grace's house at the time, and Mrs. Grace had a new baby. She would not marry when she grew up; she would paint, and stay with the mother. She smiled as she thought of all these big, strange men as a mother might at the vagaries of her children, and an old gentleman opposite smiled back in sympathy; it struck her a woman would not have done so — sure, there was another difference.

She got out at Richmond Street, and hurried along the South Circular Road —hurried, because there were lonely patches of building ground, and a long way between the lamp-posts. She hesitated at the beginning of one of the small avenues near the Harold's Cross end, then went on again to the wide street with the shops. There she ordered some things at the grocer's, to be sent at once, insisted on seeing them placed in the errandboy's basket, made some purchases in the provision shop, which she took with her, and set out home. A drunken drab at the comer flung a foul epithet at her, then spat at her, as a prelude to a torrent of incoherent filth. The child paled and broke into a run, wondering at the rage of soul, the wanton vileness of it, shuddering at the light it threw on places in the world she was just awakening to. It was like the bad dreams she sometimes had at night — dreams filled with awful specters, that came hurtling out of the gloom, tugging at her with insistent, tearing hands, until she grew sick with terror at the things in the world inside herself, of which it was so hard to speak. She paused at the last house at the end of the avenue. One could hear the wind crooning in monotones to the big trees along the canal bank at the end of it; the air blew damply, too, from the water. The blind in the parlor window was held slightly askew, and dropped straightly as she hurried up the narrow garden path. A smaller girl opened the door, and questioned her anxiously with serious eyes, whispering:

"Mother has been so anxious."

The room was a lodging-house parlor, but it was home, and it struck warm to the child as she entered it; for the high chair at the fire held the mother, her fingers playing over a curly head laid against her knee. In nine cases out of ten the mother makes home. She laid the parcels on the table and went over to her; the woman met her with love-light sparkling and burning in the wonderfully bright eyes, glistening white teeth showing through her parted lips, and a smile that seemed less the play of eyes and lips than a wonderful illumining of the whole face, as if the mask had become suddenly transparent to let the spirit flash through.

"I was anxious, dearie; those horrid streets!"

"I didn't come through them, Mumkins. I came in the bus from Sackville Street. No," in answer to a query on the mobile face, "he hadn't it, but I got it since. Oh, yes, he's quite well. I fetched some racket balls, and then went to Sackville Street."

"My poor little girlie, my own one — all that long way! Why, you must have gone ten miles to-day. Let mother take off your boots; put up your footikins."

The child looked at the figure in the loose crimson dressing-gown, noted the labored movements with a loving, awesome look in her eyes and laughed a refusal, pushing the mother gently back into her chair. The mother's long, black-brown hair, straight and fine, hung loose below her waist; the elder laddie — a solemn-faced manikin, with eyes like brown velvet — had been brushing it, as she darned stockings and told them stories, or crooned Welsh hymns or Spanish folk-songs, her own troubles dozing in the background. The other little maid took away hat, jacket, and boots; opened the parcels, counted the eggs, and put the cooked beef on a plate, with quiet, old-fashioned deftness. She asked:

"There is a ring, Mary; did you order anything?"

"Yes, take them in. There is a tea-cake for Mumsie; we must toast it."

They spoke no more of the day's events; that topic was reserved until the little ones were tucked in bed, when the child-woman and the womanchild sat and planned, and sighed, and loved one another by the dying fire. When the tea was being cleared away the door-bell rang, and a slatternly maid brought in a basket addressed to the mother, and a paper to sign. It filled the room with perfume, and the children crowded round it until the maid went out. The mother read the address again, and opened it. Feathery moss, then flowers — such flowers! — orchids like fairy blooms masquerading as insects, roses glowing with color and heavy with sweetness, covering the fruit underneath; a gigantic pineapple, nectarines, purple grapes as big as plums, custard apples, and a basket of green figs. The dainty lady flushed, and her hands trembled as a child's will, when it examines some wonderful toy. She hid her face in the roses, touched the enchanted blossoms with tender fingers; told them the names of the fruit with eager-rushing words, and the places she had seen them grow. The child watched her, noting the flitting color, the dark stains round her eyes and temples, with the gripping fear that is always a part of a love as near idolatry as was hers for the mother. She wisely kept her own counsel when the mother speculated as to the giver, and perhaps on grounds of conventional morality and strict integrity; nathless, handsome Jack L'Estrange, deep in the books of Jew and Gentile, was scarcely honest in his generosity. Be that as it may, he would have risked that again could he have seen the dainty lady with her brown face buried in the roses.

CHAPTER III

IN ONE OF THE suburbs of Dublin, on the sea-line, that would take one to Kingstown harbor, were one to follow it, two tall, narrow houses stood facing a long field that was bounded by the sea-wall on one side, and the road along which the tramway ran to Dublin on the other. Standing in one of the upper windows, one could gaze across the wall, to Sandymount Strand, and the cockle-beds; and beyond them the treacherous quicksands, ever shifting; and Howth, defined as a ripple against the horizon. At night the fog spirit used to come sliding along the surface of the pearl-gray water, creep to the wall and, leaning over, send her shrewd, salt breath across the field to the houses.

All day long little feet pattered up and down the stairs of the house nearest the sea; sometimes a woman's voice hummed snatches of out-of-date ballads, or Spanish dance tunes. It was a curiously furnished house — every available inch of wall in the unused drawing-room upstairs was covered with choice watercolors, rare engravings, old miniatures, or fancies embroidered on silk. Two cabinets held stores of old china, much early Dresden, rare Sèvres, and some figures of exquisite porcelain of Rabelaisian subjects. Quaint seals, pouncet-boxes, Chinese puzzles, ivory carvings, a rosary and a missal of Marie Stuart — a veritable museum. It had been let furnished. The deck chairs covered with striped rugs and ponchos, the furs and books in the rooms downstairs, belonged to the tenants.

Every forenoon a child used to stand at the tall iron gate leading to the road and wave her hand back to the central face at the window. Its tender lips would part and show the dazzling teeth that seemed the high-light of the brilliant smile that came with such a radiance, sparkle, and love-worthness, that it made all other smiles seem poor things in their relativity. The child used to carry it away, invoke it at will, call it up as a thing existent in itself, without need of eyes, or mouth, or features about it — rich in its possession.

She had changed a little: the tail of hair was thicker and longer, the face paler, the forward pucker of brows more frequent, the gaze more often introspective, yet no less penetrating, when turned on man, woman, or object of interest.

Easter mom, cold, damp, with gray mists rolling in from the sea, hovering over the meadows, and creeping round the house. The blinds were drawn down, and a wisp of sticky black crape hung limply from the knocker. An errand boy sat on the step, and as he cried he rubbed a clean patch round his eyes with his red knuckles. A red-haired slattern was sitting on the last step of the stairs rocking with little inarticulate moans, whilst the tears trickled down her dirty face. The sound of sobs, deep sobs, with a hiccough in between, and the convulsive choke, that tells when the limit of what a child can cry has been reached, and exhaustion sets in, echoed from the parlor off the hall. The children had fled in there, stuffing their fingers into their ears, when the men came to screw down the polished lid, with the brass plate, after their last look at Mumsie. The Mumsie, with the strangely pinched nose, and the eyelids so sunk round the eyeballs; the still, white Mumsie, lying in the middle of frills pinked out like a ballet-girl's petticoat. Yes, Mary had said that to herself, with an impulse to laugh; she had bitten her wrist till her teeth drew blood, in her effort to conquer the inclination. The Mumsie that struck so curiously cold, so that the baby cried when they lifted her up to kiss the quiet face. Yes, they had run in there when the men came, and the Major, with big Bill Blake and a few others, had carried it down, and taken it away to the train to lay it with the ashes of his forbears.

The little maid, a strangely old-looking little woman, sat with her arms round the boys; the second little maid held the baby, and moaned, "Oh-ah, oh-ah," over it, because she could cry no more — and there was another silent little figure in a corner. The red-haired slattern came in and laid the cloth; the man in possession in the kitchen toasted bacon and scrambled eggs with a skill acquired in campaigning, and effaced himself as much as possible. The pale sun stole in furtively through the slits in the Venetian blinds; no dance in its step that Easter day. The church bells pealed joyously, and each peal was like a whip-cut, dealt in mockery at the pain gnawing inside; the child felt she could shriek with laughter at their glad "Christ has arisen, alleluia!"

She could imagine them, kneeling there, screeching with simulated bliss — ugh! It was a matter of complete indifference, — nay, not indifference, — sullen, rebellious resentment! She did not care one bit, not one bit, if the stone had never been rolled away in that far-off Easter time; for were not they bearing away the little mother, who was nearer and dearer than anything that was in, or had ever been in, the world? and she was all that mattered, after all.

A few months later the sun was shining warmly, and the sea blew kisses to the burgeons and buds and tender shoots on the trees in front of the house, where the little mother still walked in spirit.

Flaring sale-bills were plastered on the gateposts, and a shabby man in a shiny-seamed coat and old-fashioned horn spectacles paced up and down the footway, ringing a doleful bell. The auction was compulsory. A group of seedy-looking men smoked and talked in front of the railings. A big woman with crinkly hair waved a pot of frothing porter from the doorway. Every room was dismantled, and each piece of furniture had a number pasted on it. The table in the front room was littered with small things divided into lots. Women in sealskin jackets that looked as if they had suffered from some skin disease, and rusty scarfs of real lace twisted round their necks, and gold drop-earrings, gossiped and drank in the kitchen and on the stairs. Their coarse voices, with the worst of Dublin accents and the idioms of Liffey Street, rang through the house. Ke-link, ke-link, pealed the bell through the salacious jests and raucous laughter, like the ghost of a belated muffin-bell that had strayed by mistake into the spring.

Up in a back bedroom the children sat, with awe-struck eyes staring out of their wistful pale faces. The second little maid sat on a box near the window, and held the baby's head to her breast; her eyes stared fearsomely over the flaxen rings of its hair to the bed, where the third little sister lay, breathing quickly, with the shadows creeping round her mouth. Mary stood by the bed, and her lip curled as the little nun, with her soft face framed in her snowy coif, prayed as fervently as if a great sinner were passing away. Once Mary's face worked as if in agony, for she remembered — God, how it hurt, too! —

how the little one — she could see her, a quaint, erect little figure, with a beaked nose, and short, curling upper lip, with tears in the deep hazel eyes, standing at the gate, her face all a-quiver, for her boot was broken, and the gray lining showed, and the others had refused to take her out with them. She had inked it, and came in triumph to show them that it would not really show; besides, she was so tiny, no one would notice her. They had still refused — God, what little snobs they had been! — and though Mary had begged her to forget it afterwards, and given her a coveted paintbox to make up for it, she herself would never be able to forget it, or forgive herself for it — never! and now the little one was drifting out to the mother.

A laugh pealed out; the bell kept on, bringing scalding memories of winter teas round the fire, with Mumsie in her chair, and the little one bending her dear, beaked nose over some drawing or other...The bell stopped with a jerk; there was a sudden hush through the house; then steps through the hall, and the door banged to. The lead-blue lids quivered and the dim eyes opened. A look of listening, that seemed conveyed by the muscles of the face rather than the eyes, was expressed on the child' s pinched face. The door opened: the father came in.

"They have gone; it's settled," he whispered to Mary, and stooping, gathered the ewe-lamb of his flock to his arms.

A smile wavered over the little face, and a strangely hoarse whisper of —"Pappy, my old pappy dear," fluttered through the stiff lips. The boys cowered together, hugging each other tightly. The girl at the window cried silently, and the sudden stillness in the house below seemed to Mary like the holding of a great ear, listening for the coming of something that needs a finer sense of hearing than the ordinary to catch its passage. The door opened once more; a second nun came in and stood at the other side of the narrow bed. She looked closer, then she began to recite the *De Profundis* and the kneeling sister responded. The Major laid his burden and his head on the pillow, and sobbed aloud, and the red-headed slattern stole out with an "Ochone, Holy Mary!" to draw down the blinds once more and shut out the spring.

CHAPTER IV

Five years have passed.

"Dee di doodle dan, deedle, didle, doodle, doodle, doodle —" a gasp, and a tremendous splutter.

"Dee di doodle dan, an' dee di doodle day!" warbled a very mellow voice, as its owner flashed in a tub of water, dying away finally under the assaults of a large sponge — then an interval of silence. A fat woman, with a hooked nose in a long white face, came to the head of the stairs, and took advantage of the quiet to rap on the door and call:

"Major, there's a man in the hall wants to see ye, from Geoghegans the tailor."

A voice called through the bedroom door, "Eh?" She repeated it.

"Tell him I'll call in the afternoon." The woman mumbled as she went down again to the inspiriting strains of "Washington Crossing the Delaware." A girl with questioning dark eyes looked out through the sitting-room door on the first floor as the landlady passed; she half smiled as she heard the confident melody come marching down. The woman was coming up again; the girl drew in her head.

Sharp and prolonged rapping on the door above had the desired effect; this time it opened, and a pair of singularly beautiful eyes, in an ugly, humorous face, peeped out. The owner had wound a bath-towel into a turban round his head — wound it artistically, as an Eastern might, with a pride in his fashion of wearing; or a Western, with leisure and an eye for artistic effect.

"He sez he wants to see ye himself."

"Tell him to go to the devil — well, wait a minute; I'll give him a note."

"It's no use —"

The door shut with a click, and as she toiled down again, the sweetest crooning came forth from the room, heartbreak and tenderness, dropping like honey from an overfilled comb:

> "It's all round me hat I wear a green ribbon,
> It's all round me hat, for ever an' a day;
> An' if anybody axes me the rason wy I wear it,
> I tell him cos me thrue love is far, fa-a-r aw-a-a-ay!"

All the vowels melting like butter on hot toast. The girl was bent over a book on the hearth-rug; two little boys were blowing smoke into a picklebottle full of water, and observing the effect on some "pinkeens" as the woman entered.

"Take some paper an' a pen up to yer Da, Miss Mary, an' get him to write a note, or see the man, an' not keep him standin' in the hall!" muttering in an aside: "The divil a button he cares av id waz full o' thim."

There was a sudden rapid patter of feet above; the ceiling seemed to sway, the chandelier jumped ominously, and the cut-glass lusters on the mantelpiece — that had a dusty array of visiting-cards and unopened bills stuck in the frame of the glass — and the tea things on the tray joined in with a dissipated jingle. The Major was dancing "the rattlesnake jig" to his heart's content.

"Musha, my God thin, it's a light heart an' a thin pair o' breeches he's got this day. Miss Mary! Arrah! the ceilin'll be down this blessed minit, Major!" She hurried upstairs, following the girl as quickly as her breadth and bulk permitted, and hammered on the door.

"Dad," cried the girl, "do stop; you'll have the place down — the chandelier's rocking! Can't you listen?"

The door opened. "What is it now? All right! Splendid air that! Joe Burbank set Melbourne mad with it when Melbourne was Melbourne, before the damn Yanks exploited it. Oh, all right! get me some paper. What! ye have it? Well, wait a minute."

The note was written, and taken down with a dish of bacon and eggs that had been brought up some time ago. The Major descended finally to the strains of "Jackson's Morning Brush." He used to say:

"The beauty of this air is, that it fits one's mood, which is, thanks be to God! not regulated by any damn commercial considerations of finance. Taken quickly, it is rollicking, divil-may-care, with the dew of morning in its freshness. And it bears the true test of all real Celtic airs: taken slowly, in a minor key, it just becomes heartrending in its pathos."

Perhaps it needed the Major to give it the true twist — the Major, who could whistle the birds off the bushes, and drive a blackbird to despair with the flute-like finish of his pipe. The girl had been standing near the window, gazing attentively through the dingy white curtains; she turned her keen face and said:

"There is the man again; he has been watching the house on and off for some days. I believe he's a "bluebottle" (writ-server)."

The boys jumped up from the table.

"Let's see. I saw him talking to another man at the corner — the same man who came on a car with Captain Hackett," said Miley.

"By the Lord Harry, then," cried the Major, "it's that old scoundrel Malloy. What an infernal nuisance! I had most particular business — an appointment at twelve. Put on your things, Moll; you'll have to go with a note to Hackett."

The girl flushed, and examined her left boot; it was burst at the side. She said nothing, set her lips tighter, and asked:

"Were you to get any money by going? You might finish those sketches. The rent is overdue; my boots are finished, but Lacy wants something on account be —"

"My dear girl, don't I know all that? Isn't that just why it's such an infernal nuisance? I'd have a cheque like a shot if that da—"

The girl had left the room, and the Major went back to his interrupted occupation of showing the boys how to make a deadly pike-lure. Up in the bare room, with the dingy honeycomb quilt on the hard little bed, the girl was kneeling, drawing together a hole in the heel of her stocking; she could not dose it altogether, for that would make it bag at her ankle at the back; just enough not to be seen. She was going to wear a pair of kid slippers; the boot was impossible. She looked a quaint figure, in a heavy black velvet hat that hid her forehead and made her nose look too big, and a jacket that had shrunk in the sleeves and pinched her breast. She looked anemic; her back often ached, her growth made demands on her ill-nurtured strength, and often made her brave spirit answer churlishly. A few minutes later she was walking swiftly down the street. It was a true Irish day, soft and warm, with a clear mistiness that made one's clothes feel clammy and one's cheek deliciously cool and soft — soft and warm; even the mud under one's feet seemed both. It was a good walk, and when she got to the top of Sackville Street the docks were striking noon. The church bells had pealed the Angelus unanimously, but she could hear the city clocks striking, one after the other, for many minutes. She smiled; it was an Irish characteristic, but one could always depend on the "chapel" (the use of the word church in Ireland suggests a Protestant building) bells better than the official timepieces. She bowed with quaint sedateness to two well-dressed big Irishmen outside the Gresham, and paused a moment on Carlisle Bridge to look up the river, with a smile of pleasure on her sensitive face. She knew many of the people she met by name. In College Green she looked steadily in front of her as two first cousins of her own came towards her — in delicate deference to their snobbishness, for she knew it embarrassed them to acknowledge her. She went into the hall of a large house in Dawson Street. The porter, sitting at a table, saluted her with the deference of a well-trained, old-time soldier, and she mounted the stairs to the first floor and rang. A manservant opened the door.

"No, Miss, the master's not in" — adding, with a quick intuition of her doubt, "indeed he is not, Miss; he went out with Mr. Martin. I think they expected the Major. No; I don't know at all when he'll be back; he said nawthin."

The rain was falling with a soft, almost caressing persistency; she slipped the note into her pocket — well, there was nothing for it but to go back, a generous two miles. She hurried along, almost breaking into a run at times. The baker had said yesterday he would supply no more unless he got something off the book. The grocer might refuse any moment; the poor boys! Strange how Miley's curls had a trick of flicking her memory! It almost seemed as if they had an elfish quality of detaching themselves from the little bullet head and converting themselves into tiny brown moths, that brushed her lips as they flew along with her. It was a weary little figure that mounted the stairs; the smell of a good cigar offered a grateful antidote to the steam and soapsuds in the basement. She opened the door; the Major put up a deprecatory left hand — he had beautiful hands; she had inherited them from him. His mouth was askew, one eyebrow elevated; his whole face was a ludicrous caricature of an acquaintance. The Major always twisted his face to match the lines he drew. He put in a last careful touch with held breath, held the sketch at arm's length, and smiled with appreciative satisfaction.

"I never did a better thing in my life."

The girl's eye sought a drawing, fastened to a board, on an easel near the window. The Major avoided the hint. He had no heart whatever for the six character-studies he had promised a North of Ireland friend, who wished him to use his genius to some practical purpose, and was willing to pay for it. It was an extraordinary thing, how the beastly money-grubbing took all the delight out of one's work; made an infernal task of it.

"Out!" he cried. "Just like my luck! no, he wouldn't know where they were going to; I was to have gone with them. Let me see; you'll have to go out again — "with an air of assumed distress; in reality he was in a particularly sunshiny mood.

"I am tied by the leg as long as that beast sticks there — let *me* see" — he puffed vigorously, sat down, and wrote two notes.

"This is for Rick Burke. If you don't find him take the other. It's for Furness; there are two of them. Man I mean is a big man; cheery voice, long, curling mustachios —" gives an imaginary twirl, making a face resembling the late Victor Emanuel. She looked at the envelope: Furness, Esq.

"Don't you know his initials?"

"I never saw such a girl for asking questions; you were cut out for a sea lawyer; your poor —" something in her face checked him. "Office is a big, new, red brick building. Shortest way is up Dame Street and back of Castle. You'll have to hurry. Try and see Blake first, though."

The kitchen-door at the end of the hall opened as she went downstairs. The landlady beckoned; her arms were shriveled from washing; a cup of tea and a round of toast stood on the comer of the table near the fire.

"I wet a cup o' tay for Patsie, Miss Mary, an' he never came in" (a lie invented on the spur of the moment). "It's a pity to waste it, these hard times; just sup it up. So yer on the trot again, alannah! Faith, it beats Bannagher, an' Bannagher, they say, beats the divil, why the Major does isn't do better, wid his gra' talents. He'll have to make some alteration, for Murphy is getting rampageous. I sed to him, sez I, 'sure I can't press, for the Major is a rale gintleman! I think they do think less av the ould stock; them that's been in America.'"

"'It's too many av them,' sez he, 'you've got in Oireland.' 'Ye can't have too much av a good thing,' sez I. 'guess a good thing in itself is just a bad thing av ye can't sell it or swap it,' sez he. Don't ye fret. Miss Mary; but just give the Major a hint. I'm afraid o' Murphy whin he gets the drop in."

The girl shut the hall door wearily, and started the same road again. She walked on without seeing anything, until she came to the Gresham; the hall-porter went to look for Mr. Blake.

"No, he is not in, Miss."

On again to Dame Street; there she looked up at the figure of King Billy. She had a dislike, quite unmotived, perhaps racial, to that equestrian statue. She glanced into the castle yard when she came to it; a fair-haired Sassenach boy was looking out of the guard-room window. She knew the room; she had been up there once. A Highlander was pacing up and down the inner courtyard;

it always looked orderly in there. A hundred fancies flitted through her brain as she hurried along, buoyed by her dreams. She knew every turn of this old locality: Smock Alley, that was where the old theatre stood, before the Royal was built; Golden-Lane, where Mangan had wandered, maybe as wearily as she. She had a definite brain-picture of him — a sensitive, tormented face, with golden hair, like a woman's, under a steeple-crowned hat. He drank — strange all the nicest men she had known drank! Poor O'Hara! the tears filled her eyes at the thought of him. So many strange fancies and inexplicable stirrings worked in her of late, and there was no one to tell her what they meant. She could have asked him as well, ay, better than the little mother, if he had lived...

She remembered how once, when she was being prepared for confirmation, the nuns used to get uneasy at her queries. The examination of conscience on the Seventh Commandment was so strange; it made her ashamed, as if someone had stretched out a dirty finger and put a smudge, an evil-smelling smudge, on the white robe of her soul. Aunt Frances, too, had taken one of Aphra Behn's plays from her, and told her she must not read such things — they were unfit for her; and *Tristram Shandy* too; she had thought Uncle Toby entertaining, and she could not remember ever to have seen one bad thing in any book. Even if she had, one never need remember horrid things! She used to shut her eyes and leave them outside, and say: "Jesus, make me forget it!" She had books, schoolbooks, on botany and zoology; and yet it was a sin to think of quite natural things if they touched on men and women. Once she had asked Sister Aloysius, a big sister, with funny, twinkling eyes, and a very long, flexible upper lip, Who had manufactured all the things that were sins? Did not she think the old Fathers of the Church had rather nasty minds? She had heard Sister Aloysius say to the Reverend Mother, "That child is difficult to direct; she won't take anything on trust."

She had spoken to her dear O'Hara once, as they sat on the sea-wall at Kingstown, looking out across the dancing waters in the bay. He used to fetch her early on Sundays, and they spent all the day together. He told her tales of brave deeds, and recited beautiful poems of tender women and the magic of love. It was earlier, on that same day, when they had stopped at a little inn for lunch, that he had taken a fiddle from a blind man, and played at the roadside, until a crowd of Sunday promenaders gathered around them, and he made them smile, and rub their eyes furtively as the tears came, and fill the "dark man's" pannikin with pence.

Just at first she had felt ashamed, because she was dressed as a little lady — her mother's daughter — until she had caught his keen blue eyes, through their long-slit lids, questioning the quality of her soul: they made her feel small and ashamed of herself, as if she were one of the people he used to call "huckster-souls, with garments of cotton-backed velvet;" and she had drawn herself up, and held the tin in her little kid-gloved hands. Some one in the crowd whispered that they were French refugees from Alsace-Lorraine. Indeed O'Hara might easily have led to such a conclusion, with his keen, soldierly face, hawk nose, and close-cropped head, and his trousers cut as a French Zouave's, and gaiters such as no one else in Dublin wore. It was so quiet sitting there, only the water crooning in undertones, and the gulls circling from white to gray, and gray to white. She had felt as if she were in some grand cathedral, where no unclean thing could enter, such as she had visited in dreams. She had told him of her puzzled thoughts, asked him why men and women were less simply clean than the animals? He had pulled his long, drooping mustachios, each hair as if fine-drawn gold, and he had put his arm round her, and his eyes were troubled as they rested on her little serious face; and he pressed it to his shoulder, saying with the drawl that was peculiar to every one of his kin:

"The parable of the unclean spirits in the Gadarene swine, *ma mie* has never been correctly annotated. The beasts couldn't stomach them; they committed *felo de se*: the human beast can stand anything. In questions of decency the swine can give him points. It don't do to dig too deep in your own depths, little lady! You come on primitive deposits, that turn into ghouls in the dark, and rend you with the cruel enigma of your own creation. You can make a temple of your soul, little one, — a beautiful white temple, —to which, when I am dead, and, if I get my deserts, damned, some man will crawl on hand and knees to shrine himself. But the foundations have been laid long before your time; don't *you* go down prying into the vaults; no man, still less a woman, can do that and keep sane. I kiss your little brown hand, princess! Now I'll sing for you!"

Her poor, dear O'Hara! and some ladies had wondered that the little mother, the wise little mother, with the great dean child-heart, had let her go about with that disreputable Captain O'Hara.

Her outer eye had marked all the turnings; she had reached her destination.

A clerk stepped forward with an inquiring air. She asked for Mr. Furness.

"Mr. Robert Furness?" he queried; she hesitated. "There is Mr. George coming up the warehouse." Her quick eye took in every detail of the clean-shaven face, smooth hair, and natty figure of the man coming towards them. North of Irdand! was her mental comment.

The odd, cold, sick feeling, compound half of shame, half of suspense, clutched at her chest, as it always did on such occasions. She threw up her head, with the direct look that was almost a challenge. "

I have a note for Mr. Robert Furness!"

The clerk walked away.

"My brother. Is it anything of importance? anything I can do?"

"I don't know —" with puzzled hesitation; "it's not business; it's a private matter. I think my father, Major Desmond, sent it. I'm to wait for an answer."

"Come inside!" opening the door to a comfortable office, with a big fire. He held out his hand for the letter, and cut open the envelope carefully. "I know your father, have known him for years, a remarkably clever man — wasted. I fancy you made a mistake; it might be for either of us; your father perhaps forgot my name for the moment."

She flushed until cheeks and brow pricked with the blood, for the description given was not of this man, but of another, looking out from a pen and ink sketch on the mantelpiece.

Shiftless poverty had many stratagems; but how they made her cringe!

The man was studying her over the letter, his lips drawn into a severe line. There was a photograph on his desk of a dowdy, sweet-faced woman, with her lips laid to the curly head of a child on her lap, and one long, thin hand on the shoulder of a little girl at her side. It caught his eyes as he sat down to reply. He hesitated; looked round.

"Your father promised to do some sketches for me; he has drawn on account already, nearly all. He says they are almost finished."

The girl's eyes did not falter, but a look of repressed pain gathered in them. There was a moment's silence.

Very well, I leave it to you. If I advance the rest you will see that he completes them — to the best of your ability, of course. Very well. You are not very warmly clad, child," he said, laying his hand on her shoulder. "I have a little daughter about your age (she was five years younger). I hope you mind your studies. Knowledge is power, ye know."

The short-clipped Scotch vowels, and the kindly pat of hand on her shoulder sent her out into the damp streets, where the lamps burned dimly, with a warm glow in her breast.

The whole aspect of the waning afternoon was changed. A girl's laugh rang out from a doorway, about which a group of white-aproned women were gossiping; a flash of fire-flame, and a smiling woman pouring out tea in a parlor behind a cobbler's shop, quite touched her. It seemed but a few minutes' walk when she found herself climbing up the steep steps of Hoey's Court. She knew the house in which Swift was born; it was let in tenements — had a fine staircase. She liked all that part of the city. The ghosts of "silken Thomas" and Lord Edward Fitzgerald used to meet her there sometimes, for her white-letter days were spent in the library of the Royal Dublin Society.

It struck her as humorous that she could not take a 'bus (not many running when the outside car was so cheap), with money in her pocket too.

Anna Liffey was shrouded in silver mist as she crossed the bridge again. An outside-car pulled up with a jerk as she stepped onto the curbstone. A big, burly man tumbled off. His head was like an unkempt Irish hedge; his eyes gleamed and danced with restless fire; his hat was right on the back of his head, and he spoke with a quick, running stammer that seemed more as if his thoughts were too quick for the words to follow than a defect of utterance.

"Where's your father, where's your father? At home! Jump up; that's right. Always forget the number. Thirty-three." He hurled the address at the driver, and they turned and headed up Sackville Street.

"We 'rout the badger out. Rick," he called to a fair man on the other side of the car; "rout him out, the beggar! What's he doing at home, little woman, eh? What! Bailiffs, confound them! Malloy, the scoundrel! He served me last time; we'll circumvent him," rubbing his hands gleefully. The jolting of the car and the soft breeze in her face made her drowsy. She had eaten little or nothing all day except the toast.

Bill Blake — one time commander of a Waikato regiment, known to the Māoris as "The Pakeha Devil," "The Wizard," because he had twice escaped out of their hands by demon agency, as they thought, being ignorant of the tricks of the Davenport Brothers, maddest of all the mad men with Berserk blood in Ireland — looked at her, and slipped his arms round her shoulders. His eyes burned as he felt the wet jacket, and travelled down to the mud-soaked slippers. "It's an infernal snarl, that's what it is; an infernal snarl!" he growled to himself. "She's like the dear lady a bit about the temples. It hurts, confound it!" and Big Bill stifled the sudden emotion that seized him at the memory of a chivalrous, hopeless, past love by an invocation of oaths weird as terrible.

"Pull up, Gubbins, at the big shop near the Gresham! Little maid's dead beat. Rick; get down!" as they stopped. "Get a chicken, pheasant, anything cooked, tin of soup, grapes; pitch them all into a basket. Damn their eyes, if they stop tying up." Gubbins, the jarvy, noting the impatience of every word, broke tactfully in with a humorous story of a Yorkshire man, who thought "he could tache little Miles o' the Curragh a thing or two about a horse."

She woke to find herself lifted down to the pavement before her own door. The third man seemed to hesitate. Bill Blake gave a wild cooee! in the hall as soon as they entered, and the door above opened to let down a stream of firelight. The Major looked out and cried: "Lord love ye, Bill, darlint, yer a sight for sore eyes! Eh? Rick, old man, back from the wars, covered with glory! I see you picked up the little woman on the way!"

The Major's keen eyes took in the third man as he greeted the others, with his heart wrapped up in his smiles. "Faith, I was forgetting, Paddy," cried Big Bill. "My young friend Featherstone, 'Jim' to his pals; my old friend. Major Patrick Sarsfield Desmond."

"You must be a son of one-eyed Featherstone of the Diehards!" exclaimed the Major, as he shook hands. "Got your mother's eyes, though. She was a Thunder, crossed Ormonde; there were three of them. I danced with them before ye were born, me boy! They were darlints, but she was the pick o' the basket —"

The lad flushed to his light, fair curls and smiled. Big Bill yelled with delight, "I told ye so. Drop Paddy in Shanghai, and he'd tell ye the pedigree of every white man in the sink."

"Remind me to tell you a story about your father some time. We were coming home from the Crimea —"

The man called Rick had put a chair for Mary, and was smiling down at her, saying: "You're getting along, little woman; plaited up your mane. Last time I saw you you hid your face in your locks like a witch, and sat on my knee. Well, I've been stitching up Tommies ever since. How old are you? What! just seventeen?"

A look of distressed surprise shot out of the half-closed, sleepy gray eyes that travelled swiftly from the thin face with the bloodless lips to the wet, small feet. There was a sharper note in his voice as he said:

"You ought to make Miss Desmond change her things, Paddy; she's wet and overtired; she's not looking very robust."

"God bless my soul! She's as fit as a fiddle. Game for anything, aren't you, Moll? Run away and change your things. Call for some glasses on the way—"

She toiled upstairs with chattering teeth, and took off her shoes, sponged her little red, cold feet, — the mud had found its way between her toes, — and turned over the few things in the drawer. She found a pair of old stockings, too short in the legs. She drew in her under lip and held it tightly as she smoothed her hair and went down. Mrs. Murphy was beaming as she met her on the stairs with a decanter of whiskey and some glasses on a tray. "I got it for the Major. He'll settle for it afore he goes out," she whispered.

Smoke and laughter and glad voices rang through the house. The boys had come in, and sat together in a corner of the sofa, taking in the scene quietly. The Major was clearing things off the old square piano. The lad sat down and sang with a voice that was like a silver tuning key to rushes of melody. It crept into the girl's heart, and her face flushed and her hands trembled and got moist, so that she rolled her handkerchief into a little ball between her palms. Her skin looked dear in the lamplight. Dr. Rick watched her, muttering under his breath — "Transformed, by Gad! imaginative, emotional — the Major's daughter, if she's cursed with beauty into the bargain!" He took up a pile of books on a rickety little side-table, — Fongué's *Undine* with translation notes, a German grammar, *Silvio Pelico* in French, Carlyle's *Hero Worship* — asked with raised eyebrows and lift of finger, "Yours?" A nod of head in reply; and whilst the others asked for Irish melodies, famous drinking songs, and bits of opera, this wildest of army surgeons, reputed misogynist, drew her to talk of her efforts at culture with more deference than he ever extended to the wife of his commander-in-chief.

He managed, perhaps designedly, to rouse a belief in herself, and the worth of pluck in man or woman.

One of the boys went out to reconnoitre, and came back with the intelligence that Malloy had vanished, and his colleague was deep in a political discussion in a public-house round the comer.

The Major called for his coat, gloves, and hat, and as he brushed the latter on his sleeve trolled gaily:

> "Hurroo says she for element,
>   a drop of drink's no detriment,
> Shure I eat because I'm hungry,
>   and I drink because I'm dry."

He felt in his pockets with a perfect bit of acting, then said: "Lend me a couple of sovs. Bill, old man. Kept in the house, you know, by that confounded—"

The big man roared as he handed them over, as he had done all the days of their comradeship, and their eyes met — old pals, old friends, with a love for each other that no knowledge of weakness or sin could lessen; and perhaps the light in the Major's, that leaped to answer the light in his, was such that not even the dead lady had called it up. For where two men love as these two comrades did, perhaps it is a love of a more unselfish type than man ever gives to woman — woman who, even in the hour of her surrender, is always something of an enigma to him.

"Good-bye, little lady," said the doctor. "Put a word in your prayers sometimes for a vagabond sawbones, and get some iron. You've got brains and a big heart, but it takes blood to pump it."

Big Bill tipped the boys, and they rattled downstairs to whistle for a car.

There was a new light in her eyes as she stepped to the table; it made the Major uneasy; dulled his bright mood as a breath on freshly polished steel; recalled her womanhood standing on the threshold. He put down a sovereign. Seeing protest in her face he put down another half sovereign, and patting her on the head said:

"God bless you, dearie; say your prayers, boys!"

"Moll!" he called back from the stairs, "what about F.?"

"All right," she called, going out; but mad, buoyant Bill Blake had pulled him down the stairs with a whoop, crying: "The enemy is in sight! charge for the car! now for it! drive like blazes! go it! Sold again, Malloy—"

She could hear their laughter above the crunching of the gravel and the horses' hoofs, for they had left the hall door open in the rush. She went down to shut it, and met Mrs. Murphy in the hall.

"They're a gallows lot. Miss Mary!" she said, smiling broadly, "an' your Da is the worst of them all, gallivantin' and scamanderin' an' screechin' as if it were a wake! Did he lave any word? Murphy has just enough in to be cantankerous; just a weeny drop more an' he'd be in a beautiful humor."

"It's all right," answered the girl; "you can take two pounds off the book."

And upstairs the boys were opening the basket Big Bill had filled so lavishly; and the philosopher, as she called the graver lad, and she calculated with the astuteness of a clever finance minister trying to doctor the budget, whom they could soften by judicious installments.

First, the washerwoman and the baker; Miley must go to Lacy for her shoes, and he could have a cap; Phil must have two pairs of socks; "What?" she could not hear when he whispered right into her ear. Would she go with him to buy something for Nora and send it to her? Ay, that she would; and she ruffled her hand tenderly over the crisp curls that clustered so lovingly to the little bullet head. Her little gossoon, with the glorious eyes, and the lovable, weak Irish mouth; who lay so close to her heart, and gave her so many misgivings.

Later on, when he laid his curly head against her knee, and the philosopher toasted chestnuts on the bars, all the pain was eased out, as when one puts a burnt finger on a cool place. Next week's worries were shoved out of sight, with the Irish ability to forget; which is a wise dispensation of Providence, to balance the keen capacity for suffering and the measure of disaster that is the birth-portion of every Celt. Mary Desmond sat gazing into the glowing embers, seeing strange castles in the fire, luring dragons, and a knight in virgin armor, pricking along the road of life to strains of romantic music — her own knight, with her favor on his breast, and ready arm to turn aside the fiery ploughshares that lie in the path of every damsel.

What she did not hear as she sat and mused was the great cry for love, love, love, that is as the voice of the wind, calling over the waste of the world's waters; or the vague, never-ceasing hum in the hemispheres above that is the music of the aerial world, seeking ever for answer to its call, and finding none. What she did feel as she sat with the light caressing her face was the little, trembling thrill of the senses that stir in the secret fibers of a girl's being; a stirring and half-awakening, the outer sign of which is intense self-consciousness and tremulous delight; the inner, a fearsome realization of a wonder-world of strange feeling that is the passing from girlhood to womanhood.

THE BLOSSOM IN THE BUD

CHAPTER V

MID-SEPTEMBER, SATURDAY AFTERNOON in the cove of Cork, therefore market-day. A long line of asses' carts was drawn up to the sidewalks; others clattered down the narrow, steep, straggling streets. They raced in response to the repeated "prods" of pointed ash plants, and the guttural, "Garrn, garm ow o' that now!" of youthful drivers; or the sedater thwacks of some blue-cloaked, white-capped woman.

Crowds of emigrants mingled with the market folk; a quick ear might have distinguished the guttural Kerry accent, the short-clipped Northern vowels, between the soft-singing lilt, with its rising interrogative cadence that makes every assertion a question, peculiar to the South. Peasants from the wilds of Connemara, from the stormlashed coast of the West, were talking "the Irish."

Spike Island was so wrapped in a golden haze that it suggested Hy Brasil the Blest, rather than an English-governed convict prison; the wharfs were all bustle and hurry, to an extent unusual in Ireland. Emigrants of all classes, some with bundles of clothes and bedding, and gossoons bearing wooden trunks, were streaming out of the lodging-houses, "convenient to the say." A group of shy-eyed, tearful colleens in the midst of relations was gathered outside the door of Miss O'Brien's shelter — some of the flower of Irish girlhood, their dark hair gathered back from almost invariably lovely brows, guileless of hats.

Comedy, pathos, passion and tenderness, meanness and cunning, the fleeting expressions of primitive feelings, changing and interchanging on the faces of an Irish crowd, as sun and mist on a typical Irish day.

"Be me sowl!" ejaculated a dry little man with a keen, light-blue eye, "it's the Widow Nolan's boy!" smacking the boy (a man of thirty) on the back.

"Begor, it's Dinny Fitzpatrick!" cried the boy in delighted greeting. "Sweet Kildare, short grass, for ever!"

The public-houses — every grocer's shop had a license for "tea and spirits" — were doing a roaring trade. Tears and whisky mingled with farewells. Here and there, in the grocers', bashful girls accepted "a glass of the sherry wine," for luck's sake — the Irish lower-class girl has to come to England to learn to visit a public-house.

The town clocks were striking two when a girl came along the quay alone; a ragged "caddie" followed her, with a trunk on a hand-truck. She looked up as the hour struck; a flag was running up a staff, and the name of an Anchor liner became visible as it fluttered out on the sea-going breeze. A quiver ran through the crowd, a tightening of breath that was almost a sob, transforming all the units, for the moment, into brothers and sisters of common fostering.

Her face was very white and her lips compressed; but her eyes looked fearlessly ahead, with the same questioning look in them that had caused Captain O'Hara (long since dead, and buried one gentle spring morning under a blossoming pear-tree, that scattered its white blooms on his coffin) to drawl, the first time he made friends: "Singular eyes, little maid; you'll go over some grass in your time before you get that question answered."

She gave the boy a shilling and touched his curly head caressingly, stepped onto the tug, into the space set aside for "intermediate and steerage passengers." It struck her, as things will, in inconsequent flashes, that in all her vagabond, hard-up life she had never travelled other than first class. Well, this grass had got to be gone over as well as more to come! A voice called out: "Pass Doctor's muster there." So there was to be a perfunctory medical examination on the way out to the steamer. She had a confused vision of swiftly receding wharfs, dotted with people, trees, church spires, and fleeting clouds, behind her, yet visible; of the shape and hang of a frieze coat in front of her; and the outstretched tongue of a red-headed lad. She caught the doctor's name, her own county, the son of a "gombeen" man. He was just in front of her: he had a self-satisfied little face, — was asking questions brusquely. She felt herself smile, for he had grafted what he believed to be a real English accent onto his original middle-class brogue. He stared at her inquisitively and put his hand on her arm; she slid it aside and looked at him with an expression that made her curiously like the Major in his most bellicose mood. He passed her; she leant against the railing and watched the water. A band, that had accompanied a town councilor on his way to collect Land League funds in Western States, struck up: "Though the last glimpse of Erin." Mothers were sobbing over departing children, and wives clinging to husbands; a burly priest with a htunorous mouth and kindly eyes was wishing a batch of his parishioners "Godspeeds," with an undercurrent of admonition thrown in. There was a burst of laughter as a tipsy cattle-dealer pulled out a string of "drisheens" (a Cork delicacy, white puddings with tansy). "Irish shamrogues!" cried a vender of sods as neatly cut as for a lark's cage: "Musha, thin, take a bit iv the ould sod wid yez, for luck!" And indeed a lark in a cage or a sod of black turf were common enough belongings. And when the voyage got rough, and the hatches were battened down, the sods got swept out with the sickness; and the larks like many another Irish (human) lark got crushed against the wires of its cage. "Oh, God bless ye, alannah machree; it's a sore heart I'll have till I get wurrud av ye! Oh, holy Mary, Mother iv God! look down on us this blessed day! but it's a sore day!"

It reminded Mary Desmond of "keening" she once heard in Mayo, in the God's acre of "The Church by the Lake." The sobs of a comely peasant girl, leaning over the rail next her, made her chest hurt; she touched her on the shoulder, and added a sluthering brogue to her own soft tongue, that was English in its genesis, and fostered for the sake of the mother.

"Don't cry, girleen; don't ye want to look at the old counthry as long as ye can?"

She led her to the other side of the tug, put her arm round her shoulder, and watched the sun striking white sparks off the houses, that were each an Irish home, fast fading into a blur of green and white.

The steamer loomed up suddenly above them, as a monster rising out of the ocean, every porthole a menacing eye; rows of pink faces that seemed to look down on them from an immense height and run into a conglomerate face. They filed up the gangway, showed their tickets, and crowded to the side to look down to the tug. The tug, that seemed to Mary as insignificant as the steamer great; a tiny, absurd object tossing on the water, with a ludicrous band playing "Come Back to Erin" as if the players were getting sick into their instruments; and a crowd roaring up with that in their voices that might have made God Himself sorry, as they called Him to endorse their blessings.

They were overcrowded; the stewards found it difficult to find berths; it was late before Mary could get her things arranged for the night. The passengers were mostly objectionable. She seldom spoke to any of them, and perhaps they found her manner repellent. In the evening she used to come down after eight o'clock and watch the steerage girls; there were some fifty young Irish girls, many barefooted. They mingled with the steerage passengers in the daytime, but after eight o'clock came down to their sleeping quarters, which were separated from those of the intermediate passengers by a latticed partition. One "limb of a girl," as the stewardess called her, used to sit on a pork barrel and play the concertina. She reeled off jigs, reels, and plaintive melodies with equal facility. The girls footed it merrily, and the crowd at the lattice grew as the strains of "The Priest in his Boots" followed "The Little House under the Hill," or gave place to "The Dish of Nettles." And when the shipbell told nine the music hushed, and the "limb of a girl" led the Rosary, and the "Hail Mary" in English was often answered by the "Holy Mary" in Irish, and the crowd melted quietly away. And once, when an irreverent youth from Maine State thought fit to indulge in indelicate comment, he was subdued for a day after by a short but pithy interview with the Captain, who was of the opinion that "Irish girls of that kind bring a ship luck!" though he was a Birkenhead Baptist himself.

She had noticed a tall, hale old man, with a Whitman head, square-toed Wellington boots, fine black broadcloth clothes, a shirt of unstarched linen, with very narrow black silk tie. He was travelling with a well-bred-looking young Englishwoman. Some evenings after they had got well on the voyage, she was standing watching the girls — she always called good-night to them; looking up she found him considering her face.

"It's a great religion for an emotional people, when the civil government is anything else!"

Mary nodded, "Yes, it's the only one for them."

"I suppose you are Irish; I saw you come on at Queenstown?"

"Half of me."

They went on deck, and from that out she spent most of her time with him. English born, he had run away as a lad; was an electrical engineer, an American citizen, a bit of an astronomer, and a great deal of a philosopher. Had been home to see his native town; was taking a niece out.

The night before they arrived he talked to her of his life, and Mary felt, as she had done often before in desolate hours, on finding a helpful passage in a book, that he was accidentally talking to aid her. Before they went below he said, putting his hand on her shoulder:

"You are bound to be lonely, for you probe life too deeply; you take nothing on trust; your head is too coldly analytical to give you a chance of happiness as long as that big, hot heart of yours calls in you. In love, as in all else, you will be like one of those rare wine-tasters, of whom it is said they can taste an atom of leather in a cask of wine. You will always taste your bit of leather unless you find the right man; and he would be an uncommon specimen. The rising generation is a poor thing — brute or decadent, or a cross between the two, — few whole men. But unless you do find him, go alone — you can — and in some things you will always have to. You will never keep in any Church —you couldn't, with your nature, and *be honest*. I am sorry we shall be too far from you to give you even a glimpse of a home now and then, but keep your brave heart—"

Mary could never recall her first impression of the entrance to New York harbor; the impression of her second entry, years after, when the colossal statue of Liberty had been erected to guard it, was vividly present to her; but the first was nebulous. She must have sunk into a dream, only to awake to a realization of a sea of upturned faces gazing at the steamer.

She waved aside the express delivery men; it was delightfully familiar to read Wells, Fargo, & Company on a man's hat; it made her feel that she would not have been astonished if Juba Bill, or Jack Hamlin, or the Rose of Tuolumne had stepped forward and bade her welcome. She asked the man who wore it where she could leave her trunk until she knew its destination, and he answered her in the accents of Dublin Bay, guiding her to the central depot. Money was precious; she decided to walk to the business address of a distant connexion.

It was a clear, warm morning; the inland breeze fluttered the flags of the different steamship companies gaily She picked her way along the dirty sidewalks; fruit-shops, ship-chandlers, tobacco-shops, — with a Highlander mounting guard on the pavement outside, and "Cigar Store" over the door, — saloons and eating-houses of all kinds, to suit the fluctuating population of the harbor.

Many inquiries made to very uncivil policemen, whose facial characteristics reconciled her to the caricatures of Pat in the English comic papers, brought her to a large building. She went up in a luxurious lift, "elevator," the boy called it, and entered a private office. The genial-looking little man at the table read the Major's letter of introduction twice through, whistled softly in perplexity, and looked at her again. Then he took her to a map on the wall.

"See, here we are. Now, when you leave the office you have got to go straight so; that will bring you to Broadway. There you take a 'bus; tell the conductor to drop you at Fourteenth Street. There's the fare, and I'll give you a note to my wife."

When the girl had gone, he opened a cupboard and mixed himself a cocktail carefully and deliberately, and when he had finished it he said: "I'm damned! looks straight, proud, strong-willed, thoroughbred to the bone, and — entirely impossible."

And perhaps the summing-up was the conclusion at which Mary Desmond herself arrived before many weeks had passed.

She walked all day, mounted dozens of stairs, knocked at scores of doors. There was work, not plenty, but here and there a place for anyone with one certain tool that they could use skillfully in their grip. She applied at the dry-goods stores where they needed young ladies; they were polite, but decided; she would not suit. One day, in despair, she mustered her courage, and asked a sympathetic little Jew, who had offered her a chair, "Why?" He looked astonished, but smiled and said:

"You've chust come across? I regoned so! Well, if you want to know, you've got too mooch 'style'! "Yes," in answer to her look of frank amazement, "we have no use for 'style'; if you were 'stylish,' it would be anozzer zing; zat is chust wot you are not. Give me your address; peraps somezing might happen."

Mary stole a look at herself in a long glass in an entry in Broadway. It seemed to her that she looked very inoffensive in her tailor-made tweed; but she forgot that one only sees the envelope of oneself in a mirror; that there the play of soul and spirit is lost.

Years afterwards, when she knew the working world of London and could judge it fairly with New York, she used to look back and laugh at her efforts — and, truth to tell, compare the business men of the great hive at the Thames' mouth unfavorably with those of the newer city. For through all her futile efforts she met with invariable courtesy, although her "vagueness" as to what she could do must have been trying to harassed businessmen.

If she had only known one thing! Languages were no use without shorthand and typewriting to supplement them; yet she persevered doggedly. She was scarcely miserable, because she had not time to think of her position, and she was too bewildered by the feverish whir of this monstrous international sifting sieve, silting ever fresh polyglot particles, too often discarded by the older and wiser nations.

Life seemed less concrete, less inside the houses and warehouses; it was everywhere, pounding like a gigantic steam-hammer, full speed, in the air, in the streets — insistent, noisy, attention-compelling. Trains above one's head; one caught glimpses of domestic interiors, intimate bedroom scenes, as one whizzed past second stories in the early cars. And one could hear the conductor's "Hurry up, all aboard!" through the street noises and jingle of the road-cars below.

In the city one met men crossing the streets in their white shirt-sleeves; one saw them sitting on the counters, smoking, in the wholesale stores; it was a new note in a whole scale of screaming novelty. In the evenings men and women sat on the stoops and verandas, the red glow of cigars or cigarettes gleaming like fireflies between the light gowns; their whispers and laughter crept down into the streets and became part of the atmosphere. Restaurants and ice-cream stores were open all night, and the horse-cars ran, and people sauntered about serenely at two in the morning; night was but a subdued edition of the day. Mary felt that the clocks in America must surely give two ticks to the one of the sedate old timepieces at home. The very air was a stimulant, a nervous febrific; the noise seemed to assume the character of a national fanfaronade. The dignity of the "help" was blazoned at each street-comer, where the citizen of the New World mounted into elaborate brass-nail-studded chairs to get his boots cleaned. One took one's choice of the news of the world in papers in French, German, Spanish, Russian, and divers other tongues, from tables in the street. The apothecary began or ended each block, and notices of root-tea, boneset, or sarsaparilla at five cents added a strangeness to their windows. Swedish draymen, German *delicatessen* handlers, French confectioners, Chinese laundrymen in every street, whilst Biddy from Limerick, and Pepita from Naples, waged war as they raked with curved irons in the refuse-barrels on the sidewalks of the poorer quarters.

Mary soon learned not to criticize; learned to step warily on the thin ice of American sensitiveness; learned that although as a nation they assume the right of criticizing the Old World with a New World frankness, the national susceptibilities are tender as an open wound; one is loath to touch them.

One day when her eyes were growing weary with constant questioning, and the future looked very black, a little Jewess in the house in which she lived came to her and said, smilingly:

"My uncle wrote to me about you the other day; he has a dry-goods store in Fifth Avenue; I see you remember; he took a real fancy to you. He wanted me to help; I wasn't sure if I could, but I guess it's fixed now. You go right along to this address," handing her a note, "and give this. You won't mind my telling you, but you've got to blow your own trumpet if you want to get on in Amurrica. You've just got to get along whatever way you can; put out your elbows and shove; just say to yourself: 'Well, I've got to get there, and if I don't hustle someone else, I'll not alone get hustled myself, but I'll get left.' It don't do to get left in Amurrica!"

CHAPTER VI

ON THE THIRD FLOOR of a Titan building, down near the ferries, some fifty women of all ages were thronging to their day's work; the lady superintendent had not arrived; her desk was empty. The windows looked across at a wholesale glass warehouse, the office of Frank Leslie's illustrated papers, and, farther down, the organ of Fenian Ireland.

Mary Desmond leaned against a desk and watched the women as they trooped in — girls of sixteen, women of thirty; shabby, well-dressed, "stylish," dowdy, pretty, homely, all sorts and kinds. They divided into cliques — Brooklyn girls, Jersey girls, uptown, and Hoboken girls; the Brooklyn girls bore the reputation of having the most "vim" in the office. Two sisters came in, very pretty, tawdrily dressed in cheap finery of smart cut, with paste jewelry and a taking air of finding life good. The one with a dimple hummed a snatch of a catchy song, in vogue at Tony Pastor's, as she took off her fall and stringless bonnet. She stood up a piece of looking-glass against her ink jar, and proceeded to pin each curl of her bang into a square bit of paper; then powdered her nose deliberately with chalk on a bit of white cotton stocking-leg. Mary laughed at this striking evidence of working in "the land of the free"; thought of the likelihood of the young ladies in an English insurance office beginning the day by adorning their foreheads with paper devices to catch the wily curl.

Nine o'clock; a sudden stop in the conversation and work began. Inside: the click, clickety-click of the typewriters, and dull pound of india-rubber stamps, varied by the scratching of the pens; outside: the thud of the printing-presses opposite, rise and fall of the elevators, and click of door at each stoppage alternated with the rumble of trains and shriek of sirens and steam whistles. The room was already close.

Mary had mastered the routine in a short time. Each week was the same: applications to check, accept, or reject; entries to make in red or black ink in divers books, and check in the O.K. ledger; write policies for fresh issue, and call over the lapses. Scratch, stamp, call; whilst the door swung open every now and then to admit a boy with the mails — the agents have been on the war-path in the Wild West; the bags are heavy. Whenever the lady superintendent leaves the room there are whispers, and a shaking of backs that denotes suppressed laughter, at the desk in front of Mary. A girl called the "chipmunk" has a new story, and the other Jersey girls are watching its effect on the Brooklynites.

The stamping machine behind seems to have got into Mary's brain; her line of work is slack; she spills some ink on her fingers and goes up to the lavatory. The elevator seems a soaring haven of restful quiet; up six stories, past doors that appear to shelter relays of patent agents, notaries public, and commissioners of oaths, right to the top. She washes her hands, steps out onto the roof, leans on the parapet, and gazes out to the river. Brooklyn to the left, with a patent drug in gigantic letters that seem to stretch right across it; and the river with freight barges, wherries, steam packets, and crafts of all sorts, darting to and fro; the gray river, bearing its burden oceanwards. It grew to be symbolical to Mary of restless, hopeless, tragic life, drifting to the Isle of Death. She drew in the salt air in long, deep draughts, and went down again.

"John Brown desired to insure his life for forty dollars; he is forty-eight inches round the chest, — bully for you, John! — and five feet eight and a half high. But John Brown is a publican, and this office is conducted on strictly teetotal principles; avast, John Brown! What does she know of J. B.?" She racks her memory. "John Brown's body is marching to the grave." No, what on earth is it? Oh! "they hanged John Brown on a sour apple-tree"; so they did; she swung her foot in time to the tune.

The girl next her whispered: "Sakes alive! are you crazy? You'll have the boss down on you in two sees."

Fortunately a horn blew somewhere on the river, announcing the lunch hour; Mary sat on her high stool and watched the others as she did every day. Those who went out put on their hats and trooped out in pairs; the others gathered in groups; the dimpled sister, named Cora, was always the center-point of one cluster — there was a mine of amusing slang. Scraps of many conversations reached Mary.

"Met such an elegant fellow on the boat this morning, mustache —! oh, a daisy. —Had a good time last night? —You bet! —What did you wear? —Was Fred Davis there? — Oh, the cutest shoes and an elegant waist, too cunning for anything. — He did; he gave her a perfectly lovely stemwinder, with her name in pearls on the back. —Whisper, girls! I've got such a killing story! —" heads in a bunch and whispers.

Questions, answers, broken by the everlasting, "Is that so?" and the "Pearl one, plain two, keep your silk untwisted! I think he's just too lovely; he's too cute to live when he preaches; we had a splendid time; did you have tea? from the religious element, who were strong on fancy work. The story finished amidst shrieks of laughter, the "chipmunk" said quaintly as they died away:

"I never knew an elder yet who couldn't give a python points on hugging. I just feel as if I want something; mommer didn't give me any cake; come round to the baker's for some crullers."

"Say, Cora! Ad Jones was asking for you; I guess he's sweet, ain't he?"

Cora made a grimace; she is engaged in the delicate operation of wiping the chalk off her eyelashes with a wet third finger.

"Lands alive! He's engaged to a girl in Jersey City; father's a real estate agent."

"Who? Ad Jones? You don't say! He used to come to the rink. Was too toney; went in for English style: 'aw'fly bad form, don'tcher know — haw, haw!' Great Scott, Sadie! you are a time putting on that fall; come along, do."

"She's a daisy; she's a darling, lum, tum," sang Cora, as she snapped her fingers, waltzing out.

For a week she had listened to them; the conversation had always run on the same lines, sometimes in more objectionable directions, when they discussed cases that were described with the biblical directness of American reporting, or told stories, in which the wit was not winged enough to excuse the vulgarity. They worked steadily all the afternoon; occasionally there might be a titter, and the fuzzy little curls on Cora's neck and round her pink ears would tremble as she laughed at some note of the "chipmunk's" Yet those two were the best workers in the office. Most of them had homes and worked for pocket or dress money. She paid her landlady four dollars and a half for a tiny room and very indifferent board; that left her fifty cents for her washing, and for that she could only send six articles. Well, next month she would put down her name for extra work after five; and with a German lesson or two on Saturday afternoon, or perhaps on Sunday, she might pull through. Meanwhile — a brave heart. The worst of it was, that there was no interest in the work; it grew mechanical; entry after entry, hundreds of them: Murphys, O'Reilleys, Bradys, Browns, Joneses, Robinsons, Gomezes and Mendozas, Mtillers and Griiners, Russians and Poles, with a hatful of consonants — a grotesque tale of overcrowded mother-countries, *wandertrieb* evictions, enterprise, or expedient flight.

Winter came with the bitter cold of New York and the marrow-searching quality of its winds. She was standing one morning at Canal Street, in the midst of heaps of dirty snow and refuse; crossing seemed hopeless, with the never-ceasing line of freight-wagons. Perhaps something about her forlorn figure appealed to a big, fair giant on top of the first of a fresh train of carts. He pulled up his team, and called down: "Run along, Sis!" heedless of the blasphemous yells of the drivers in the rear. She laughed up a thank-you, and half slid, half walked along; the snow melted and dripped and fell in blackened splotches from the elevated railroad on the dirty streets below. Sodden discomfort and misery on every side; Mary Desmond needed all her dogged endurance and brave heart to keep her up. She lacked the gaiters, and rubbers, and warm clothing the other girls had, however poor they were; she was working extra as often as possible; but what she earned meant so little when clothes were doubly as dear as at home. The office reeked with hot air and damp clothes; most of the girls had colds; sometimes her back ached until she felt shivers of ice and fire playing up and down her spine. She could not have sworn one hour after the other as to anything she had written.

She used to avoid Broadway going home, the men stared so, — used to go along Bleeker Street and Lower Fifth Avenue until she reached Thirteenth Street; her house was in Seventh Avenue, between block twelve and thirteen — it was like living in a sum. Uncle Hiram and Aunty Sadie, as the boarders called them, were Down-East Yankees from the State of Maine. She was a lean, squaw-like woman, with peculiar snakelike, flat, black eyes; yet sometimes they could emit a quick red gleam. She always had a chunk of gum in her jaw. Mary often met her standing on the stairs, chewing pensively as she mused. Then she used to rouse up, move the gum with an adroit twist of the tongue to the other side, and glide silently away, with her head on one side, and a worried pucker of brow. Uncle Hiram drank in bursts; lie always went about in his shirt-sleeves and a large straw hat, chewing a piece of stick. He used to tell good stories. Aunty Sadie had stuck to him like a buttered bun, through good and evil, striving, poor soul, to make the best of things. Lying had become second nature to her; as the drummer said, she was "kinder lonely unless she romanced." She would come into the breakfast-room knowing perfectly well what was lacking, shift her piece of gum, and say in a sad sort of way, "I hope you have all you require!"

"I'd like to see some butter!" the shipping clerk would venture. She would gaze at him absently, murmur, "Well, I want to know—" and glide noiselessly away. Most of the boarders were decent, hard-working people, many from their own State: there were a budding doctor and his mother, a law student, and a drummer or two. Mary seldom got home until the others had finished, for which she was glad.

She used to get books from the Apprentices' Library, and, when not too tired, wrap a shawl round her shoulders and sit with her feet on the register and read. Perhaps it was her sense of humor that saved her; kept the horrors from creeping in, the vulgarity and coarseness from touching her inner self. Humor is like brine; it keeps the things of the flesh from tainting. The "hired help," a fast-looking woman over thirty, used to chaff the male boarders as she waited at breakfast, and go away on Saturday afternoon in a French hat, silk gown, and sealskin sacque, to reappear on Mondays — she gave her services for nothing, otherwise. Uncle Hiram always shared his particular "bake" of Boston beans with Mary on Sunday mornings, and gave her the reversion of his paper — a wonderful Sunday edition, with a specially written Sunday sermon, an odd mixture of Rabelaisian reporting and family advice.

It was just before she got extra work that she made friends with a girl who had interested her from the first. A pale, slight reed of a girl, delicate as an early wind-flower; eyes blue, full, and soft, with the look of an appealing child. Super-finely delicate skin, with the bloom of a baby. Her hair was gathered into a careless bundle low on her neck; her head was peculiarly shaped, so developed at the back that it seemed weighed down, so that it rested on the nape of her neck — a long, graceful neck. A babyish nose and very short upper lip, showing small, sharp teeth that rested on her nether lip that was a thick little scarlet line, above a small chin melting into her throat. A queer girl's face; it reminded Mary of a passionate, precocious baby. She was a favorite with the wild set, although she said scathing, sarcastic things enough to them — witty things and reckless things, broken by a racking cough. She kept paregoric in her desk, and sometimes French sweets. When she had money she spent it lavishly — bought roses and forced violets, and dined at a good restaurant, until she had none left; then went without with a jest.

The first evening Mary stayed late this girl was there with two others. Septima, that was her first name, put on her hat and asked Mary if she wanted some tea; they usually got it in from the baker's and shared a pot between two. Mary flushed painfully; the girl added, as if she did not notice it:

"You will find your extra money on the desk, with a receipt slip in your name; it is convenient sometimes to get it at once."

When eight o'clock came, they went out into the drizzly night together; she hooked her arm into Mary's to keep herself from slipping; they got to know one another a little as they walked home.

"You live in the block near my street," she said; "we can always walk home together if you like. Good-night."

CHAPTER VII

Christmas Eve — A White World

MARY DESMOND TURNED OUT of Broadway into West Fourteenth Street; the snow lay thickly and crisply on the ground; the clear air cut with the keenness of a cris. The electric light threw everything into brilliant relief. As far as one could see, a thoroughfare of white light and black shadow; a stream of laughing, sauntering humanity, a blaze of light at Macy's on the left, a globe of light farther up at Haverley's theatre on the right. Well-dressed men and women, with children clinging to their arms, laden with parcels; the inevitable cardboard envelope of candy, stamped with the magic name of Huyler, slung on one finger by a loop of ribbon. The merry jingle of sleigh-bells, gleams of bright color in the hats of the occupants and tassels of the horses' trappings; colossal negro coachmen, with handsome fur capes; cheap Jacks crying novelties. A monster wooden champagne-bottle, with a pair of down-at-heel elastic boots showing underneath — a pathetic ending to the brilliant gold top — bumped against Mary, as it stepped on to the sidewalk to exchange a greeting with a gorgeous cracker. Cold, light laughter, the lilt of children's voices, the smell of good cigars, and to Mary an atmosphere of strangeness that attracted, although an overpowering sense of loneliness crept in with it, and hurt, so that the drayman's "Run along, Sis!" struck a warm memory. She had a glimpse of a familiar face under a scarlet cap in one of the train of sleighs going up Fifth Avenue; of course, Cora, with whom she quaintly called her "best gentleman friend."

Someone caught her by the arm, as she tried to skirt the densely packed crowd of laughing people at the comer of Sixth Avenue, outside Macy's store; a compact mass, so tightly wedged that either getting in or out of the store seemed impossible.

"There you are. It's rather a farce to wish you a Merry Christmas away from all your own. How do you feel? You look real sick."

Sep! Mary scarcely knew her. A bunch of violets in the fur at her neck, a mass of Jacqueminot roses in her hand, and a lot of tiny parcels slung over her arm. Her eyes shone brilliant as stars in her odd little soft face; her cheeks were deliciously pink; something vibrant, glad, emanated from her to Mary and thawed the gathering ice in her.

"You were not at the office to-day," said Mary; "I was afraid you were ill."

"No," she laughed, — such a cheering ripple of a laugh; "I took French leave, — 'Gather the roses while ye may.' I guess happiness is just real mean, anyhow, and you've got to catch on to it when you get the chance. Something turned up unexpectedly. I have had a real good time."

The smile was feverishly bright now. "Just a real glorious time. I was going to look for you. Come right along home with me; I don't somehow want to be alone just yet."

They turned off Sixth Avenue into Thirteenth Street. She ran up the narrow steps of a clean-looking house and opened the door with her latchkey. It struck warm as they entered; they went up to the top. There was a large, square, carpeted lobby, with white porcelain German stove, a deckchair with cushions, a wicker rocker, and a little Japanese table with books, which gave it the air of a tiny sitting-room. Two doors led to rooms in the front and one to a room at the back.

"A rather nice Hungarian has that room; he's a violinist, seldom in. The man in the other only appears about once a month, so I have the place to myself."

Her room smelt like a bed of violets. A long three-cornered bookcase filled one comer; a lavender silk tea-gown with ribbons and lace lay across the bed with a lace petticoat, and silk stockings to match the gown. An absurd pair of tiny silver-embroidered Turkish slippers lay on the floor. There was a beautiful engraving of Dorè's "Paolo and Francesca da Rimini" on the wall over it.

"Come right in, take off your sacque, and go and sit in that chair near the stove; you find some new mags on the table."

She came out in a few minutes and put the roses on the table; opened a high tin box next the door, saying:

"This is my housekeeper, — a cunning arrangement, isn't it?" took out a saucepan and lit an oil-stove.

"Now, I am going to brew some spiced wine; you rest. They will send some soup from round the comer; such a dear little colored boy brings it." It was good to sit in the warmth, with the perfume of the flowers filling the air delicately; to lean one's head against the cushions and doze; Mary was almost asleep, when Sep roused her.

"Supper is ready, you poor, tired thing! Taste my wine. My old Aunt Harriet sends me a dozen now and then, and I keep a spice-box by me. I don't ask you if you can make your dinner of this, because I know what your kind of boarding-house is like. The soup is real good, isn't it? Then we'll have some rolls, and a bit of chicken, and some of Aunt Harriet's bakework. You look better already!"

There was something feverish, infectious, in her gay mood. It was as if the nerves in her frail body had been strung to a pleasant vibrancy by some cunning hand. Something electric, magnetic, came from her, so that Mary felt it reacting on herself. She sat with a tiny blue and white bowl of caramels in her lap, and watched the odd, quivering little face, through the smoke of the cigarette Sep was trifling with, blowing one ring of smoke through the other as she made it. Her tiredness vanished; they talked and made confidences. She had a little money every quarter, very little, it did not last long; this was a feast, she said with a laugh, because she was glad. She drew as much from Mary as the latter cared to tell her of her home life. They compared fathers.

"I guess mine is the Amurrican edition," she said; "less genial; he is death on patents (she pronounced it pattents), always boards with maiden ladies; rouses expectations of matrimony in their virginal bosoms. They think he's real elegant. You should see his Turkish dressing gown, dyed curls, and velvet smoking-cap. Yes, I have brothers and sisters; the boys are engineers out West; I have *one* sister, a hateful person, in Hoboken; two others are school-teachers in Maryland, and there is a little one," her voice broke slightly, "with the Dad; the boys pay for her; she is clever, goes to school. Yes, there *were* more of us. Dad was always prodigal, and the mother was old-fashioned. The modem Amurrican woman would sooner adopt a baby than mother one. Not much home life! Well, not in N'York, except amongst the Germans, perhaps. How long I have been in the office? On and off two years. I go away and come back when I want; one of the principals is a kind of connexion. I have passed lots of exams. I tried teaching for a spell" her little face puckered behind the smoke. "I reckon I did have a good time at it. I was only seventeen. The mistress got ill, fever and ague; they wanted an immediate substitute to run till the end of the term. I put on a white bunting, trimmed with Madeira work, and a gipsy hat, with poppies and corn-flowers, — cutest hat I ever had, — and went to see the committee. They were mostly middle-aged or old men; I guess the hat did it, and I was seventeen. I got the school. Such a pretty schoolhouse, with pine woods at the back; about thirty girls. Oh, I had a celestial time; the boys chopped wood and carried water for me, and all the mothers sent me cake and hardbake, pine tea and chill recipes. Fred Wood used to drive me to meeting in a buggy. I liked Fred; I have a lot of his letters somewhere. They had a camp-meeting, such fun," her eyes danced at its memory. "The minister was quite young; called one day, took me in hand when he found I was reading Bob Ingersoll, wrote me eight-page letters on sermon paper. All theology? What do you think? The end of him? Oh, he got Then there was Gus Reed. Mrs. Reed was a spiritualist; we used to seance in the front parlor — Miriam was a medium, Gus was a skeptic; we used to sit in the porch, he was great at astronomy—"

"And fond of the schoolmistress?"

"Well, he just was, poor Gus! I'm always sorry I fooled Gus. He gave it to me straight, too. There was good solid grit in Gus. I recited 'Archie Deane' on breaking-up day; the boys had me out three times. A man then wanted to take me West to recite, but mother was afraid. I went off laden with hampers, recipes, and farewell verses. Perhaps that was my best time. After that I was secretary to a blind preacher, a writer, in Connecticut, boarded with Uncle Reeves. He is a peculiar study. I wish I could take you to him; you wouldn't find his prototype across the pond. He ploughs, sows, and does all his own farm-work. Ruth and Annie help him; Sadie does the housekeeping. Ruth and Annie are big women, like Greek statues, wear no stays, sandals in the house, and knickerbockers and short skirts in the fields. They read Greek and Latin, shoot, fish, and swim, and recreate with mathematics. I read Euclid with Uncle Reeves. I guess they killed Aunt Sadie. She was a professor's daughter from Boston, a lovely musician — her harp is in Sadie's room. She plays the violin, goes out to the woods in the dark, and improvises crazy tunes; is a scared-looking thing with weird eyes; writes poetry. Mother used to say she favored Aunt Sadie; poor auntie! She fell in love with uncle in an imaginative moment, — Thoreau was a friend of his, — and then the loneliness and the rough life on the farm killed her. He calls it 'the life beautified.' Well, I guess you're tired; you look just too noble and strong for anything, but if one could crack that shell of yours I guess the kernel inside would be real sweet."

It was not till Mary was lying in her little lumpy bed, thinking over the evening, that the question came to her with puzzling persistence: What had happened to make this singular girl so vibrantly happy?

CHAPTER VIII

Christmas Day.

MARY FELT TOO TIRED, too shabby to go out. She stayed in bed, for she knew Uncle Hiram would come up and knock at her door, and ask her if she would have some of his Boston beans. He baked his own "lot," as he said, and always shared them with Mary. She was a favorite with Uncle Hiram. She had chosen a book of Norwegian peasant tales, by a man with an unpronounceable name, at the library, and snuggled down in bed to read them. Soon she forgot everything: the disagreeable atmosphere of her surroundings, her lack of almost all that made life pleasant, the vulgar attentions of the shipping agent, the staring ogle of the drummer. She was away in the fjords, and up in the saeters with Arne; sitting on the cliff with Marit, to the despair of the yapping dog, watching for "the happy boy." Away in a magic world of soul witchery and marvelous, impossible peasants. Later, when the name of Björnstjerne Björnson became familiar, she always associated it with a solitary Christmas in New York. Everyone was in to a noisy, early dinner; they were all hurrying off to matinees and lectures, so she went up again to her little room. She read and dozed all through the afternoon and, when the dusk had gathered closely in it. Uncle Hiram came up and cried at the door:

"Missy, missy, I guess it's kind o' lonesome lying in thar; you jist come down and jine us; there ain't no strangers."

She bathed her face, for Miley's curls had cropped up so vividly that they had tickled her eyes until the tears had come.

The whole family were gathered in a big front room. Mary thought she had never seen so many rocking-chairs; they were eating ices, in spite of the cold, and peanuts, and drinking Swedish punch. Mary had some tea; Uncle Hiram tried to persuade her to "lace it with Old Rye." Blossom, the younger daughter, played and sang coon songs, or some of "Lotta's" ditties, in a thin, sweet voice, and they all joined in the chorus. She played the accompaniment to an old-fashioned ballad for an elder married sister.

"Penelope used to sing that, way down Cape Cod; a niece of mine," said aunty, pausing in her rocking.

"Do tell!" cried Uncle Hiram, stopping to spit (they called it expectorate). "She was a real sweet girl, was Penelope!" rock again.

"She married such a homely fellow," sighed Aunty Sadie. "I can see her now, before me; she had an Indy muslin gown with sprigs, a Quaker-gray mantelette, and a white chip bonnet, with her hair all crinkled on her pretty forehead. They were Friends, were the Blossoms; mighty strict they were too. She broke her heart when he was killed down South—"

They chew, and rock, and muse silently, and Mary's thoughts fly off to the dead Penelope and her love-story before the war. The daughter-in-law calls her back by saying:

"Sing that song I like, Uncle Hi, do."

And Uncle Hiram and Aunty Sadie, with her squaw-like head held on one side, and her chocolate-flowered gown clinging to her thin frame, sing a doleful love-ditty about weeping willows and riven hearts; so that the fancy came to Mary that it must be the voice of one of those quaint hair memoriam brooches embodied in tune; and as she considered this strange couple, she wondered how they looked when they were young, and if they had loved one another. Someone stopped a chair and said:

"Sing Phoebe Brown's song, Mommer," starting to rock again; indeed, all the chairs are swaying noiselessly to the music.

"Phoebe Brown was a Marylander, an old sweetheart of mine," adds Uncle Hiram, as they search for the music. "She used to visit our way to her mother's kin. I was real sweet on Phoebe; we used to go to meeting together. I allus liked fair women! Phoebe had blue eyes, and hair the color of a ripe corn-cob, and she married a Primitive Methody. Sakes alive! how music do bring back things! It's kinder like table-rapping; calls up the sperrits."

He stopped his chair for a moment to send a well-directed volley of tobacco-juice into the cuspidor; then started again. Mary sat as at a play, and watched them as they chewed, and rocked, and grew ever more doleful. And Aunty Sadie sang, "Under the willows she's sleeping!" with tears at her own pathos; and they struck up a revival hymn with fervor, grew reminiscent, and talked of corn-popping in days gone by, and huckleberrying, and old sweethearts, and of little children — always the pick of the flock buried down Maine way — until Aunty Sadie, with her lies, and makeshifts, and struggles, faded away, revealing a soft, true woman' s soul underneath; but when Mary went up to her room after supper. Aunty Sadie and her greatest crony were sitting close together with an upturned tea-tray on their knees, and a pile of cents in the middle, playing cutthroat euchre.

Her black eyes were glistening eagerly, and her face was as hard as a Fiji idol's; and as Mary passed she heard her say with a vicious rasp, "What! three pips, and left-bower — well, I want to know!"

Mary used now to call for Sep every morning, and wait whilst she breakfasted in a baker's in Sixth Avenue — a pot of tea and a roll for six cents, with grapes or a banana added.

"Your appetite is not typically American," Mary once said. "The most ethereal-looking women eat enormous breakfasts, dozens of things, out of little white dishes set all round their plate."

"Yes, I don't see how they can. They've got to pay for it though; dyspepsia is the national disease, it makes an amateur apothecary of every Amurrican," laughed Sep.

They generally worked late, and walked home together. Mary had lost some of her bright, child look; she was turning over a great many pages in the book of life, and readjusting moral values. Once, in a lonely hour, she took her doubts, and whispered them to the wired square of a confession-box in a church of the faith of her childhood; for her brain was bewildered, her heart heavy; she was creeping back, along the lines of evolution, to the bedrock of things. But she found no comfort, only struck her hand and bruised it against the granite wall of ecclesiastical authority. Everything was small in comparison to an offence against that; sins against herself, against her neighbor, against humanity, might find atonement; but absolute submission to the authority of the Church, or no mercy. She stood at the end of the dark aisle, and looked up towards the altar; the red glow of the sanctuary lamp threw the gilding on the tabernacle into relief; I looked with a regret, and the realization that henceforth she must wander outside. From a little child she had loved to think of Christ — the Christ that was so sensible, so human, so little of a doctrinaire; but she had always found the Church instead.

She turned out into the night again. It was a sodden night, with a sickening smell of foul suds; for the steam puffed out from the laundries in the poor street in which she found herself, and seemed to hang about the doors in a cloud, unable to disperse. The chemist-shops and drinking-saloons alone seemed prosperous. Far ahead of her, looking into a shop window, the profile of a man's head stood clearly defined; vividly beautiful, in the sordid ugliness around her. The features were pale and pinched, the eyes hollow, the hair, a bright red-gold, hung in curls on his collar. The look on his face was familiar to Mary. She whispered to herself, "hungry," and hurried on. He was staring into a baker's, close to him; she could see the faint down on his upper lip; his boots were broken, his pea-jacket buttoned right to his throat. Her extra pay was in her pocket, she felt for the half-dollar, and laid her hand on his arm. He looked down at her with surprise — he was unusually tall — and raised his cap. The color rushed to her face, and her voice shook a little. She shoved the money into his hand, and said: "Please take it. Sometimes I am hard up too, and should like someone to help me. Don't refuse, will you?" He looked at it and her.

"How do you know it isn't my own fault? I may be the worst tough going."

She smiled, shaking her head.

"That hasn't anything to do with it if you are hungry!"

"Thank you."

A few moments later he overtook her and said: "Give me something for a mascot. I was in despair; perhaps this is the turn: a bit of pencil, — anything, — so long as it is yours."

She felt in her pocket; yes, she had a pencil, a little German-silver thing of no value; she laid it in his hand; their eyes met, and they both laughed.

Three weeks later, going to work one morning down Broadway (Sep could not stand the back streets), she saw him coming towards them, decently clad, with his mane cropped. He recognized her, with a hesitating move towards his hat; she bowed and smiled, and he raised it with a glad look. Mary had to undergo a fire of cross-examination from Septima, and all through the winter, whenever they went that way at that hour, they met him, always with the same flashing smile of greeting. She would have missed it — it gave a pleasant impetus to the day. Late March was upon them when she missed him for three mornings; she wondered if he were ill; then one evening she found him waiting for her outside her own door. He said, diffidently, "he wanted to have a talk with her; would she come with him and have tea, or something, please?" They walked on to a confectioner's, and he ordered some tea. He looked eagerly and timidly at her; it puzzled Mary then, as often after, why people seemed afraid of her at first. He told her he was going home, down South; everything was all right now; he wanted to thank her; he knew where she lived; he had seen her go in one evening. They talked of Europe — yes, he would probably go there soon. Mary Desmond was not then, or later, a woman that a stranger would ask for confidences. Men, women, and children confided in her, but they rarely tried to peer into the secrets of her own life. The making of ordinary small-talk was always difficult to her; she talked better to one person than to several. She was conscious of it herself. She remembered how, at the few rare dances to which she had gone whilst staying with relatives in Ireland, when she had been told sometimes that she looked more than pretty, men had let their eyes rest on her with an unmistakable look of admiration and got introduced to her; and gradually she had felt their disappointment. She was not amusing — life pressed too heavily upon her; she had not as yet acquired a keen enough sense of its ironies to treat it humorously. She wanted to talk to this boy, yet she felt like a solemn old owl; the lad stooped and kissed her hand as he wished her good-bye. Blossom, the unmarried daughter, screamed to her as she passed their door —

"I guess you've got an admirer, Miss Desmond; wait till you see the flowers upstairs."

Mary felt a little sorry as she bent over the green white bells of the lily-of-the-valley and the varied purple of the violets in the pretty basket on her dressing-table. The handle was tied with a satin ribbon; there was a line in pencil on it: "A little thank-you for a big service!" Nice boy, she thought — if she had only thawed more!

CHAPTER IX

SEP HAD PUZZLED MARY lately; sometimes she was in wild spirits, and came to the office in a pretty gown and absurd little patent boots, with what the girls called "Spanish insteps," and left early. Sometimes she had a week of depression, in which she worked languidly, with dull eyes; her cough was troublesome too, or she stayed away.

"You bet your bottom dollar, there's a man in it," said Cora — "serious case, temperature 104 Fahrenheit; patient irritable."

April came and the spring seemed to call insistently. Mary felt she could not have held out a day longer, were it not for her visits to the roof, where she drew in long breaths of the clean, strong sea air, with its vigorous smack of brine. Strange, how she felt the wonder of the season more in the close city than ever before in the country. She could hear the sap rising in a hundred imagined trees; see the buds, and burgeons, and fronds uncurl and burst; feel all the mysterious stirring, and working into life, in the world of beast and bird; the birthing of lambs and springing of foals in the meadows. The very jiva of the earth seemed to stir in her senses, making her conscious of her womanhood in some subtle way: calling, calling, calling in her, whispering and luring in her, until her limbs ached with the stress of it, and her soul was thirsty; the very atmosphere of the office was charged with it. Mary was realizing, for the first time, one of the tragedies of her sex, her affectability; the primitive element in her, untouched by its passage through all the centuries, keeping her sib to the earth and the things of it; closer to the forces of nature than man — genetic woman, answering to the call of the generative season. She was frightened at herself sometimes, frightened at the spring. It seemed to call in the night, and to make her realize herself and the possibilities hidden in her. One night she had lain down in her clothes, on her little, uncomfortable bed, and fallen asleep; and when she woke the room was flooded with moonlight, and the witch-virus that belonged to it. She had risen and undressed, leaned her elbows on the table, and looked at herself in the glass. How big one's eyes looked; how the light seemed to grow into them! She pulled down her hair in a loose, dark cloud about her ears. If she only had courage to wear it that way; how it threw the modeling of her temples into relief and helped her eyes! She peered into them. Strange how little one knew of oneself! The more one looked, the stranger the soul looking back at I one seemed to be. How white her shoulders were; how gently her breast rose, melting into the white — no, silver-white in that rare light — of her linen! And her arms, velvet-fine. She rubbed her cheek to her own shoulder, and the dance of the spring whispered again, and she moved to its beat, waved her arms around her head, and bent her body in lissom rhythm, until her feet followed, and she danced a quaint measure to her own fairness. Then she sat on her narrow bed and fell to thinking of the pity of it. Silk-fine, velvet-soft; all wasted! Out there, somewhere in the world, there were music and dance and laughter and clean love — just fancy, if someone were to come, someone whose very step would be a keynote of music, — to come and kiss her hands and lips, and lift her up and bear her away to a kingdom where love reigns supreme. She shook at the very thought of it. Fell a-thinking of all the others, just as she, silk-fine, velvet-soft, with all the white wonder of their beauty hidden under their workaday gowns until it shriveled and grew brown and hard as a last year's lemon. She wept at the thought of it, and then laughed till the tears came down at the quaintness of her own distress; shook her finger at the lady moon, and railed at her for a jade in league with the spring.

She had been busy making a new gown. Fate had been kind in devising means to procure her extra work. There had been a timely storm; no old-world apology for one — a new world storm, in which the American elements of surprise and racy go-aheadness had not been wanting. It had lifted a train off the track into a gulch, swooped down on a Swedish settlement, and deposited schoolhouse, teacher, and scholars in an adjacent lake, whirling the rest of the population before it as leaves on a fairy "blast." A flood, and the wiping out of a few frontier settlements by Apache Indians, did the rest. The latter, as Sep said, served also to restore the wavering belief of their childhood in Fenimore Cooper's braves. An agent, with Yankee snap and Irish blarney united in one enterprising body, had just visited the unhappy districts, and insured the entire populations for sums varying from fifteen to a hundred dollars.

"It's a tragic way to get my spring clothes," said Mary at lunch. "The Lord tempers the wind to the shorn lamb," said a girl with "water-waves" on her forehead, who sat under Talmage. Mary pointed out that the quotation was not Biblical, and that she was too conscious of her own insignificance to suppose that Providence organized a sort of matinee of disaster for her special benefit. Her life was beginning to endow her with a scathing quality of tongue, that made her feared later, until another turn of the wheel softened her.

Sep had not been to the office for two days. The superintendent asked Mary if she would find out if Septima were ill. She had been late herself both mornings, and failed to call; she would see on her way home. The colored girl let her in. She went upstairs and knocked at the door; no reply. She went in. A queer, heavy, sweet smell pervaded the room. Sep was lying on her side, with her face flushed and swollen, her mouth open, breathing heavily. Mary tried to rouse her, called her, shook her, lifted her into a sitting position, laid her down again. Then she took off her things and left them outside; lit the stove, and put on the kettle. She undressed her; the girl had lain down with most of her clothes on under her dressing-gown; an empty paregoric bottle lay on the floor. She filled a water-bag from the tap in the bath-room, and put it to her feet; found coffee in the housekeeper, and made a potful, extra strong. Then she put a towel under Sep's chin, and forced some through her teeth. She moaned and struggled, but roused enough to let Mary force a little down her throat; in half an hour she came to enough to try and see who was with her. She turned over with a cry, and buried her face in the pillow. Mary lowered the wick in the stove, leaving just enough light to keep the coffee hot, put on her things, and went home; had her dinner, a very lukewarm plate of lamb potpie, and told Aunty Sadie that her friend was ill, and she was going to stay with her. She bought a tin of soup on her way, and prepared to sit up. Sep was sleeping, breathing regularly; but she moaned now and then, and muttered a name, — always the same name, — "Carlos, Carlito," in every scale of tenderness. At midnight a man bounded up the stairs; an odd-looking man, with a crest of hair standing upright from his forehead. He clicked his heels together, bowed, and went into the room at the back; then all was quiet again. The gas went out with a sudden lapse into blackness; she lit a candle, found a night-light, and put it into the basin in Sep's room, and sat down in the chair again.

It seemed as if all the strange experiences, the new knowledge of the last months of her life, were passing in review before her. One event after the other detached itself from the chaos, and assumed its proper relative position. Women, women, women in all phases — what a part they played in it! There was a woman in her own house; she saw her occasionally on Sundays. A big, white woman, built on voluptuous lines, with deep-set, long-slit gray eyes — wonderful eyes — and thick, red hair that sprang straight from her forehead, like doll's hair, without any little short hairs to break the line. She had large white hands too, with a superb diamond ring on one finger. She slept next Mary. Every morning at half-past three she got up and dressed, and the bobtail car that passed at four stopped in the street below; when she was a minute late the driver rang the alarm-bell until she appeared. The hall-door shut, and the car jingled on.

"She is desk-lady," Blossom said, "in a morning breakfast-house down amongst the shipping; they open at four, and she's finished by nine. Comes home, goes to bed, and gets up at five. She has an evening post at one of the theatres. She has exquisite English clothes. I don't know why she boards here, but she pays Kate to wait upon her. She goes away generally for Sundays; goes to the French balls too, and Jake says he has seen her in queer places. Well, she's proper enough here, and one must live."

Mary was strangely alert, with one of those fits of introspective memory upon her in which images came flashing along. How vividly the pictures in childhood, with all their details, stages of feeling, smell, and color, stood out to-night! They danced along; she remembered the multitude of questions that used to rise in her; the deep, fundamental, undaunted, daring questions of the child-mind seeking light. The time of her first communion came back. How she had ransacked her little heart for a sin to tell! How she had swept and garnished her soul for the coming of the bridegroom! She can recall the long row of children in white robes, white wreaths, white veils, and shining tapers; the shiver of horror that swept through her at her own iniquity, because the stiffly crimped hair of a girl in front reminded her of unplaited tar-rope. The ecstasy of the actual moment, and afterwards the delicious, sleepy calm, as when one has been very hungry and eaten too much. If one had only kept that feeling of exaltation! But the years go by, and one searches into the issues of life, sees and hears much; and the second soul that sits in one, the accompanying genius that prompts and suggests, argues and concludes, points out that such moments of exaltation can be produced at will with practice. Ay, more, that they lie on the boundary line, and can easily merge into pathological phenomena. And the second voice keeps saying in there: "Nothing to do with you, all this! You have got to find your own way. You are just a traveller on a dark night with a lantern in your hand Her confirmation day, too! How the mad impulse had come to stand up in the midst of all the white-clad girls and black-coated boys and cry out, "It is a sacrilege which I am about to do; I don't believe any of it"; but she had squeezed her eyes tightly, and closed her inner ear and said: "Believe, as a little child, blindly; that is what you must do, Mary Desmond." Later on she had felt so ashamed of her cowardice, and cried out as she knelt in her room in her white gown, and turned her face to the sun (she always liked to pray to the great, invisible, all-wise Father of all, behind Christ and Buddha, and Mahomet and all the prophets, with her face to the sun). "O all-wise Father! I want to come to you, but they make me say I believe *their* teachings as a little child; and *you* know I don't, and what is the good of telling you lies?" And now that she had freed herself from the first bonds she was beginning to see a little tiny flame of light in the darkness. "Carlos, Carlito!" called Sep from the dark room in poignant whispers. The darkness seemed to draw closer, bringing a strange quietness with it, and it made, as it were, a black frame with a black velvet mount for the visions that came to her in such moments.

She could see an unfamiliar, flat country, and a dusty road, with cedar trees on a ridge to the west, and gently undulating hills, and the dawn breaking — a curious, yellow dawn. A well, with the stones about it worn by many feet, was at the side of the road; a torn cedar-tree grew by it, and next that the fallen trunk of another. The atmosphere was foreign and yet familiar, as if behind this life of hers; a memory within a memory, and the smell was the East. Every country has its smell, absolutely distinctive to those of finer sensitiveness. A lark — it reminded her of an English lark — was singing somewhere above, hundreds of insects began to chirp insistently in staccato notes, and the dawn came with ribbons and pennants and spears, floating streamers of light, until suddenly day stood smiling with his morning face under a canopy of gold. A figure came along the road, a serene figure wrapped in a coarse brown woolen mantle, with folds of white underneath, swaying as he walked with an easy joyousness of movement. He came and sat down on the fallen trunk, and clasped his hands round his knees, and drew in the morning air. His fine, dark beard curled closely to his chin, and his hair waved and ended in rings; and his face was Eastern, and his eyes glowed and smiled, wells of light. It seemed to Mary that *she* was projected into his soul, so that she felt as he felt, sitting there in the dewy morning — and it was so warm and light and serenely glad in there — no problems, they belonged outside, had no place there; it was warm and restful as when one lies awake with one's head on the shoulder of a sleeping well-belovèd on a summer night with the lattice open and the warm night air stroking one's cheek with a caress of satin; whilst the lap, lap, lap of the ocean comes faintly from somewhere in the distance, singing lullabies in the moonlight. It was so well with one; the gladness of it was as one of those unconscious moments of unreasoning happiness that come to one, one knows not why, and make one break into lilting song, so that one's feet trip to the music in one's own heart. People began to come along the road: a disheveled, haggard-eyed woman, with swollen lines under her lovely eyes and stains of wine on her crimson robe, halted, calling out a ribaldry; he smiled sadly, and she ran with a little contrite cry and crouched at his feet; and he laid his hand on her head and she wept silently. Then she rose and laid her lips to the hem of his white robe, and went her way with a peace that was in itself a joy shining in her eyes. And as the sun grew stronger Mary could see that the ground was enameled with tiny flowers, and she felt that he rejoiced, and that she was reading flower runes for the first time. Then children came tripping and climbed on his back, and up on his knees and kissed him; and he made little slits in the stalks of the flowers, and wove fragrant chains, and threw them over the little maids' heads, and gave them their tablets, and bade them begone with a caress. Mary passed along the road, and all those who drew water at the well went away with song and laughter or dancing steps. Then a youth came swinging along, a youth with fire in his eyes and a tender mouth; his steps broke into a run as he saw the man sitting at the well, and his cry of "Master!" was like a burst of melody in the woods at night. The Master whispered "Well-belovèd," and rose stretching his arms up as a glad child; and he rested his hand on the shoulder of the youth, and they sauntered across the flower-gemmed fields.

"That was Jesus!" whispered the voice. "Love, and light, and gladness! He never had many followers. Peter and Paul soured them all—"

She never knew if she slept, or saw these visionary pictures in half-wakeful consciousness. She sprang up suddenly and went into the room. Sep was sitting with her feet half out of bed; she looked at Mary with bewildered, questioning, heavy eyes.

"I thought I was dreaming that you were here."

"No; pinch me if you like. Have some coffee? I have kept it hot; and eat a cracker."

"I guess I've given you a lot of trouble. What time is it?"

"Almost two. I told them I was going to stay."

Sep drank the coffee, and Mary said:

"Let me do your hair; it must be so heavy with the hairpins in. Then I'll take mine down, and borrow one of your matinées, and lie down next you."

"You dear thing! I think you're just as sweet as you can live; and you look as if you had been in church, or saying your prayers."

"So I have," softly. "Now turn your head; you have a lot of hair."

"Mary," she said, after a while, "I've been wanting to tell you about myself for a long time; it doesn't seem straight not to. Once before I wanted to, and you wouldn't listen. Can you recall what you said about confidences? Well, do you remember Christmas, and once since? You came round one evening, and I was in the parlor; and when I came up afterwards, in tea-gown and slippers and lace frills, you hardly knew me. What do you suppose I keep that gown for, and the other frivols, like vestments in a shrine, and live by myself, and pay six cents for my breakfast and six dollars for my boots? I'll tell you — for a man — and a man who is married to another woman. There! why don't you say something? — your eyes can say enough when they want. There isn't anything wrong — I swear to God there isn't. I only see him once in a while. I don't take anything but flowers, or sweets, or just a dinner. He was married when I met him; and he doesn't care two cents about her, nor she about him; and he just worships the ground I walk on — and the whole thing is hopeless."

"Why did he marry her?"

"Because she's just lovely to look at. He's a Spaniard, beauty mad, and she just sent him off his head with her glorious body; and he was poor, and she is vurry, vurry rich."

"Well, I can't see that he's to be pitied. You are."

"There's no use saying anything against him. Do you see that?" She pointed to the engraving of Paolo and Francesca floating over a bottomless pit of flame.

Mary nodded.

"Well, I'd just see all creation cut into inchbits to save him an hour's pain; and I guess I'd go there to be with him for eternity. Now, are you going to give me up?"

"No, dear; why should *I* hold a judgment-day over you? I am bewildered; I can't understand anything just now. I seem to have lost a grip of everything since I came to America. I am confronted by all sorts of moral issues; and I haven't sifted them yet — to my own satisfaction. It seems to me, though, if you thought you were right you wouldn't have any pangs of conscience at all about it. In any case, it is bound to be a torture to you. *He* has evidently got the power of uniting the platonic with the actual."

"Oh, don't!"

"I used to think, Sep, before I came here, that the one question for every man and woman in a love affair was, Is this the half I am seeking to complete myself — the only one for my happiness? But, when one comes to think about it, that would only hold good after all for one kind of man and one kind of woman, not the many. Almost every natural man is, I suppose, for the many by inclination. Yet it might be worthwhile to pass one's whole life in the search; one's chance of happiness would be greater. Your man sold himself on the way. That is the terrible thing in being untrue to the finest instincts in one's soul — one can never confine the consequences of one's tie to oneself. Poor little Sep, like a bit of thistle-down!"

"You are a great-hearted, dear thing, Mary Desmond!"

"Am I? I doubt it. I think I am just like a little child with a puzzle; I am getting inside it and outside it, and I am not quite sure which it is — kind of playing ninepins with my old values; knocking down all my old wooden men; and I have not yet found new ones to replace them. It will be rather lonely when I get into a ninepin land of my own, where no one understands my game or wants to learn it. Your head is very hot; give me your hand; let us try to sleep."

When Mary woke, Sep was up getting breakfast.

"Time to get up," she called. "I am going to write and ask for a week's leave. I'll go to Albany to some cousins — I always have a real good time there. I guess that will fix me up. You look very peaked."

"Oh, I'll be all right when I've had my bath."

"Cold?" with a shiver. "You Spartan!"

"It never is cold," laughed Mary. "You keep your houses at such a temperature that if you didn't use ice you'd have to drink lukewarm water. I shall not be long."

CHAPTER X

SATURDAY AFTERNOON, A WEEK LATER, Mary found her waiting in the lower hall as she left the office. Silk violets in her pretty hat, real violets in the breast of her new spring jacket — radiant as the earth after a shower. She linked her arm into Mary's, and they started to walk up Broadway. Up near Twelfth Street a jaunty little man, with glossy hat, glossy hoots, and airily tied scarf, greeted them with an exaggerated wave of hat. It needed no introduction to tell Mary his relationship: he was still more like a precocious baby than Sep herself.

"Charmed to meet you. Friend of my daughter? Wonderful specimen of American enterprise, this daughter of mine. All the American daughters are wonderful! Dianas in chase of the nimble dollar, with their quivers full of arrows, tipped with the iron of horse sense. You are the Irish friend? Wonderful people, the Irish! Isle of saints; emerald gem of the Western world; land of poetry and politics! Curious run of P's — ever notice it? Potatoes and poetry, potheen and politics. You have an unkind way of keeping the saints and sending us the politicians. You supply us with mayors and policemen. Curious, but a fact! I assure you there is a large political body in America who speak with a nasal brogue. A — ah! another curious fact, my mentioning emerald gem. Man I went to see coming along — interesting man, says he can make them; verdant statement! yet there may be a patent in it. Ta-ta!"

Sep's and Mary's eyes met and interchanged a smile, and Sep said, with delightful mimicry:

"Wonderful thing, fathers! Wonderful thing, mine!"

"What State does he come from?"

"South Carolina; the mother was New England." The spring slid into the summer, and the office became a furnace; the girls lived on ice-water and slices of melon. If it had not been for the blessed breeze that one could catch in snatches on the roof, Mary felt that she would have had to give in. Jimmy, the elevator boy, used to shake his head in patronizing sympathy as he took her up to the top. The delicate bloom of her face wilted in the stifling air; it almost seemed as if one were inhaling something astringent with every breath; it had a drying quality, and a glow struck back from the pavements and burned through the soles of one's shoes.

One Saturday afternoon towards the end of July she fainted, sliding quietly off her stool. As the work was slack the superintendent gave her two weeks' pay and bade her take her holiday. She dragged wearily homewards; she had no sunshade, and although she walked along the shady side of the street, the pavements burned, and the air glowed as in an oven. The little colored children alone seemed to revel in it; they tore round Washington Square on roller skates, or buried their lovable black faces and glistening teeth in great topaz-pink slices of melon. All the "colored ladies" on the stoops, or lolling in the doorways, or gossiping from the windows had muslin "waists" or print matinees, whilst her beige gown stuck to her shoulders. No season is favorable to genteel poverty. The way home seemed endless; she got there at last, quivering in every limb, and toiled wearily up to her room. The law student met her on the stairs.

"Home so early?" he asked.

"Yes, I broke down; so I have got a couple of weeks' vacation."

"Is that so? Going away?"

"No; I am afraid they must be spent here; but the rest is good, anyway."

"Don't know so much about that; depends on how you get it. You must use my veranda. You can bring down your own chair. It's cool there all the afternoon. The sun shines straight into your room; you won't be able to bear it."

"Thank you, I will."

Her room *was* hot; everything in it always felt warm to the touch, even when she did not get home until after sundown. She could not sleep in the mornings either, in spite of the awnings. She took off most of her clothes and flung herself on her bed; it was good to lie and doze, even if one's head seemed to throb in time to the dance of the moths in the sunrays, and one's body to be a patent heat-absorber, and one's hair clung to one's head, and one felt sticky and yet dry — heat-dried. She recalled how someone had said on the voyage out:

"N'York climate! It isn't a climate, it's hell — hot hell in summer, and cold hell in winter, to punish you either way!"

She was glad the student had offered his veranda; it was cool there. She would be dull, not to go anywhere, but it would be good to just rest and nothing else. Sep was away at Cape Cod; had gone after one of her despondent fits. She had not seen anything of her own connexions; they had been to Europe, and spent the summer at Newport. She dropped off to sleep.

It was late when she awoke; she dressed listlessly and went down to dinner. Aunty Sadie met her on the stairs, shifted her wad of gum, stroked Mary timidly on the shoulder, and begged for a dollar. Mary paid her a week's board; it was not due, she seldom owed it, for she often advanced as small a sum as a quarter. Aunty Sadie used to glide up to her in the morning as she came down to breakfast, deposit a worry with her in exchange for a trifling loan, and steal silently away. "Poor woman!" thought Mary; "she leads a tortured existence in which the three furies masquerade in the guise of poverty, debt, and makeshift."

She spent hour after hour on the veranda. Sometimes the law student would come and talk to her, or lead her to talk, or bring her a book; sometimes he would sit and smoke silently. When the dusk fell he used to play to her — he was a fine musician. His reticence fitted her mood; she had grown silent herself lately. She was making up her mind to go back, to try London. Everyone had said her chance was better in America, when the need of earning her living had become imperative. The Major was in London. Well, in its way it would be as foreign as New York. She must devise means of getting there. She had a great yearning after her own people; after all, there was no one like one's own. Peggy must not come out to her, as they had planned at first. How pretty Peggy had grown! She could see her quite plainly as a quaint little girl, crying over the baby near the window when the little sister was dying. And now she was grown up and liked pretty things and comfort. No, it would never do. She ached to see the boys too. On the last Friday of her holiday the student said to her:

"Come to Jersey to-morrow. You haven't been there; we can go by an early boat. I know every inch of the woods, and all the unspoiled places. Then you can rest all Sunday, and be fresh to start work."

Mary hesitated; the old home ideas of propriety, the chaperon idea, cropped up; but she wisely put them aside and consented. She woke early, with some of the old childlike excitement at the prospect of a treat. She had bought a muslin gown from Blossom; that clever young person used to invest in what she called "a web of muslin" and make it into gowns; but she "couldn't seem to take to this one nohow!" so she sold it for a trifle. Mary looked at herself as she fastened it — it became her. The feeling of being becomingly dressed, of looking well, restored some of her old brightness and self-confidence. She smiled as she thought of the power of clothes — thought whimsically, if the State would only bathe everyone compulsorily every day and dress them in new purple, they would all live up to it. Uncle Hiram opened his eyes when she came down, and patted her kindly with his great hand (it roused comment amongst the male boarders that, whilst she permitted such familiarities to Uncle Hiram and Aunty Sadie, she repelled all their advances), and went to fetch her coffee, exclaiming:

"My, missy, I didn't know you! You should always wear light things; it do make quite a considerable difference; not but what you don't allus look kinder high-toned. Eh, mother! don't our little lady look real sweet?"

Aunty Sadie pinned some roses in her waist; and she was conscious of an expression of surprise behind the student's glasses. On looking back to her American experiences, she always remembered this one day as perhaps the pleasantest. Nothing particular happened; nothing particular was said' they sat in the woods and listened to the sea in the distance; talked of books, exchanged ideas. Their arguments were always impersonal. They had come home through the dusk, and shaken hands on the stairs, and she had said:

"Thank you so much; I have had a lovely day!"

And he had laughed and replied, *"Nix zu bedeuten Frauldin!"* one of the standing jokes in the house since a German boarder had stammered it in reply to the apologies of a raw "help," who had upset a plate of chipped ice on his head. She hummed a little tune as she undressed, and slept the dreamless sleep of a tired child.

She dozed all Sunday afternoon in the rocker; the student had gone out early in the morning, and it was evening when he came into the room, nodding a silent greeting. He sat down to the piano, and improvised as the mood seized him. Later, when he did come out on the veranda, she saw that his clothes were dusty, and his face lined with weariness. She remembered that Blossom once said he used to walk right out into the country; in the general opinion of the house he was a "crank." The moon mounted higher; the sumac leaves cast flickering darts of shadow on to the veranda; a little whispering breeze rustled through the trees. Mary sighed involuntarily as she thought of the office. He turned, saying softly,

"Your holiday is nearly ended, little lady!"

"Yes," answered Mary, as she stood up to say good-night; "and I owe you a thank-you; you have made it nice for me."

"So? Well, perhaps it has been my holiday too!"

And he put back a little strand of hair that had blown loose on her temple, and turned and gazed down again into the shadows; the shadows that lay closely in the four squares of the block at the back, closely as in a vault.

It was years after, when Mary had grown wiser in the ways of men, that it struck her that perhaps her lack of consciousness of herself as woman, and man as man, may have made her a little careless of the law student's feelings.

CHAPTER XI

Sep came back to the office; but she often missed a day, and ran the gamut of all moods. As the "chipmunk" said:

"Her temper is like an eating-house potpie! You never know what you'll strike on next." When she wanted Mary the latter responded warmly and fully; otherwise did not force herself upon her. Sep had told her that *he* was going to Spain in the fall.

"With his wife?" asked Mary.

"No," she had replied.

Mary had drawn her own conclusions, for the girl talked often and eagerly of places in Spain. To have remonstrated or argued would have been of no avail. Sep was of the kind to fight her own demons, and would have resented interference; so Mary felt she could only wait and help, if possible.

Then one day Sep failed to appear again. Mary felt unaccountably, strangely anxious. She had to work overtime, but she hurried on her things, and went home in the elevated cars. A dull feeling of uneasiness gnawed at her chest; it seemed to be in the air about her, to choke her, to fleer at her; she could not shake off its dreadful oppression. Aunty Sadie met her at the door, and told her a colored help had been round twice for her.

"I reckon your little lady friend is sick," she added.

Mary turned back without a word, and ran to Thirteenth Street. She knew in some subtle way that her going, or not going, would make no difference — not the slightest difference. It almost seemed to her as if Sep herself said so, with the cynical smile rippling over her baby face. The door was ajar; she ran upstairs; the landlady, a fat Frenchwoman, with grizzled white hair turned back over a cushion, came to meet her.

"A-ah, Mademoiselle, vous voilà! I am glad you are come."

She talked volubly, but sensibly.

"La pauvre! she has taken too mooch of zis villainous paregoric. You can say vif me, she have the custom to take it, for her pains, ze neuralgie, you know it! I told Monsieur ze Doctor so; he have gone to get somezing. He vant ze papa fetched; you can find him for us, hein?"

"Yes, Madame, I'll go for him; but let me see her first!"

Madame turned to whisper to the Hungarian, who was standing in the lobby, and Mary went into the little room. It smelt heavy; Sep had a blister on her neck; her head was slipping; Mary put her arm under the girl's shoulder to raise her up, with the tears filling her eyes. As she drew her hand back she felt something hard, a little bottle; she closed her fingers over it. She kept it concealed as Madame returned. The doctor was running up the stairs, followed by a nurse. The landlady came down after her, and beckoned her into the parlor, closing the door.

"La pauvrette," she cried, "she had trouble! it is not worz wile, n'est-ce pas. Mademoiselle? to speak of Monsieur to her familee; it help nozzing. Zis package was on ze table; it is directed to Mademoiselle."

"A book," Mary said.

She got into a street-car and stopped at Twenty-second Street. She did not know the number, but thought she could find the house. She had waited outside, on New Year's Eve, whilst Sep had gone in with some things for the little sister. She asked for the father; he came with an air of jaunty surprise. She made him understand, but had some difficulty in preventing him from blurting it out to the child. And it was not until the maiden ladies had braced him with brandy, found his gloves and silver-topped cane, and she had declared bluntly that she would not wait another second for him, that she succeeded in getting him under way. She felt a hard irritation and dislike for this selfish, chirpy little man; his absurd baby face brought back Sep — Sep with her birdlike daintiness, incisive, cynical tongue, and frank Bohemianism, with the odd strain of Puritanism ever at war underneath — Sep, who wore lace petticoats to the office, who always had flowers under her little flower face. She let him go upstairs, went into the parlor, and looked at the little blue vial. It was not so tiny after all, as if it had no neck. "Poison," in tiny red letters, and "Laudanum" underneath. She debated a moment;

then thrust it into her pocket, went upstairs, and sat in the chair and waited. The nurse came out and shook her head. Madame went downstairs consoling the pauvre papa. The hours dragged; the doctor came and went. He returned finally with a brother practitioner, a man with an atrocious, twanging voice, who gave orders like a drill-sergeant. The married sister came up with her husband and went down again. One thing they were all clear about — she had had neuralgia, had taken an immense quantity of paregoric, probably on top of some laudanum; and her heart was weak too.

At half-past one it was over. Mary went downstairs; the door was open, for the colored girl had set it wide to let the poor departing soul go out without a struggle. The law student was leaning against the railings smoking, with his hat tilted over his eyes and his hands thrust in his pockets. He threw his cigar away as she went out, and said:

"I came round at twelve to see if you were coming back, then I waited. You are shaking all over and are cold" — he pulled her hand through his arm. "You must have something hot to drink."

Strange New York night! with its lighted streets, running horse-cars, open restaurants and eating-houses, and people sauntering along as if it were their day. Mary had often leaned out of her window in sleepless nights and watched them. Wondered where they were going to, when they slept, why they were out when all the world and his wife were abed? She never had any very clear recollection of that night, but black coffee and fin-cognac always brought it back to her — perhaps that was what the law student gave her. She lay down in her clothes and heard each hour strike; at eight, as she was bathing her face, someone came to her door and went away again. She opened the package — Sep's Dante, with her name in full, Septima Evangeline, and, underneath, Mary's own name, with "from Sep" added, and yesterday's date. Lower down she had written —

"Love is stronger than death, for death has a limitation: death can but kill one, love may murder two."

She found a basket of white flowers outside her door, with the law student's card. "For your little friend," was written in pencil underneath his name. He must have been out early, she thought; it is very good of him. She took them with her; the blinds were down; an odd fancy came to her that Sep herself met her on the stoop and went up with her, leaning heavily, as was her way, on her arm. Up to look at her little, straight, white, dead self, and that she said:

"Not much of a baby now, Mary mine! Look, how the softness is stiffened to dignity! You didn't guess the iron underneath; same old iron! came over in the *Mayflower*."

She told the superintendent as soon as she got to the office; was sent for to the manager's room and told it over again; and at lunch-time she had to repeat it to the girls — and all the time the little blue bottle lay in the bottom of her pocket. Cora let her bangs go uncurled; the "chipmunk" cried over her entries in the O. K. ledger; and the whole office subscribed — even Jimmy, the elevator boy, and the male clerks in the department below — and sent a white cross and a violet lyre to put on her coffin. And a reporter wrote an obituary, as only an American reporter can, with the heading: "Cut off in the white flower of her youth; verdict, death by misadventure." It passed into different papers, under various headings, until it reached a climax as: "Paregoric on the War-path."

The pendulum swung back slowly but surely; the office regained its cheerfulness; only Mary missed the little square shoulders, the whiff of violets, when the breeze crept in; the quaint cynicisms and pretty attentions. Her back ached always now, and sometimes, when she worked overtime, she roused with a start to realize with a feeling of terror that she had copied a whole page without seeing, so far as she could recall, a single line of it. At first she used to read carefully down to see if she had not been writing the last line *seen* over and over again, — but no, each entry was correct. This got to be a regular thing, and once she found herself at her own door, with no memory of anything after Canal Street. All that lay between, — the crossing, shops, people, which side of the street she had walked, — all was absolutely a blank; that half-hour of her existence was nil. It frightened her, and the longing for her own called in her blood; her stomach began to revolt at the coarse, ill-cooked food, and sometimes, when she was up on the roof, the homesickness tore so at her heartstrings that it was almost beyond endurance, and the waves played a *ranz des vaches* outside.

One evening she went to see a doctor. He sounded her chest, asked her many questions, and wrote a prescription, saying:

"I can only give you a tonic. You are very finely strung, the climate here adds to your nervous irritation; you want rest; get back if you can. No, I won't take a fee, child, I'll feel hurt if you mention it; you are only a guest in New York, anyway."

She took her watch and called into the establishment of one Ephraim Moss. It was a dirty little den, with a heterogeneous collection of clothes, jewelry in dusty trays, and bundles of silk handkerchiefs. The outlines of a woman's profile showed through the dusty glass of a door to the back.

He opened the watch, closed it with a snap, and said: "Two dollars fifty."

Mary calculated mentally — ten shillings.

"It cost fifteen," she said.

"Ah, buying is one zing, selling is anozzer. Ze people here who vare zilver votches vare Zherman zilver."

"I wouldn't sell it, only I want to buy some medicine," she added weakly.

The little grimy man caressed the end of his fleshy nose, and looked at her over his glasses. "You are ill, alone here? We Chews take more care of our vimmens. I vil give you dree dollars!"

Mary nodded. He gave her three dirty bills out of a leather bag. She thanked him, and turned into the street again. She had only gone a few steps, when she felt a touch on her arm. A girl with a glorious face, full-lipped, deep-eyed, magnificently modeled, and, it must be confessed, grimy, was looking at her. She held out another dollar and said:

"Yes, you must have it; I told my husband; it is all right."

CHAPTER XII

One noon hour in September, Mary went out and turned down Broadway. It was thronged with men; walking was difficult; but she found it impossible to listen to the gossip in the office: the eternal confidences about gentlemen friends, or scandals gathered from the daily papers. She was stopped by a jovial "Hillo, little woman!" and found herself face to face with her first acquaintance in New York. How much she had learned since the day she took him her letter of introduction! He looked sun-tanned and immensely cheerful. He turned back with her.

"Well, how is the world using you? We haven't seen much of you; been all over the place; you look seedy."

"I am." The tears got into her voice — a short silence.

"Would you like to go back?"

"Yes, but that seems a bit hopeless just now."

"Not a bit of it! I can work a pass all right. When would you like it for?"

"Oh, any time; I have nothing to keep me a day."

"All right, little woman! buck up, and I'll fix it for you. Good-bye."

Some days afterwards she found a letter on her desk when she arrived in the morning: a first-class pass on the S.S. *Sicily* running from New York to London, a cattle-ship, carrying a limited number of passengers; sailing Saturday, 30th September, A.M. Ten days more. The words danced up and down in a bizarre way — ten days — they came and went (as words written in certain chemicals will appear and vanish as they are held to the fire) between her entries; danced across the policies, seemed to be stamped inside her eyelids. She calculated that, given the usual extra work, she would land in London with a little over two pounds in her pocket. The time went quickly; she asked permission to terminate her work on Friday night. There was no difficulty. Her place could be filled up on Monday morning; one writing machine was as good as another. Sep had been her only intimate; she was too "toney" for the wilder set in the office; too impatient of cant to be popular with the religiously inclined. Her only farewells were made to New York City from the top of the roof, and to Jimmy the elevator boy. She gave him her Shakspeare. He shook hands; his keen little face, with its look of supreme self-confidence, was momentarily soft. He wished her a real good time, and guessed she would hear of him some day in the future, when he had worked his way up — he was going to write his name in the annals of America, or know why. She liked Jimmy.

Uncle Hiram and Aunty Sadie were "real sorry"; the law student uttered his habitual laconic "Is that so?" but he came to her room the evening before her departure, and asked her to spend it on his veranda.

He had put two old Venetian glasses and a bottle of wine, with some biscuits and fruit, on a small table. He played all the evening: played in silence, but Mary felt that he was playing to her. Then he had come out on to the veranda, and bent his long, gaunt, hollow-chested figure down, and looked into her face, saying: "You are glad you are going? You needn't answer me. It is in your eyes and round your mouth. Your face is a marvelously sensitive register of your feelings." After a pause — "You are going to be remarkable in some way! You have magnetism, tenderness, understanding; but yet one feels that you may grow aloof, outside all goodness, and beyond all wickedness, on a lonely pillar of your own." The moon hung high like a silver paten in the blue above. He touched his glass to hers and wished her luck, and then he said, half as if to himself, — sometimes she scarcely knew if he meant to address her or not, —

"Yes, I wish you all luck. You will go into others' lives as you came into mine, and you will go out of them as you go out of mine. I doubt if you will ever know exactly what you can be to other human beings — perhaps if you did you would be less. No, I shall not see you in the morning. Sometimes on a walking tour one gets belated; the gloom envelops one suddenly, as if one is caught by a dark, close blanket flung over one's head. One is walking wearily along in the gloom; the fear of the unknown makes one's steps falter, and one's heart dismayed; suddenly somewhere out of the shadow a little strain of melody pierces to one, a strange, haunting little tune, with courage and love in every note of it, and an elusive quality that defies one's efforts to seize it. But one forgets the gloom, the fears and weariness and bewilderment that are driving one off the right road. One is saved for the time being, but — one never makes one's own of the little melody. I will say good-bye now, and God keep you! When you go upstairs, open your window and I will play to you."

And he rested his hand on her head for a moment, and then turned, and she left him gazing into the great four-square in the center of the block of houses, that stretched away like a black vault between them.

At noon next day she stood on the deck of the *Sicily*, leaning over the rail, watching the cattle-jobbers. Their brogue came up as a smell of home; a little colored boy was selling matches, showing his white teeth as he laughed. As they swung round, and everything receded gradually, she felt a throb of gladness at the thought that her face was turned towards the Old World once more, and if she had any regret, it was a. purely personal sorrow at leaving a little of the white shimmer of her youth behind her.

CHAPTER XIII

St. James's Park.

THE END OF OCTOBER; a mild, warm Saturday.

Two soldiers and a couple of girls were rowing in a boat; one of them was singing a musical ditty, and it floated across the water through all the other sounds. Whenever there was one of those hushes in the traffic that sometimes come with startling suddenness, one could hear the quick, rattling thud of grounding arms, and the measured beat of recruits' feet in the barrack-yard. The sparrows twittered and shrieked; the staccato quack, quack of frightened ducks struck harshly, then trailed away as they flew across the pond.

Carriages, cabs, hansoms, crossed and intercrossed, and streamed past the palace gates in two files. Nurses, children, loafers, crunched along the graveled walks, or sat and talked, or nodded or slept on the seats. Mary Desmond was sitting in a side path near the water. Her face looked inched, more impassive, as if its sensitive quickness of expression had been arrested, numbed by some outside influences. She was hungry and tired. She had walked all the way from Bayswater to Regent Street; to an office with a great name for its philanthropic aid to women workers. She was weary when she got there, and she sat and waited until her turn came.

"No certificates? that makes it so difficult."

Mary had intended to say how sore her need was, had planned how she would say it; but the alert, clean-scrubbed-looking Englishwoman, with the metallic voice, cultured accent, and attentive but abrupt manner, made her realize all at once how little really it concerned anyone. She felt the racial difference keenly, — felt how irrational Irish people were, with their interest in everything and everyone's troubles, their expansive confidences, their almost childish want of reticence. No; one had to knock and send in one's card at the door of Englishmen's hearts. The woman ran down her book with her pencil.

"You wouldn't care to try a place as help to an old lady? She keeps a woman for the rougher work, but you would have to do all the lighter things — read and mend, and exercise the poodles. It's in the country. She only gives a year £14 — No? Well, you see, without experience it is almost impossible to get a residential position. I really don't think we have anything at all likely to suit on our books. Yes, there is a society of that kind. Miss Brown, find the address of the Society for the Promotion of Employment for Women. There it is; good morning." Sharp rap of pencil. "Next, please!"

She was to meet the Major in the Park. She dragged slowly down Regent Street. This monster city, with its irregular streets, the slums elbowing the aristocratic squares, that made it so difficult to find one's way, bewildered her. Some of the adventurous spirit that had acted as an incentive in her first venture was quelled. London seemed gray, repellent. It seemed to lack the color, the polyglot atmosphere, that made New York a sort of sample-card of the cosmic panorama. (Later she changed her view.) It was lonely in New York, but it was beginning to grow on Mary that loneliness in London would be more cruelly absolute. She could scarcely define the difference, yet it met her everywhere —in the trains and omnibuses, the offices to which she climbed in search of work in answer to advertisements. There was less frank, human freemasonry, as it were. She felt that she would not dare mount one of the stairs here and boldly ask for work, as she had done in New York, relying on her need and her personality to awaken an interest, even though only momentary. It was conveyed to her in some subtle way that individuality, unless backed by wealth or interest, counted for less in this great repellent prison of a city, where each man and woman looks with a certain distrust at every unknown person.

She almost laughed to think of how she had looked up the names of the city members who could sign reading tickets for admission to the Apprentices' Library in New York and chosen one at haphazard; how she had got leave to go out one afternoon, and entered the magnificent offices in Broadway which he occupied as head of a great safe company; the courteous way in which he had received her, put aside his writing, and, after a few kindly questions, filled up the order and smiled her out as he might a duchess. Intuition told her that she dare not risk experiments of that nature in London — no, it was certain that one felt more at home in America. One had not that crushing sense of being of as little account as one of those white duck-feathers that fluttered and rose and drifted a little way, to be caught and rolled over and over, at the sport of the breeze. She felt so stupidly tired sitting there — so stupidly tired. A man came by; she felt his eyes run over her. He passed, tapping his stick on the gravel; came back, — tap, tap, — passed; returned; sat down on the other end of the seat and said, "Ahem!" She could feel his eyes. An overpowering, violent sense of irritation seized her. Why should he come and stare at her? She had never even looked up; only seen his hateful, splay feet, with their tan gaiters. She turned and looked at him. Ugh! what a beast! As if there was a woman living who could see anything in that flat, white, flabby face, or the gray curls twisting round the brim of his hat. Perhaps her eyes expressed her thoughts, for he got up and walked away. She looked at her little gloved hands lying in her lap. How heavy they lay; how heavy she felt altogether, as if she were cased in lead, and might easily— just as if she were to wish it ever so little — easily sink right through the seat! She crossed one foot over the other, — it was an effort, — and fell to considering it. She smiled; she always had to smile when she looked at her own feet. It was like meeting two good-humored little acquaintances. Funny how individual they got, how much of oneself is expressed in one's boots! Ay, if all the numbers of the same make in the world were to be piled in a heap — she had to laugh again at the thought of this extraordinary heap — she would be able to pick out her own. "Poor little patient feet, your boots are wearing out sadly; naughty little left boot, always wearing out first!" She got quite confidential with them, downright sentimental; in a few minutes more she would have been weeping over them and herself. Then Big Ben boomed out twice. Half an hour late — poor Dad! he never could keep an appointment!

There he was, poor old Dad! He looked older, less full of the joy of life, less buoyant. Her heart rushed out to him in a sudden gush of sympathy.

"Any luck, little woman?" he asked as he came up.

"No; going to another place this afternoon. It is difficult —" she was going to add, "when one has no fixed calling," but the reproach implied might hurt, so she broke off. Her ever-clearer seeing into the tangled issues of life was making her tolerant. The inner voice that always had its way in there whispered: "After all, where is the use? Life is short; you can't judge anyone; you can't do it fairly, unless you go back through all the ages of each man's existence, weighing the life and circumstances of each ancestor, and perhaps if you could do that you would only be narrowing the responsibility to a point in the will of the great First Cause. Look to yourself, Mary Desmond," it kept whispering; "no man can do more than toe the line that is between him and every other man's soul!"

"Damn difficult! I thought I could have managed a letter for one of the papers myself." He stopped to look at a well-dressed woman coming towards them, with a military-looking man; turned round and gazed after her with sparkling eyes —

"There's a darlint for you. Superb figure! First really handsome woman I've seen since I crossed the Channel. I'm hanged if the women are as good-looking as they used to be!"

And he launched into enthusiastic descriptions of lovely women he had known — women who had made havoc of hearts in the'sixties — with many a tender epitaph to their memories. Drew Mary's attention to queer effects of light on a building near the exit; paused to make a scathing criticism on a new infantry uniform, putting everything seriously unpleasant out of sight with an easy philosophy.

Near the Houses of Parliament he pointed her out a shop where she could get some tea; slipped a florin into her hand and went his way, his hat cocked knowingly over one ear, and a spring in his step and a light in his eye that beguiled every cabby to hail him as a likely fare.

CHAPTER XIV

Saturday night in Christmas week.

GOODGE STREET, RUNNING INTO Tottenham Court Road, was ablaze with light and bustle, and seething, laughing, shopping humanity. It was too early yet for the rush; troops of girls were going home from their work, linked arm in arm in groups of three or four, casting pert challenging glances back over their shoulders to the salesmen. The butchers' shops were one gory spectacle of meat and skinned rabbits. The blue-aproned youth, whose curls looked as if they were anointed with suet, were screaming:

"Buy, buy, buy rosy meat, rosy meat, rosy meat; fine bunnies, bunnies, bunnies!" more in anticipation of custom to come later on than anything else. Wreaths of holly and ivy and Japanese lanterns dangled from the stalls. An umbrella vender, twirling an antique on the palm of his outstretched hand, was amusing the crowd by assigning each gamp to a political parent. So that the virtues of a fifth-hand Fox's paragon frame and the opinions of Brummagem Joe were paradoxically united.

Mary Desmond came along; she walked very erect, though her steps lagged. Her face looked drawn; only the brave eyes, with the question in them, looked straight into the world as ever. She smiled with a quick flash of amusement that creased out the tiredness marvelously, as the raucous voice reached her of a man who was holding forth on the merits of burdock, as a specific for everything, from the mucous membrane to the spleen.

"Listen, my friends, to wot one of hour greatest Hinglish potes says abat this wonderful plant. Listen to Byron on the burdock."

Earlier in the day she had been sent on a message. She had gone on the top of the 'bus, although the conductor had looked surprised. She had sat and listened to the chaff of the driver and conductor, had endorsed the opinion of the latter that Christmas was a fair sickener, all very well for them as 'ad plenty of money, an' a bloomin' fraud for them as 'adn't."

"Look at the traffic!" he had appealed tragically. The pavement was thronged. Parcel vans blocked the crawling line of 'buses. "Curious," she thought, "the city was like a great heart; a block in one of the big arteries sent a shock right through all London; could be felt even in one of the veins at Hammersmith." Her head got dizzy at the thought of the great human ant-heap. How that conductor chafed! He was a pessimist, and the driver was a confirmed optimist. Did anyone really care for Christmas? She would, if she had plenty of money, and could give lots of things away. But she had no concern with all the pretty things in the windows ablaze with light.

Suddenly there was a hoarse cry, and a crowd pressed forward from a narrow side street. She shrank back, to find herself pushed against the steps leading to a door; her shoulder was bruised by the impact.

She could see a policeman's helmet bobbing up and down in the crush. The traffic was stopped higher up by the ever-increasing curious crowd. How they swarmed, like hounds on a hot scent! She got up on the step. A group of women were pushed towards it; they had baskets on their arms, and were laughing and chatting. The policeman's whistle pierced the clamor; voices were raised in hoarse abuse, with a kind of half-hushed remonstrance on the part of the crowd near the dense knot, above which the helmet kept bobbing up and down.

"Did yer see Mrs. Casy yet?" asked the most youthful of the group, a pale girl of the coster type.

"Yuz, me an' Jim went larst night. Ee was nussing the little nipper."

"Is it a boy?"

"In course it is."

The whistle blew more insistently; hoarse cries reached them, and the women were thrust nearer as two more helmets pushed their way through the crowd. Oaths, cries, a woman's exhortations to her man to go quiet, made Mary pale. She felt the fierce excitement of the crowd communicate itself to her; their faces gleamed orange and scarlet and purple in the light of the lanterns. The women went on with their gossip, too inured to scenes of the kind to mind; they stepped up on to the lower step, and continued calmly:

"It 'as a lot of black 'air. You should see m; ee was whistlin' to it same as if it was a bloomin' blackbird. I 'eard m say to Jim, ' Ee's a fair treat, ee is, ee ain't no mug; ee just winked at me same as if ee knew.'"

Jim larfed. "Garrn,' sez ee; 'they don't know mor 'n a puppy. It was blinkin' at the light" 'You eat yer 'at,' sez ee. 'I oughter bloomin' well know wot me own kid's adoin' of. 'And them glasses, an' we 'drink 'is 'elth.'" The women laughed in chorus."

"I made 'er some gruel —"

The crowd had ebbed into the side street again; the man's voice had dropped to a raucous reiteration of foul words; the woman's sobs reached Mary through the mutter and laughter of the crowd. There was a quartet of helmets — two at the head and two at the feet. Mary caught herself saying this as she hurried on; her face was wet. That poor woman! Four angels round my bed — two at the feet and two at the head — head, bed, said, lead — yes, lead, she felt like lead. One seemed never to be able to escape from the people; they swarmed about one like flies. She ached for solitude. It seemed years since she used to long to mix with crowds; to find exhilaration in the sight of multitudes; to fed her pulses throb to the beat of all the myriad feet. The reality was different. The sordid squalor forced itself upon one; the great, aching pity one had for each unit was only another cause of pain, for the people in bulk repelled one.

She went on until she came to a large house in Gower Street, with a brass plate on the door, "Aston House." She turned the handle of the door and went in. There was a glimmer of gas from one jet in the hall, which was bare and gloomy, with a narrow mahogany table against the wall, and a wire letter-rack. Mud-stained footmarks, in all stages of dryness, marked the dingy linoleum. The hum of many voices echoed through the house, almost as in a school. She remembered a day long ago when the laburnums were raining gold, having stood under the windows of a national school and listened to the children spelling c-a-t, r-a-t, s-a-t; but these voices were more metallic, and they dropped their aspirates and softened their r's.

She left her hat and thin jacket in a room at the end of the hall; it was such a climb upstairs to her cubicle. A puff of hot, close air, the smell of overcrowded women, struck her as she opened the door of the sitting-room, made her feel faint, flushed her face. The long table down one side of the room was crowded with girls mending garments, trimming hats, employed variously. They gossiped and laughed, whispered and giggled as they worked; another group talked in a comer near the piano; a quieter circle sat round the fire. A girl, with the head of an exquisite Greek youth, and an extraordinarily clumsy figure, in an "aesthetically" made olive-green gown, with a hanging lace collar, and necklet of beads, was reading stolidly through the din. Sometimes, as a common word or vulgar jest floated out, she would look up with a curious, wondering look, and then go on with her reading. Mary sat down on a stool near her feet, and looked up at the title on the back of the book, *Dante; for Beginners*. A big, red-faced, coarse woman, with a paradoxical air of good breeding, lay in an arm-chair, and slept heavily; she gave a half-snore every now and then. Her nether lip hung, and there was a subtle smell of some drug clinging to her. A girl looked up as Mary sat down; a hard, smallfeatured girl, almost Slavonic in type, with high cheek-bones; she had black brows, that were thickly smeared over two bony ridges, jutting over her little, round, twinkling brown eyes, making them seem abnormally deeply set. Her shining brown hair was brushed uncompromisingly back from her brow, and no trace of the day's toil marred the exquisite propriety of her dress.

A large pasteboard box stood on the table before her. It was divided into several compartments, holding beads, buckles, and bits of satin and buckram. A German phrase-book was propped up against the back of it. She was working with incredible swiftness, catching up the beads deftly on the point of her needle, and whipping the satin over the buckram. She made exactly the same number of stitches each time, tossing the bows as made into another box. She moved her lips as she learned each new word, and shifted a slip of paper every now and then over the German column to test her memory. She looked at Mary Desmond, a long look that someway softened her face rarely. A girl with a tousled head, who answered to the name of Ryan, or Pat, sat down to the piano and "vamped" a waltz. The refrain — it was vulgar and rather stupid — was eagerly taken up by the noisy set at the head of the table. Most of the girls wore black gowns of good cut, and had abnormally round, small waists. The Narcissus-headed girl looked up now and then, with a curiously cold, contemplative expression on her face, as if she were studying some strange form of lower animal life. One felt it was quite outside her; her beautiful eyes gave nothing of herself away, admitted nothing into her soul.

Mary's head throbbed; it was her first Saturday night in the house; she had been out the former one and had come in on a Monday. On other evenings there were not so many girls; many worked later on other days. She got up and went upstairs; the gas was turned down in the big back room on the third floor. The four jets without globes gave a poor light, and hissed as they burned. The room was divided into squares by iron uprights and cross rods, with hanging curtains — four shillings a week for each cubicle. There were seven in this room. She got inside the Turkey-red square allotted to her. It contained a narrow bed, a diminutive chest of drawers which served as dressing-table and wash-handstand, a square of glass on a nail, and a chair. A leather frame holding the little mother hung over the bed. She took out the half-sovereign paid her for her week's work as extra Christmas hand in a stationer's, and added up on a bit of paper. Four shillings for room, and a penny for insurance. She had cleaned her own boots and saved twopence. Seven breakfasts at threepence — one and nine; seven suppers at twopence-halfpenny, but she had been obliged to have a cup of cocoa, at another penny, to get them down — say two shillings. Altogether, seven and tenpence. The blood rushed to her face, and the sick feeling that was associated with money in so many different ways clutched her chest. Iast Sunday she had dinner and tea — another tenpence — eight and eightpence. Her washing would be a shilling, that would leave her fourpence for dinner during the coming week, and all wants! Wants! Heavens! she needed everything, almost everything. It would buy paper and stamps. She must write to Peggy. She missed her bath more than anything, but she could not do on less food.

Last week the Major (poor old Dad, he was in desperate straits himself!) had given her two shillings. Yet she had not been able to afford sixpence towards the tea fund. It was stupid to mind; yet it hurt, because the others thought she was mean; even the genteel woman with the faded eyes and long ringlets hanging on her shoulders, and the remains of a silk-velvet bodice with futile trimmings of old bead lace, gave that much occasionally. She told Mary her story. She was the daughter of a Norfolk squire; had run away with the groom. He ill-treated her; beat her in his cups; but all the same she could not leave him. "He was my fate," she said resignedly; "yet I don't understand it." Her people had taken her boy on condition that she should never try to see him.

"He is at Marlborough," she said proudly; all my brothers went there." She had a little dry cough, and used to weep silently. Mary felt sorry for her — she was such a raveled shred of a woman — and always talked to her when she went down to warm herself.

Jones, the bookbinder, and the melancholy paster worked together in the cellar amongst the packing-cases. He had made a long wooden stool for the poor thing to stand on. Jones was a freethinker and a socialist; used tremendous words, and called Mary "Missy"; but she always fancied that, on his lips, it became the English equivalent for *citoyenne*. They got to be friends; he had a Socratean head; quoted Tom Paine, Garibaldi, and many others of whom Mary had never heard. He had asked her to make his tea for him one afternoon, and, if it would not be a liberty, "to do him proud" by sharing it with them. (The poor lady paster was a constant guest of his.) Mary felt he had sacrificed cherished principles by his manner of asking her, and consented gladly.

It was bitterly cold up in the shop. She sat right in the draught of the door, and she used to feel as if she had an icy band clipping her waist. The women never shut the door behind them; the men were a shade better. At the end of the week Mary had acquired an unreasonable dislike (not to use a stronger word) for prosperous middleclass Englishwomen. Their peremptory voices, certainty of purpose, determination to get what they wanted, and their entire want of consideration for the shop-girls, made her long to get up and run them out of the shop by the shoulders. They shoved and pressed, shrieking out what they wanted, and why they wanted it. One woman had tapped Mary on the shoulder, and called in her ear:

"Get up; I am in a hurry, do you hear? and tell me how much these cards are."

"I am not serving. Madam; it is not my business."

"Such airs! it is insufferable! what the masses are coming to I don't know," muttered the matron as she caught another girl. Mary shook her head impatiently at the recollection. Why could not she forget it? It was so small to mind. She laid her head on the pillow and dozed; she felt faint. She had only been able to spend twopence a day for a midday meal, out of the florin, as she had been forced to buy soap and some darning-cotton and other trifles. Supper was only bread and cheese, or bread and sausage. Sometimes her stomach refused it, and she had tantalizing visions of dainty food — a snipe, browned to a turn on deliciously soaked toast, as the Major had often done it. He might have held the *cordon bleu* had he gone in for it. The counterpane smelt sooty; the soot seemed to stick in the hard, cotton honeycombs. Honeycombs! The very word suggested warmth and sweetness! It was cold up there, but she could not stand the noise downstairs. Her thoughts went to the boys and Peggy. Peggy was governessing — quaint, pretty Peg. Baby Noreen had gone out of their lives; been adopted by relatives in South America. She shivered; her back burned. Someone came into the room; she could hear the shouts of laughter downstairs as the door opened, and far away, out amidst the rumble of vehicles and the Titanic, monotonous hum — that is, the London voice — the melancholy notes of the "Lost Chord," played on a comet, came up at intervals. She found herself smiling at the pathetic accentuation of the melody; conjured a vision of the player. She felt sure that he had a red nose, a pimply red nose, and down-at-heel laced boots, and a rusty coat — the kind the tailors' advertisements name Prince Albert —bound with shabby braid, and he felt what he played; was immeasurably sorry for himself; tears of gin-and water stood in his eyes and touched the passers-by, for the man in the street is always a sentimentalist. She stirred uneasily, and opened her eyes. The bow-maker was looking in, holding aside the hangings.

"We are neighbours," she said; "I have brought your washing. You ought to take off your boots; they are wet. You look very tired — let me."

She had an unusually deep voice with a resonant note, and distinct, careful enunciation. It struck Mary that she had studied to eliminate all commonness from her speech.

"Oh no — please not! I am tired — that is all; I am not generally so stupid, but my back aches."

"Ah, part of our woman's disability. Our backs, or our nerves, or our hearts — always something. You are not coarse enough for the struggle. You look like a tall vase of Venetian glass serving as a porter pot. Did anyone ever tell you so before?"

"Yes, in other words; the girls in New York used to say I was too 'toney.'"

"So you have been in America? I am going there some day, when the time is ripe."

"To work?"

"Of course. Am I not one of the eat-your-bread-by-the-sweat-of-your-brow allotted? Have some hot water? It is emptied for us on Saturday nights."

She brought it in a foot-bath. There was a cheery, helpful directness about her; her plainness vanished, and the small eyes seemed to enlarge as she let them rest on anyone she liked. The hot water eased Mary's feet and seemed to brace her whole body. The bow-maker popped her head in again; she reminded Mary of a robin peering out of a figure-of-four trap.

"I have a friend who has a mania for making felt slippers. She has sent me two more pairs — that makes four; take a pair off my hands; I must get rid of them somehow."

She dropped them in. Mary opened the drawer, found a pair of stockings past mending, but clean; she washed out those she had taken off and hung them to dry on the rung of her chair, did her hair, and went into the bow-maker's cubicle. She was writing a letter on a board, with paper and envelopes fastened by elastic bands. She had a candle of her own, for the four gas-jets gave a dismal light; one had to do one's hair in the mornings by guesswork. As she had the cubicle with half the window, she was able to fasten a hanging book-shelf to the woodwork. Mary read down the titles of some of the books — Shakspeare, the Bible, Carlyle, Stuart Mill, Darwin's *Origin of Species*, Marcus Aurelius, a Latin *Principia*, a German grammar.

"Wondering, eh? Knowledge is power. No one need be ignorant in this big Babylon of ours. I used to go to the Birkbeck, but a man taught me the rest. The man was worth ten Birkbecks; he drew one out instead of larding one with bits of educational fat."

The gong sounded. She pulled the top of the window down an inch and paused to look out to the murky blue, with the irregular, misshapen clusters of chimney-stacks clumped against it.

"Do you like cities?" she queried of Mary, in her sharp, decisive way. "I hardly know, once I thought I did."

"I love them and I hate them. Look out there as far as you can see; roof after roof, smoke-curl after smoke-curl, each rising from a hearth, and under each roof a human being or a cluster of them; each a knot of suffering, or sin, or sorrow, or work, or fleeting joy. When I shut my eyes and recall the district in which I work — Whitechapel — my heart aches, aches until I fed as if it is crying tears of blood; and it calls, calls like a child in there — I will never have a child." The phrase, or the tone of it, struck Mary as curious, and she looked with keener interest at the other's strangely moved face.

"And I feel as a woman must when her child craves milk and her breasts are dry; for I know that were I to divide myself into atoms, and sell each atom for a piece of silver, it would avail nothing to stay the misery there. Do you know Poe's *Tale of the Beating Heart?*"

Mary nodded.

"It always reminds me of London. Hundreds of murdered hearts, throbbing and throbbing with an appealing call —"

All the passion had died out of her voice; her face resumed its stolid calm.

"We must hurry down; Saturday is always a scramble; most of the girls are in to supper."

They made their way to the basement, to a clean, cheerless kitchen. Two long tables were laid for supper. A sour-looking, middle-aged woman in a print gown was heating coffee over a gas ring; the range fire was out.

"What's on to-night, Emily?" called the girl who "vamped."

"Bread and cheese and pickles, or sausage, or fresh herring!"

"Lor! hold me up, Carry; wy, oh wy this burst of generosity?"

"Three charnces for your money; the committee'll have a fit. Four 'errin's this way, please! miauw! I'm sure this sassidge purred — Puss, puss, kitty, kitty! Don't you be so rude! Oh, dear! make way for a real lady—"

Banter, laughter, bickerings, the clatter of plates and tongues, coupled with the fresh, abandoned laughter of healthy Cockney girlhood at the end of a week's work, secure of a holiday. In a lull, one heard whispered confidences, in which "My young man sez," was the dominant note. Mary found the art student leaning against the door-lintel, looking on with the same passionless face. The scene excited Mary. Its palpitating life dominated over the feeling of disgust at much of it. After all, the vulgarity was only relatively different from that of the upper or middle classes. The wonder was the flock of girls themselves; bread-winners of all sorts. Meanwhile, the bow-maker had cleared a side-table, and was laying their supper with deft, quick fingers. She made Mary some cocoa. The art student joined them.

"It's my own, you must have some; it's better than the house supply," she said.

They ate silently and quickly, for other girls kept coming down, looking for places, calling greetings, quarrelling, and joking, until the room got unbearably close. Finished, they wrote their names on a slate and went upstairs. A ringing laugh met them in the hall, a laugh that incited to echoing laughter; so much of joy, of reckless, devil-may-care humor lurked in its music. It did Mary good; she caught herself smiling in response as she entered the room. An unusually tall young woman, with square shoulders and a smart, plain ulster with large horn buttons, was standing in the middle of it. She threw back her head and laughed again, showing small, irregular teeth and a dimple in one cheek, and a little soft bit of fullness under her chin. She had a handsome face, a face impossible to pass without a second look; full, curling red lips, with humorous twitchings; long-slit blue eyes curving upwards, with intensely black lashes. Other women might have had all these, but it was the look of vitality, of exuberant youth, of womanliness, of sex, that caught and ensnared. She drew off her gloves, showing small, well-kept, white hands with rings; unpinned her hat, a pretty velvet hat with plumes; violets rested on her rippling brown hair. This was not then a fashion — just a way of her own. She had another bunch at her throat. Some of the girls volunteered to help her. She laughed and submitted, as to a right, to have her coat carried away for her.

"What, Miss Brown? try on the gown? Why not? Beastly hard lines to have to fag like that, after hours. Unusual order — should hope so! Hope you get unusual pay."

She unbuttoned her bodice and let her skirt slip, showing a pretty petticoat.

"Very low, is it? Oh, well, I'll get behind the screen in case of shocking anyone, whilst I tuck my sleeves down." She popped her head out. "Give me my puff out of my pocket!" She stepped out in a few minutes in a yellow satin gown, trimmed with crystal trimming. There was a lull, then cries of frank admiration. The art student followed the lines of her figure with awakened interest, saying:

"Of course her waist is absurd, but she is a magnificent creature."

She looked triumphantly handsome, and peeped into the mirror with naive delight at her own beauty. The girls were outspoken in their criticisms.

"I'd go on the stage if I had your face and figure, I know," said the Ryan girl; "catch me looking for a place as buyer in a warehouse! You've just as good a figure as Addy Conyers, and a deal better face."

"Cawn't do it, dear girl, cawn't really; family considerations, don't ye know?" She stood and chaffed, as the dressmaker arranged the ribbons. More girls came in; most of them had eggs, rashers, tins of bloater-paste for their breakfasts during the coming week. Mary forgot her tiredness, watching this panorama of working-womanhood.

CHAPTER XV

Mary slept heavily, and woke early, before the first bell rang, for many of the girls were astir, dressing hurriedly to catch early trains to the country or outlying suburbs, to spend the day. She lay with closed eyes listening to the rustle of clothing, splash of water, and opening of drawers. Tired bodily, her brain was alert, and picture after picture kept dancing before her eyes. It seemed as if her life was to run in extremes; as a child and girl she met only men; now she met only women. How should she meet her Prince? Would he see her in her shabby garments? He would need keen eyes to find her amongst the crowd of working-women in this monster desert of a city.

It was strange how little men cared for her. Was it her unguessed-at shyness, the jealousy of her soul-self that made her cold; or what was it that made them pass her by for less well-favored girls? Love! She could love; she knew so well all the warm, white fire that was closed in the shell of her heart. If only her Prince would come and lay his ear to it; he, too, could hear the music of its dancing flame. She longed for quiet sometimes; quiet to listen to the dreams in herself. There never was any quiet; there was something indelicate in this constant intimate contact with other human beings. One breathed their aura, as it were, coarse or vulgar, or whatever its nature — one was only protected by a curtain of Turkey-red. That was, after all, the great differentiation between the classes and the masses — the possibility of solitude. She dandled this thought as a newly discovered idea, was pleased with herself, stretched out her arms, admired her wrists, peered curiously at the little crisscross lines in her pink palms; if only one could read them. She sat up and tacked a white frill in her bodice. She remembered a time when she would have thought this a sin. Funny idea, when one came to think of it, with all the artificial arrangements of time, too. What an odd girl the bow-maker was; what a grip on her soul she had; how secure of herself; she wondered what the man was like who had taught her. There was an odd, reverent note in her voice as she spoke of him. And the Evans — what a contrast! And all the others, a whole hive of them; only bees brought back visions of straw skeps and red clover-blooms, the scent of hives and the hum of summer; this hive smelt of London, the true London smell — humanity and soot.

She went downstairs; the girls had a Sunday look, put on with their finery and extra curl of fringe. The fire in the big room was sulky; the pale-faced woman was warming her thin hands before it and bade Mary a gentle good-morning. She had been to early service. The art student had donned a pretty gown of wonderful make; and the others stood in groups, and chatted or grumbled at the weather. Mary was conscious of an air of criticism in their attitude towards her. It puzzled her then, as it puzzled her for many years to come. She was isolated from necessity; her very pride in herself, her keen intelligence without trace of cunning or worldliness, her independent judgment, and her concentration were all stones in her path. There was something individual about her that repelled the ordinary person. The little sordid things of life seemed to become visible under her keen gaze, so that those dealing in them became uncomfortable. Had it not been for her great-heartedness, and the desire of love in her, Mary Desmond ran a risk of developing into a superior person.

The bell rang again. The lady superintendent, a pale little lady, with an expression of physical pain about her mouth, a dainty lace cap always slightly awry, took her place at the head of the table. She tapped smartly to ensure silence, and knelt down with her face to the window. There was an uneven ripple of responses; the girl in front of Mary was busy rolling some straight bits of her fringe round leather curlers, and hiding them under the frizz. The sun stole in with a wan gleam, and touched the short hair of the art student; and Mary thought, so a Greek John the Evangelist might have looked as he laid his head on the Master's breast. The governess appeared to find comfort in the words, but most of the girls fidgeted impatiently: the last Amen was unanimous. The maid brought in two urns and a wire basket of eggs. She took out one and placed it on Mary's plate.

"This is not mine."

"Your name's Desmond, ain't it? Well, that's wot's on it."

"Miss Desmond" was written in pencil. Mary flushed and looked at the bow-maker; she was eating her breakfast silently, and later on she denied all knowledge of it. Breakfast over, most of the girls went out. At first there was a trooping up and down stairs; then a subdued Sunday dullness seemed to fall on every spirit. Mary was glad to stay in. Her boots were broken, and the furtive sun had crept behind a gray fog. The bow-maker lent her a book; she was going to a meeting in the East End, but might be back to tea. She looked very reliable and very plain in her comfortable coat and close felt hat, and Mary regretted her absence. There were few in to dinner; and later on in the afternoon, Mary, the art student, and the Evans gathered round the fire. The sad-faced woman was playing Schumann softly. The fire had burned to a rich glow, that was reflected off the red wall-paper and slid along the mahogany. A little woman — Mary had noticed her often, she always bade "good-evening" to everybody — came in and swept up the hearth. She was a stunted thing with a look of premature oldness on her thin, white face — a common little London face. She walked as if she were bandy-legged, or had suffered from green-bone in her childhood. She was the first inmate of the house, always nursed everyone if they were ill. The first and second fingers of her left hand had thick, horny, gray ridges, speckled with black, upon them; she was an upholstress at Maple's. Everyone called her "little Miss Green." The art student sat on the rug and leaned her head against Mary's knee; the little upholstress brought out a large bag of chestnuts — she did every Sunday — and put some to roast on the bars. Miss Blake, the red-faced woman, joined them, and Mary told them bits of New York life. She could talk well when in the humor, and to a sympathetic audience — suit her stories to them. The governess sat in the armchair, and Addie Evans lay back in a rocker and let the little woman peel chestnuts for her.

The dusk gathered; gushes of laughter rippled through the room at her imitations of an old newspaper woman on lower Fifth Avenue, and the splendid cheek of an elevator boy called Jimmy, who had declared himself Mary's humble admirer, and confided his determination of running some day for the presidency. The art student smiled with quiet humor; she never laughed, for which Mary rejoiced, for emotion and laughter too often mar the beauty of purely classical faces, and it was an exquisite thing to have this rare head to look at. The door had opened softly, and the bow-maker stood listening to the end of a story; then she came behind Mary and touched her cheek softly with some violets, giving them to her with a smile as she turned.

"I wish I had your gift of story-telling," she said, seriously; "I could use it."

"You mean publicly? Oh, I couldn't. It is only when I am in the mood, and to people I feel in sympathy with, that I can let myself go like this — one antagonistic person would lame me."

"Curious! I like opposition; I like to dominate it — to feel I can turn it to my own purpose. One opponent won over is worth ten partisans. I must have a handle of my own to turn, even if it is the handle of a crank."

"You look tired," remarked the little upholstress. "It beats me, why you go down there an' give them classes on yer one free day. She gives classes to men," with an awed stress on the word "men." Most of the girls in the house had a different note when talking to, or of, men. "My young man's friend told me; ee's a soshulist, an 'ee 'eard 'er. Ee says you speak wonderful!"

"Who spends her Sundays, little Miss Green, in carrying up breakfasts, playing at nurse, sweeping up the hearth, and roasting chestnuts for other people? How is your young man? I thought I saw you in Buston Road last night."

The little woman looked young for a minute.

"Oh, yes; ee'swell, thank you. We was buyin' a carpet — such a nice one, Brussels, nearly new."

"You must be getting along if you have come to the carpet. When is it to be?"

"Easter," with a shy smile. "'My young man is to get a rise then, an' ee won't wait no longer."

The governess asked gently, with a pathetic interest:

"Have you been long engaged, my dear?"

"Seven years it was a week come yesterday," was the quaint reply.

"Great Scot!" said the Evans, "seven years! I never was engaged longer than a month!"

"But you are not little Miss Green!" said the bow-maker gravely; and Mary wondered at the warm note in her voice. "She is a wonderful small person in her way, — no, you go on roasting chestnuts; I decline to be shut up, — a female Jacob. You must know, little Miss Green and her young man were to have been married five years ago. They had bought all the furniture, and were going to name the day, when the young man's mother got ill — a long, painful, expensive illness. The doctor suggested workhouse infirmary. Then that little person there took an attic in the house next door, and nursed, and washed, and tended her, after her own day's work, like a daughter. The furniture was sold, bit by bit, until the little home was as far off as ever; but they buried the mother decently. Then they started again, till little Miss Green fell ill, and spent a year in and out of hospital, and lost her place in the warehouse. Then, when she did get to work again, her young man broke his arm, and was out of work for months in a big strike; and if he didn't starve it was not because of the fund money, for that gave out for the single men long before the strike ended. But you can guess why, if you know the stuff that makes up little Miss Green —"

The maid came in and lit the gas, and pulled down the blinds with a rattle, and set the tea; and little Miss Green stole out with her face aflame; and the governess said devoutly, folding her hands:

"It's beautiful how the spirit of Christ manifests itself in the lowliest of His subjects."

But the spell was broken, and the bow-maker said sadly, with lowered voice, to Mary:

"I have lost faith in miracles."

"You mean —"

"That he is consumptive and scrofulous, and she has been ill-fed and overworked all her days; and all the brave heart in her won't save the kiddies from their fate."

"I'll make her a present of a clock — black marble, with a gilt Cupid; I won it at a raffle," said the Evans. "Just think, seven years; seven years to one man!"

"You have never been in love," remarked the governess, solemnly, "or you would not measure it by the flight of time."

"I? I not in love? Why, I am never out of it; but it doesn't last. I go crazed about a fellow for a few weeks, think of him by day, dream of him by night, you know. Put his photo in a frame — a silver heart; it's always on my table. Look at it first thing in the morning, before even I look at myself. Then one morning I forget. It's all over! I take it out" —with a dramatic intensity — "and leave the frame empty till I put in another."

Breathe close upon love's ashes,
It may be flame will leap.

"No!" laughing frankly at Mary's look of astonishment; "don't know the author. Man I knew well, awf'ly nice fella, used to quote it. It's rot, you know; far better get some sticks and a bellows, and light a new fire. Who'll toast tea-cakes? I bought some, but I won't risk my complexion. You will. Miss Green? You are an angel! I admire, if I won't emulate you."

They all laughed: there was something infectious about this creature, with her frank egotism and magnificent physique. Mary reasoned that, as she had dined, she ought not to have tea; but the temptation to stay was too great, she must suffer for it during the week to come. Her employment, too, would end the first week of the New Year. Well, the fire was warm, and there were two beautiful things in the room to gaze at. And as she looked up into the eyes of the bow-maker, that were considering her with a grave question, she said, with a smile:

"Let us make haste to laugh, lest we should have to weep."

Later, when she and the bow-maker were alone in the big room, and the bells were calling in many-keyed voices from the churches around, and the big house was quiet, they sat at the fire and talked, it was the bow-maker who rested against Mary's knee. She took one of the latter's hands, and laid it on her own broad palm, and said: "Strange hands, with a satin touch, and something magnetic in them; like your eyes in a way. I used to be a bit afraid of you, when you came first. Oh, yes, I saw you the first evening. You are a little repellent; but when one gets over that, one wants to go to you, close to you, and show one' s heart. I don't often; it is weakness. So many people are like old-fashioned caricatures: they go about with a scroll curling up from their lips, explaining themselves. Reticence is power; making confidences is like planting stray seeds in one's garden — one never knows what venomous weeds may grow out of them. You know German, don't you? You might give me some lessons — your own terms."

She drew out tactfully the state of Mary's affairs, puckered her black brows together, and then she said, quietly:

"I, too, know what the struggle for life means. I will tell you my story. My father was a sea-captain in a small way. I was born in Wapping. There were two of us, a brother and myself. When I was thirteen, old for my age — I had kept house for him from eleven — he married again. She killed him in three months — some women's tongues have a corrosive quality. In three more she turned me into the street. I went to a neighbor's; she kept a tiny greengrocer's shop. I read down the advertisements in the papers. I answered one, in a factory such as I am in at present. The proprietor was a Jew; he had no place for learners — he wanted skilled hands; but something sharp I said to him as he dismissed me made him call me back. He questioned me, and as he found I could write and add decently, he took me on at a few shillings a week, to check piece-work and tally the hours. I found afterwards he had discharged a boy to place me — the boy demanded more pay. I helped the woman in the evenings and on Saturday afternoons for my bed and board. In two months I asked him for a place as skilled hand. He refused. I gave him notice and entered another fectory, and took home piece-work myself — one gets to be very quick at it. Then I picked up Yiddish. In a year I secured a place as head of a room of workers few of whom spoke English. I attended classes for bookkeeping, did piece-work in spare time, earned decent wages. I left myself no spare time. At seventeen I met a man,, a German, who changed my life for me. He is a socialist, — that doesn't mean tub-thumping in Hyde Park, — a man in ten thousand, a man with some of the Christ in him. I was too poor, too plain a thing to dream that he could ever think of me with more than a kindly interest. Then one day — God! how that day worthens all the other days! — he took me, and told me that he loved me — me, poor, plain, ignorant, ugly —"

Mary looked at the face, transfigured by a wonderful light, and marveled at it — wondered if the man had ever seen that look on her face; for, if so, he would never see her plain again.

"I could have kissed his hands, kissed my own, because he had lifted them up to his neck. I became sacred to myself, because of the something akin to divine he awoke in me. And he took me to him, and told me that he had spoken because he knew that to feel that he was all mine, even though the exchanging of our love was the first step towards renunciation, would comfort me in my loneliness and guerdon me through all my life, — be as a strong sweet wine to sustain me, if I grew faint on the long road ahead of us. And he — even now I cannot fathom it — he needed in his human weakness to know that I was at heart with him. And we talked all through the long, warm summer night, up on Hampstead, with the never-quiet roar of the city surging like an ocean at our feet, and the night-winds crooning over our heads in the trees. He said that one needed to sing the one great heart-psalm of one's life in God's free air. When morning broke — God! how wonderful it was! Down below us, bathed in mist, a city of silver shadows, and the dawn marching up exultantly with a hundred golden spears and waving banners of crimson. I stood in the shelter of his arms, and my whole soul cried out with the glory of it — every fibr and thread and nerve of me. And in that supreme moment we were one complete being, soul dovetailed to soul — our wedding and renunciation in one. Then he went down the hill towards the river where the ships sail out; and once the woman in me called out, but I struck my mouth and crushed it. And later, when the bells and whistles were calling the toilers to arise and go forth to a fresh day of labor, I, too, went down to the working-place to take my place in the fight."

Mary was silent while she spoke, but she drew in her breath sharply as she ended, as when one has listened breathlessly to some mighty orchestra climbing to a glorious climax; then she put her lips softly to the other's hand.

"And you will never marry him?"

"Marry? No. Men such as he belong to humanity — to the cause to which they have consecrated themselves. They must be celibates, tied to no one woman; at the service of all suffering womanhood; father to the orphan little ones of the whole world. Families may mean holy ties, but they may also mean growths of parasitical tendency, sapping the vigor of a plant or tree."

Mary remembered the quietness of her voice, as she had said, "I will never have a little child."

"Will you see one another?"

"I think not. Have you ever seen a wreck near the coast? I did once. Ever seen how they send a rocket, with a line attached, to the drowning men on board, and they come in one by one, and the strong survive? Well, he stands on the shore, and looks out for wrecks; and I am the line that does his bidding. So I help him best. Solidarity is the keystone of woman. To be perfect as a woman she has need of a concentrated existence — home is the crystallization of herself: not so with the man. The danger today, when women are changing places with men and forgetting this truth, is desexualization. It must bring unhappiness, for in measure as woman loses the spirit of her own sex, she will feel the burden of it. Atrophy of it in man or woman makes life less worth — that is why I spoke of renunciation. As his wife, I should be selfish for him, and if I had little children, I should forget the cry of the little ones outside in listening to the cooing of my own."

A realization of the instinctive delicacy of the finer eroticism peculiar to the woman who is for the one man, not the many, came home to Mary as she listened; a wistful envy of the other's inner happiness — an understanding of the calm that was, in its essence, joy, that burned as a steady, white sanctuary-light, in the temple of this other woman's soul.

"And now, would you know why I have told you all this, woman with the question in your eyes? Because I feel it will help; because I would have you ask me if there is anything I can do; because I would have you take a good grip of your soul, and not let the love-hunger that is in you lead you to drink before the right man holds the chalice to your lips. You loving, tender thing! Better go hungry, thirsty, and love-weaned by years of solitude to your grave — and yet, — who knows? There are more ways than one of climbing the ladder to perfection."

CHAPTER XVI

MARY'S LIFE AT THIS time was too insistent; the mass of material to be observed too diverse to permit of sifting. She worked all day, came home faint in body from insufficient nourishment and clothes. Then the life in this great hive pressed in upon her; lives within lives, scandals, whispers of tragedies, and quiet heroism.

There was the faded governess who played Schumann, and walked about arm in arm with Christ (He was very actual to her), on an annuity of £40 a year — who did without a meal to give her charities. The big Irishwoman who drank whisky when she had no chloral, silently, sullenly, and muttered in her sleep of Galway hunting days —who sat, as Mary heard, for half the day dozing in the back parlor of a little paper-shop off Red Lion Street. The owner was a weazen-faced little Irishman, with a horsey look; as a little whiteheaded gossoon, he had often opened the lodgegate to let Miss Honora and her raking bay go through with the Mayor — "God rest his sowl" though he shot himself when the last acre went. He used to let her sit there from a fierce, respectful loyalty to the old blood, and fetch her a "nog gin" when she wanted it; "because, faith, it was only then the poor sowl was happy!"

Her own work would cease on Saturday. She had written to the Major, and he had sent her a half-sovereign. The Evans, the little upholstress, and the bow-maker always looked for her coming, and she always found an addition to her breakfast. Her future filled her with anxiety; the rules of the establishment did not permit more than a week's rent in arrears. She knocked on Monday — it was pay evening — at the door of the superintendent's room. It was a cozy room, pretty with photographs and flowers. The art student was sitting on a stool by the fire, with a drawing-board on her lap; the little lady was on the sofa, her cap awry.

"Come in, my dear, you don't disturb me; leave it on the table, I'll enter it later on. I am more tired than usual. Take that low chair; you look fagged. You never come in here; you can, you know, when they are too noisy in there; this child does whenever she wants to be quiet." Later on she left the room, and Mary watched the girl tracing a scroll-design on the paper.

"It is for a panel," she said, looking up; "I am learning wood-carving; I shall get my certificate at the end of this year. Then I am going to try for a post, as technical instructor, in New Zealand.

"Yes, I am an orphan. My mother's insurance gave me £60 for three years. By living here I can just manage until I am done. Oh, my name is Mary Jones. I consider it a hardship to have a name like that. It isn't a name; it's a generic term. One's parents ought to be reprimanded. If it were Euphrosyne Jones, or even Mary Eliza; but plain Mary Jones!"

They laughed; or at least Mary did. There was a sly humor of an aloof sort lurking in this girl, and a certain coldness almost selfish in its exclusive refinement.

"I cannot talk to the others as you do," she said. "I have nothing in common with them; they don't interest me. It is extraordinary the difference a few social grades can make. I suppose I am really middle-class: my mother was a clergyman's daughter, my father a Sheffield cutler — a remarkable man; he lost his life at twenty-six, in a fire in one of his workmen's dwellings; brought out a woman and a child, and went back for another; he threw it down, but never came out himself. He was a cultured saint; I always place him next to Christ and Marcus Aurelius. It seems impossible to reconcile the loss of such a man for a couple of brats that would probably be just as well dead."

"I wonder!" said Mary. "Do you know, I think that is an English characteristic — that of loving things on a pedestal. You haven't the clan feeling irrespective of merit, the blood-tie, that is so strong with us. Supposing your father were — you read Thackeray? — say, Captain Costigan, wouldn't you care for him just the same?"

She considered. "No, I don't think I could."

"You are very English!" was all Mary replied. They wandered into a discussion of books they had read and pictures they had seen.

"You are Irish, then," said the girl, after a pause; "that explains your voice; it croons at one. One likes you better after one has heard you speak; I noticed it, and your hands."

When the little lady returned, and they rose to go, she kept Mary back, and said:

"I am not very, strong, you know, dear, and there is a good deal of writing to be done; some of it got neglected when I was ill. The Committee give me a free hand, so if you will help me with it you can stay on for some weeks; it will solve the immediate trouble for you. Of course you can look round for something to do in the meantime."

As Mary went upstairs, she looked out of the long window. A bright, fiery-blue star, like an encouraging eye, blinked at her out of the blackness; a big bunch of snowdrops and violets on her table beautified its meanness; and her hat was on the bed, transformed by the deft fingers of the Evans. A funny note, stuck on the hat-pin, took away every possibility of offence. Life wasn't so bad after all; and women were nice when one got to know them. She stepped into the cubicle of this errant maid — a cubicle transformed by an eider-down, a crowd of pretty toilet accessories, and a smell of violet powder, and pocket fans with masculine photographs. The Evans was in bed, eating chocolates and manicuring her nails. She pointed to a chair.

"Oh, don't mention it! You could be awf'ly pretty if you took pains: waved your hair, you know, used your eyes, or did anything but look 'country.'

"I thought I 'd like to do it for you. I am going away; one can't stay here longer than a month without working. I wrote to my sister; my brother-in-law is a very good fellow, a dear, but I am afraid of him. So I am going to stay with them for a month or so, and be good. Church twice Open that box and look at my bonnet. Isn't it a love? A little spotted veil, and that, eh? All the same I wouldn't go, only there's to be an election. Who that is? why did you strike on him?

"Good face, isn't it? That's my solicitor; my tragic, unescapable fate, I fear. He has proposed to me every year since I was fourteen. Comes wherever I am; we have our awf'ly good time together, and then he goes off. In the end I suppose I shall have to; I feel it coming. Well, I always make a point of letting him know of all my worst escapades" — she broke into a peal of laughter at some remembrance. There was a chorus of impatient "'Sh, 'sh" — the gas went out and sent Mary to bed, and the violets smelt sweetly on her table.

CHAPTER XVII

ONE DAY SHE WENT TO the Society for Promoting the Employment of Women again; it was through them she had found her last place. The little old lady had welcomed her with a despairing "Tut, tut, tut," and had given her two thousand envelopes to address for a Christian Science league — one and sixpence a thousand.

"You can do them at the table near the window if you like." She sat down to the table and worked away. Lunch-time came — no, she could not make the pretense of going out for it. The applicants who came in steamed a little; it was raw outside, and their boots made a squelchy sound as they crossed the oilcloth;

and there was a dull splashiness in the hoof-beats of the horses in the street below. Not an application missed her; she noted every one. A long tale of misery and incompetence. Occasionally a woman or girl came who had one thing at her fingers' ends — typewriting (then beginning), bookkeeping, a bodice hand.

"Yes, this agency is not really for trade, but I'll give you an address."

They often found places. But alas for those who could only say, "I write a clear hand, know a little French. — No, not enough to correspond, I fear, but have excellent references." Poor things, they all had excellent references, and it helped them not a whit. Mary remembered the Ryan girl had told them with inimitable mimicry of how she had gone to a butcher for a place as cashier in Smithfield. He stopped her catalogue of references by saying: "Cut it! I don't care a bally tanner about your morals; that's your affair. I'll take my 'davy you ' keep straight in business hours. Can you keep my books accurately? Tha's wot I want to know."

The little lady's "Tut, tut, tut" became as frequent as a hiccough. The smell of her grilled chop gave Mary nausea. Funny, whenever she was hungry she could smell beefsteak and tomatoes. She could see them; and yet when she had to walk over a grating at a restaurant the hot smell of the cooking almost made her retch. She divided the envelopes into a hundred at a time; it seemed to make them appear less. For, twenty hundred — one shilling and sixpence for, ten hundred — one side of her brain kept struggling in a vain endeavor to calculate how much that would be a hundred — pence, halfpence, farthings. How tiresome of the imps in there to worry! She knew perfectly well it was useless. She never could add up; had never learned properly; it was a defect, decidedly a lack; perhaps with a deteriorating effect on her nature, leading to a lack of balance as a check to the fanciful. One never knew. "Dear Christ, help me!" she cried, as she wrote "James Linnegar, 4 Balls Court." That was the third Linnegar, Linnegar, Linnegar; spell it with a V, and make it Vinegar. She checked an imbecile smile. Vinegar, vinegar-plant, what did she know of a vinegar-plant? Yes, she remembered a little dressmaker in Mallow used to keep one in a bottle. The memory of this quaint stitcher of garments saved her, and she laughed softly in genuine amusement as she thought of her. She was a miniature Army List; knew every regiment in the service; battalion wise; lived in a dream of uniforms, and a lilt of marching tunes. Cried as they left, smiled a welcome as they came. Loved the military, she used to say quaintly, because — "they kicked up a dust." How Peggy used to roar at that reason when they went to fit a frock on! The inconsequent voices in her brain dozed away, and gave place to a feeling of repletion. She wrote furiously, heaping the narrow, cheap white envelopes into a dingy white pyramid on the table. At half-past four she was at her last two hundred — writing with her head on her left palm, and her whole arm on the table. As she wrote the last one she laid down her pen with a sob.

"Tut, tut, tut, tut," said the little old lady. She had been sitting for the last twenty minutes with her skirt turned over her knees, showing her scarlet petticoat, making the "map of the world" on her shins as she toasted herself contemplatively before the fire.

"There, there, my dear, I must see if I can't find you something else. There are the three shillings, and now go upstairs, right to the top. Knock on the door at the back, and you will get some tea."

She muttered something, as was her habit, under her breath; for underneath the sharpness necessary to dealing with hundreds of shiftless, inconsequent applicants, there was a very good, soft heart.

CHAPTER XVIII

The sun of a late February morning was streaming into a top room in a street off Guildford Street. It was a big room, ill-furnished; three camp-beds at one side of it; one was unslept in, neatly made, the others just covered over with cheap striped rugs, A large table in the middle of the room, a writing-table in the window, camp-chairs, a deal cupboard, and some book-shelves made up the furniture. Yet in spite of its poverty there was an atmosphere of warmth and good humor about it that must have their origin in the occupants. Many handsomely appointed rooms will throw a chill over one's spirit when one enters them. A rough Irish terrier was sitting on a stool near the fire. An old sword and rods of all kinds hung on the walls, with many drawings and Vanity Fair cartoons. Several cages were fastened to the shutter, and a curly-headed lad was sticking bits of watercress between the bars, talking to each bird in a kind of hissing whisper. An older lad, with solemn black eyes, was toasting bread before the fire, turning some slices that were frying in drippings in a pan on top.

"Call Mary, Miley; the tea will be stewed."

"She's late."

"She didn't go to bed till after one."

The lad went across the lobby, knocked at a door, and called with a slathering brogue:

"Mollums, hurry up, my tummy's sticking to my back! No, we won't begin till you come."

He went back to the birds.

"Chirp, chirp, sss, sss, you'd bite, would you, you cheeky beggar?"

The terrier pricked up his ears and trotted to the door.

"Moll's coming; look at Finn!"

Mary came in, and the dog ran round and round with strange, subdued barks and growls. He was contraband, and he knew it, and fell in with all the stratagems necessary to smuggling him out for exercise and keeping him an inmate unknown to the landlady. Mary looked older. She had a suggestion of the two lines that run down from nose to mouth that one never sees except in the faces of those who have much sensibility to suffering. She laid her hat, a piece of lace for her neck, and some large sheets of parchment on the bed. There was an air of dignity that contrasted quaintly with the old-childishness when she laughed. She kissed the boys, ruffled Miley's hair, and warmed her hands at the fire.

"What time is it?"

"Gone the quarter to —"

"I am awfully late. I had to leave some last night I couldn't finish. I did them this morning, but my hands kept getting cold. Pour out the tea, Thady."

The grave-eyed lad, thin and pale, with a sensitive, dark face, complied with the deftness of a housewifely woman. Miley took some fried bread and began to invite an imaginary company to partake of tantalizing delicacies. There is nothing like a prolonged diet of tea and bread and butter to make one keenly appreciative of the fleshpots of Egypt.

"Do let me tempt you to just a 'suspicion' of pheasant? The bread sauce is made from a recipe of the famous Tabitha Tickletooth! 'just a suspicion.'" His voice was an absurd imitation of an old Irish acquaintance, and made them both laugh.

"Poor old Miley!" said Mary; "never mind, we'll have a nice supper. I'll be home early. Not that that's a bit of luck! I'll get paid for these too."

"Have more tea, Mollums? You haven't eaten your toast."

"Miley can have it later on. I always get such a good lunch. Tie up these papers for me, like a dear."

The large sheets of parchment were petitions against the passing of the Marriage-with-a-Deceased-Wife's-Sister Bill, to be presented to the House by some irrational faddists. They were exquisitely written in copperplate writing, the "Lords and Gentlemen" engrossed, and paid at the rate of seven-and-six a hundred. Taking into consideration writing, engrossing, and "no erasures," it was not high pay. They were to be hawked about different parishes for "We, the undersigned" to endorse. Well, it was all in the day's work. Mary Desmond did not mind, only sometimes it meant nightwork too. She shook her head regretfully at the lame crossing-sweeper near Russell Square. An organ began to play a "Gaiety" air; Miley used to sing the words, for Nelly Farren was the object of a boyish admiration. She sighed as she thought of the laddies. A flower-vender and a boy passed her. The woman balanced an enormous basket on a pad on her uncovered black Irish head. She was talking of an elegant wake a neighbor had given his mother. The violets, and jonquils, and golden-dotted mimosa left a trail of sweetness behind them, and the music spurred Mary's feet. There was an omen of spring in the air, so she drew in a glad breath and began to hum softly to herself; and more than one passer-by glanced back at the girl with the parted lips and swinging step, and the eyes, with their eager, glad look, half veiled in dreams.

CHAPTER XIX

MARY WAS SITTING AT a quaint inlaid escritoire in the boudoir of a house in the S.W. district. The room was hung with Flemish embroidery and old French tapestry; an Aubusson carpet covered the floor. The fireplace was built of two superbly carved Breton wall-beds. The *benitoir* had been preserved on the upper one, and the space where the blue-and-white-check curtains originally hung was filled in by an old panel of Spanish embroidery. Three oval Chippendale tables had been converted into cases for a valuable collection of rare watches, snuff-boxes, and *bonbonnières*. The portrait of a singularly lovely girl, in spite of the trying dress of the time, by Meissonier, in his early manner, was the only picture in the room.

Mary was writing invitations to a soirée — copying them out of an address-book. The address-book had somewhat the character of a human document; it was Society as seen through its owner's temperament. Mary found it intensely diverting. The entries were made in black and red ink. The red ink marked solicitors, dentists. tradespeople, chiropodists, clairvoyantes, etc.; indeed all such as were not regarded as friends or acquaintances. There were debatable persons too, of neither qualification; and sometimes Mary smiled as she came across a name entered in black, with a bracketed note in red. Some of the names were well known. One saw their doings chronicled in the smaller society papers, people who were creeping up the social ladder; the entry in red ink defined their position in this particular house. An M.P. was bracketed as "a useful man to find yacht crews"; a man in the Foreign Office had "a delightful tenor;" some score of young men "danced."

The door opened; a tall, slight woman, with exquisitely dressed blond hair, came in and said "Good-morning!" She advanced with a sheaf of letters in her hand. Seen in that light she was the remains of a very beautiful woman, the original of the portrait. She always gratified Mary's aesthetic sense. Her loose delicate heliotrope satin negligée was confined at the waist by a lace scarf drawn through an amethyst clasp; the Valenciennes flounces of her petticoat frothed round her bare instep. She sat down, and crossed her feet in little fur-lined slippers on a footstool. Everything in this establishment marched by rule; a man came in and wound the clocks, another came and saw to the plants. This morning Hiram J. Beggs, pedicure and artist for the hands, from Schenectady, U. S. A., paid his fortnightly it visit; he had just left. Hiram J. was an absurd likeness of the third Napoleon, with a striking American accent. Lady Aymer found him amusing as well as dexterous — it was so difficult to find anyone or anything amusing.

"Have you had your beef-tea?"

"Yes, thank you."

"And how far have you got, to M? You must have worked very hard. You can put them aside now and do these. I have written the gist of the replies on the backs. What time is the rehearsal, four? I have to call at Putz's and some other places, so au revolt till lunch. You will be amused at lunch. Old Colonel Stratton is coming, and —" she mentioned the names of three stars of the old Italian school of opera, "the grand and only school," as General Aymer used to say. She laughed softly as she added:

"You and I will be the only respectable women; but it will be amusing. Why is virtue so dull, I wonder? If she were only amusing what saints we would all be!"

She always left a perfume behind her, delicate and illusive. It was a strange ménage. Mary had found a definite place in it; her easy brightness, her humorous acceptance of the odd phases of life, her entire absence of constraint, and the decided way in which she disagreed with the General, had placed her on a different footing from the other young ladies who had filled the position before. She always lunched with them, sometimes dined; and since the General had discovered that she grew very white towards twelve, there was a standing order for beef-tea as soon as she arrived.

Generous, cultured people, with the fine tolerance that springs from a complete knowledge of life. Mary always kept a more than kindly thought ever after for the Bohemianly inclined General, and the dainty, gentle lady.

Luncheon was a delightful meal, followed by excellent coffee and equally good cigarettes. The operatic stars talked prettily in broken English, talked expressively with face, and hands, and eyebrows. Old Colonel Stratton told anecdotes of the great, the incomparable, the ugly Schneider, the only Grand Duchess. Told how she had laughed and said:

"When I was young, with *beauté du diable* enough for three women, no man looked at me. No one gave me a flower. Now I am old, fat, vilaine. You men, you rush after me, cut your throats, blow out your brains; c'est curieux!" Ana of the Second Empire, croniques scandaleuses, secrets de coulisses, sidelights on Court and politics; each lunch was as entertaining as a volume of the Greville memoirs.

Men with felt slippers had come at twelve o'clock and cleared the drawing-room. This was a curious long room; an ingle-nook was formed by the simple expedient of putting up a cairene, one-storied house on carved poles; the original red-and-white striped blinds dangled from the window, and an orchestrion was erected in the little room. At one end of what had been another room was the raised platform of a stage; a Steinway grand generally occupied it; to-day a harp and four chairs were added. It had a background of carved arches, with hanging Indian curtains and colored glass squares.

Mr. Thomas, the harper, and four oboe players were to come for a rehearsal of specially arranged country dances for a pastoral play of the time of Will Shakspeare in the Wimbledon woods. The hostess sat in an arm-chair in the boudoir; many of the smart people were unknown to her — merely came to rehearse in her drawing-room. Her friends peeped in and gave her greeting. Mary stood at the door and looked on — flâneurs, gobeurs, men young, middle-aged, and perennially youthful, trooped in, all well tailored; the women were smart, well groomed, all in the mode of the day, a few in that of the day after. A thin man, with long locks, sat down to the piano. A ball of a Frenchman, with an upstanding brush of black hair and fierce mustache, jumped about like a frantic black-beetle, and screamed in broken English interlarded with French.

Monsieur Goubon, ballet master, late of Her Majesty's, engaged to teach fashionable London to foot it on the greensward as bumpkins and wenches. Mary had to draw back sometimes to laugh. Her hostess smiled in sympathy. Anything more comic than this circle of stiffly attired men and small-waisted women, tripping to the pretty, abandoned, jiggety old English measure, with the smell of hay clinging to it, could scarcely be conceived. The finale was — each bumpkin was to catch his wench, and kiss her on the cheek or lips.

The afternoon sun stole in, and glinted off a diamond or sapphire brooch, or called forth the shimmer of silk. The old melody twirled and tripped, and Monsieur Goubon tore his hair, seized his head as if he would wrench it off by the ears and fling it at them; did the steps; shrieked "Stop!" lost his temper; raved as he did at his coryphees — screaming:

"Begin all over again! You are not zhentlemen danzeeng wiz ladies; you are paysans, cochons de paysans! you must not be afraid, you must not touch wiz ze feenger-teeps — zo! You must frow your arms, abandon, abandon yourzelves — allez — stop! Mon Dieu, c'est à rire! Ve vil not reerse zee embrace; but ven it come, you must geeve it — as a paysan!" he yelled with an explosive fusion of expressions that produced the eruptive effect he desired. Later in life many wondered where Mary had acquired her esoteric knowledge of society people.

Sometimes, too, she went to the House (tea on the Terrace was not then a fashion), and listened to many a remarkable debate; for it was the day of obstruction, of Parnell, of the great little leader of the fourth party, who scintillated and blazed like a tiny black diamond of the first water on the floor of the House. She always remembered her first night of a great debate; the kind of personal pride she felt in the benches where the Irish heads clustered; the so well-known faces of men unknown to her as acquaintances; the two brothers with the out-of-date profiles that suggest togas as the only fitting wear.

Perhaps no woman with a sense of humor can regard the House for the first time from behind the grille without a feeling of keen amusement. All these men look so like schoolboys; anything that is ludicrous in a man's gait, or shape of head, or little airs of importance, is emphasized on his entrance. Politics interested her, as they did all Irish women at that time. She had a singular devotion for Parnell that would have made her put her left hand in the fire to have served him. She had heard him described as cold, impassive, and she thought as she observed him no woman would have said that. She wondered that those who had failed to get at the kernel of this man's personality did not try to get at it through a reading of that of the women of his family. She always recalled that first night. How, after an impassioned speech by Sexton, the academical English of the "letta and betta" kind of pronunciation of a lackadaisical under secretary seemed at best a step beyond dumbness.

So confused are the issues of life it would have seemed almost impossible for Mary Desmond to realize that the fate of this great Irish leader, without whose name the history of England in this century can never be written, could have had any influence on her own life as an insignificant woman. Yet it had; for when they forgot all he had done for them, and sacrificed him in obedience to bigotry and the moral fetich, it robbed her of the last shred of allegiance to the old religion in the old country. Afterwards she used to smile as she looked back upon a scene at supper in the house of an Irish friend. When the notorious committee-room scenes had closed, the men were trying to justify themselves by stress of arguments, the women were strangely silent, and Mary had burst out with a passionate — "By God! if the women of

Ireland had been his followers instead of you men, we'd have stuck to him in the teeth of excommunication."

Well, life was full of interest if one only had courage. Given that and a brave heart, sure the world belonged to one. Sometimes, when a piece was drawing to a close, she and the Philosopher and Miley used to go to the gallery of some of the better theatres. It became a quaint theory of hers that one ought to see every good piece from the gallery and the stalls; that if she were rich she would occasionally hire the whole gallery, and sit a unit in the center of the first row in undisturbed enjoyment of the extraordinary impressionistic picture below. Tiers of heads, fantastic lights, splatches of color in boxes and stalls, and the puppets moving on the slanting stage with an audacious, delightful topsy-turvydom of perspective as seen from above. It was thc way to preserve the illusion, the mystery; all the coarseness of the make-up, the joins in the scenery, the crudeness of the reality, and the methods vanished, giving one an English version of a Japanese picture. Sometimes on Sunday mornings they went to quaint bird-markets in bystreets; and time rolled on.

CHAPTER XX

Christmas had come and gone five times since Mary Desmond walked up Goodge Street. She was standing, with her foot on the fender in a little back sitting-room of a house in Gower Street.

Her landlady, a very stout woman, bustled in. Her black silk skirt rustled like paper. She had small, black, sparkling eyes, and black ringlets hanging on to her shoulders; a large cameo brooch fastened a beautiful Indian shawl over her expansive chest. She held out a very fat wrist to Mary, saying, "Fasten this bracelet, there's a dear! The girls are aren't ready yet. Emmy do look that sweet in 'er blue silk, with that white flower at 'er neck! It always makes me sorry poor dear Jones can't see 'er."

Mary knew from experience what a reference to the shade of Jones meant, so she asked, "What are you going to see?"

"The new piece at the Adelphi. When I don't go there I go to the 'Alls. Jones, ee liked Shakspeare. Ee took me oust, pore dear, to see 'Amlet. I was that tired I wouldn't 'ave kep up, only we 'ad an oyster supper comin' on after. 'Jones,' sez I, 'wen we got out,' 'never no more.' Jones said, 'That wot was so interestin' about 'Amlet was that each man could figure out for 'isself wether ee was dotty or not. 'Now, that ain't my idea of an evenin' out! I don't wanter figure out nuthin'. Either I want to larf, then I go to the 'Alls; or I want to be 'arrowed, then I go to the Adelphi. Good old domestic dramer is good enough for me; I get enough figurin' out in real life without pay in' to see it. It's like Kmmy's music, all classic; two gold medals and a diploma; an' it makes me that melancholy I could fair 'owl. One momin' larst week it made me that nervous I 'ad to call up to 'er wen she was playin' somethin' she called a 'fewgo,' Back's, 'For Gawd's sake, child, play somethin' livelier! It makes me think of the drorin-room floor unlet an' the water-rate a-comin' in.' It rumbled an' rumbled in such a way that it gave me the fair miserables. I told Sarah to give you an' Miss Ope your supper 'ere. You look tired to death, pore dear; you ain't fit for trapesin' in an' out in all weathers." She patted Mary on the shoulder.

This was not without significance. A few years ago few people would have touched Mary Desmond familiarly. She had grown tolerant; had learned to discount manner for motive.

"Do that good gentleman as comes 'ere mean anythink serious? I thought ee did by the way of 'im. Ee seems to set a store by you."

Mary flushed a little less brightly than in the old days, and smiled half humorously as she said, "Yes, I think he *means serious.*"

"Then don't you go an' let no sentiment stand in your light. It's nice in a play.

One sort of expecks the 'eroine to reject the 'aughty baron's advances, and marry 'er own true love, but it don't do in real life. You know," kindly, "you ain't everyone's fancy, an' it's a good thing to feel secure an' taken care of. Old Mother Jones knows the difference."

She bustled away, with a final encouraging pat. Time had not dealt too hardly with Mary Desmond. She looked young for her twenty-eight years; but a keen observer would have noticed that the pathetic droop of mouth was acquired — was not the original intention of its modeling; some of the alert mobility that was so arrestive had gone, too, from her face. She had lost no atom of her old "style," that was so little stylish, but perhaps her manner was less assertive. She coughed a hard, short cough: November had been trying. She glanced at the clock — the hands pointed to eight; a little shadow of disturbance moved across her face. She looked at herself in the glass between the ornaments; considered herself gravely, tried to note the change since the last time she had sought to wrest the secrets of her own nature from her eyes — that was in New York. Little had happened, and so much had happened, since then. One thing had been always the same — the need to work and the sense of loneliness. The Major had gone back to Ireland. The Philosopher had worked his way into a firm, and was planning a home for himself with a pretty north-country girl. Peggy was well married out in California; a leader of social sets. Miley was living with an aunt. Yes; it was horribly lonely, she told herself sadly. She had few illusions left. She remembered, as a little girl in Dublin, she used to come upon a queer old man with a gaunt, bent frame, not a common man; he had tangled gray locks, restless, glancing eyes that darted to right and left; he held a stout stick in his hand and hurried along, turning up every fair-sized stone as he went, looking eagerly under it, muttering hopelessly if he found nothing. There were several of them; they used to haunt Camden Street and Richmond Street, and all the district between Ranelagh and Harold's Cross. She saw them constantly; the boys molested them. She had asked someone what they were; everyone knew them. "They are God-seekers," was the unexpected reply; "a sect that believe they will find a manifestation of Him under a stone, and that is why they keep turning them over." Strange people! to look for God under a stone, and yet was it so strange to go looking for God and find a stone? From the time she was a little child she had been wishing for love — Love, the God. She smiled. Ay, she had walked many a weary mile and turned up stones enough on the way.

Her work was not chosen work; it was just what came; she had no joy in it. She was ill, could not shake off her cold; yet somewhere out in the world there were pleasant things enough, could she but have a share in them. She was so sick of God's big wheel; weary of being ground monotonously. Lady Aymer was dead. Her present place as secretary to an Association was dreadful. The woman over her was hateful; a perfect type of a narrow, solidly educated, middleclass suburban Englishwoman. Mary felt that her cold eyes rested on her in disapproval twenty times a day. She asked Mary's opinion on social and artistic questions; would not be put off; then pressed her lips when she got them. She resented Mary's want of toadying loyalty; she lived with a chronicle of the doings of Royalty in her pocket, sat under an Anglican preacher, and made a virtue of having no temptations.

Mary had learned two fresh languages, sought forgetfulness in many a book; but that was so abstract, so outside, so little in touch with her dreams and desires. The door-bell pealed, and the knocker fell imperatively. Mary drew her breath sharply. There was a knock on the door. She turned and said: "Come in." A tall man obeyed; an unusually tall man; an eagle-headed man, with clear, keen eyes a little close together and rebellious hair. A clear brown skin and strong yellow teeth that showed as he talked, coupled with something vital that seemed to emanate from him, made one feel that one would be safe with him in a row, or any contingency in which pluck and resource would come into play. It made strangers take ten years off his actual age. He held out a lean, bony hand, disproportionately slight for his great frame. Mary always felt when she shook hands as if she were putting hers into a steel glove. He considered her closely for a moment; then sat down on the couch and nursed his knee.

"You got my letter?"

"Yes."

"Haven't been able to come to a decision? I thought as much; suppose we thrash it out. First time I ever did that with a woman. You are a bit of a witch to make me do it in my old age. You look very tired, except your eyes; odd eyes, alert, magnetic, with a little questioning devil in them that never tires. Struck me first time I saw you. Must be twenty years ago. You don't look your age. You were a rum little shaver, all eyes and legs — odd that I remember. Never forget anything; wouldn't do for me to forget things —might be awkward; an adventurer needs a good memory — valuable weapon.

"So let us consider. You have known of me all your life, known me personally six months. It has not been my fault if you haven't collected some data in that time. I am not a blackguard, but it would take some nice casuistry to canonize me. I would find it difficult to make the average Nonconformist, unless in business, accept me as respectable. You are the first woman I have ever asked to marry me. I am not sure I know why I am doing so, either. You are at a turning-point. You are erotic, even if you don't know it, and you haven't much religion — at least, if I understand rightly, not a practical form of it. That's bad. I'd make all women Roman Catholics. Those old fathers had a nice discrimination in femininity, they regulated your sexual emotions by finding all sorts of outlets for them. You won't be able to help yourself if you wake up, and you'll probably come a cropper. It's the best woman, not the worst, who does that. Believe me, little one, it is wholesomer for a woman to play cutthroat euchre with any sort of a decent man than to play the game of patience with her own emotions! There might, probably, be two opinions as to the advisability of your taking a hand with me; twenty as to my moral value as a partner. I have played the world off my own bat; played my own game in my own way. I have tried to give two knocks for every one I got, but I have always fought fair. As far as your sex is concerned — well, I'll own up. I have loved just as many women as I have had time to, but I have never treated one of them badly. I dare wager every old sweetheart I have ever had has still a corner in her affections for me — would prove my very good friend if I needed her. Why? Because I never loved a woman merely for the sake of my own gratification; I have always made my love a gratification to her. You'll understand the distinction as you grow older."

Mary had crossed her arms on the mantelpiece, and laid her forehead on them; she was looking into the fire; her whole figure looked weary. The mud on the little boots had dried gray; there was a black streak on her collar where her jacket had rubbed. His quick eyes noticed it just as he had come in; she had made no toilet for him, she had no wiles, no trace of coquetry, and yet to him she was full of witchery. "You don't answer. Was I wrong about you?"

"No—"

"What are you thinking of?"

"A woman I once knew, a bow-maker."

"Thank you! I flattered myself I was talking in a way to make you think of me."

Mary looked round.

"She came into my head as a comment on what you were saying. Something she once said."

"Which makes you hesitate?"

"Yes."

"How long ago? Five years? One has time to change a good deal in five years. You will never be a great woman in the sense of one of the world's successes, because your heart, and the dream in it, will always prevent your using your brains to your own advancement. If you were not handicapped by your need of loving you might be a glorious adventuress; as it is, you never will. You have a great capacity for love going to waste in you; why not turn a little of it over to me?"

A note in his voice made her turn and look at him. He held out his left hand, and she took it, and he drew her down next him; leaning his elbow on his knee, and holding his chin in his hand, continuing:

"Yes, to me. It wouldn't be for very long. Honor bright; a couple of years at most. Yes, I came from a specialist the day I wrote to you. It's only a question of not too long a time. I have a fancy to have a good sort of little woman with me for the last stage, and I think I have enough of my own cunning left to make it to your advantage. You are tired."

"Very."

"Poor little thing! Ah, I know you better than you know yourself! Well, I must know, that is all, because I, or we, leave in three weeks. I have a big deal on in Chile; we'd stop in Buenos Ayres, go on to Valparaiso, back by San Francisco. You'd enjoy the trip, eh?"

The wavering flush crept up again; her eyes glowed; she looked keenly at him. His hard eyes had a soft light in them; it caught her more than all his arguments, and the gambling instinct, the reckless desire to experiment, that is inherent in every natural woman who has preserved her instincts intact, roused in her. Perhaps — he had calculated on it. She answered without dropping her eyes, examining him with a close look as if she were trying to solve the puzzle of this man's nature:

"Very well. I don't mind."

His eyes flashed for a second, and he rose and turned her face upwards, and looked at it with an odd, almost wild, tenderness working round his cynical mouth; but he only stroked her smooth hair softly, and said, gaily:

"So you and I, Mary Desmond, are going to venture together!"

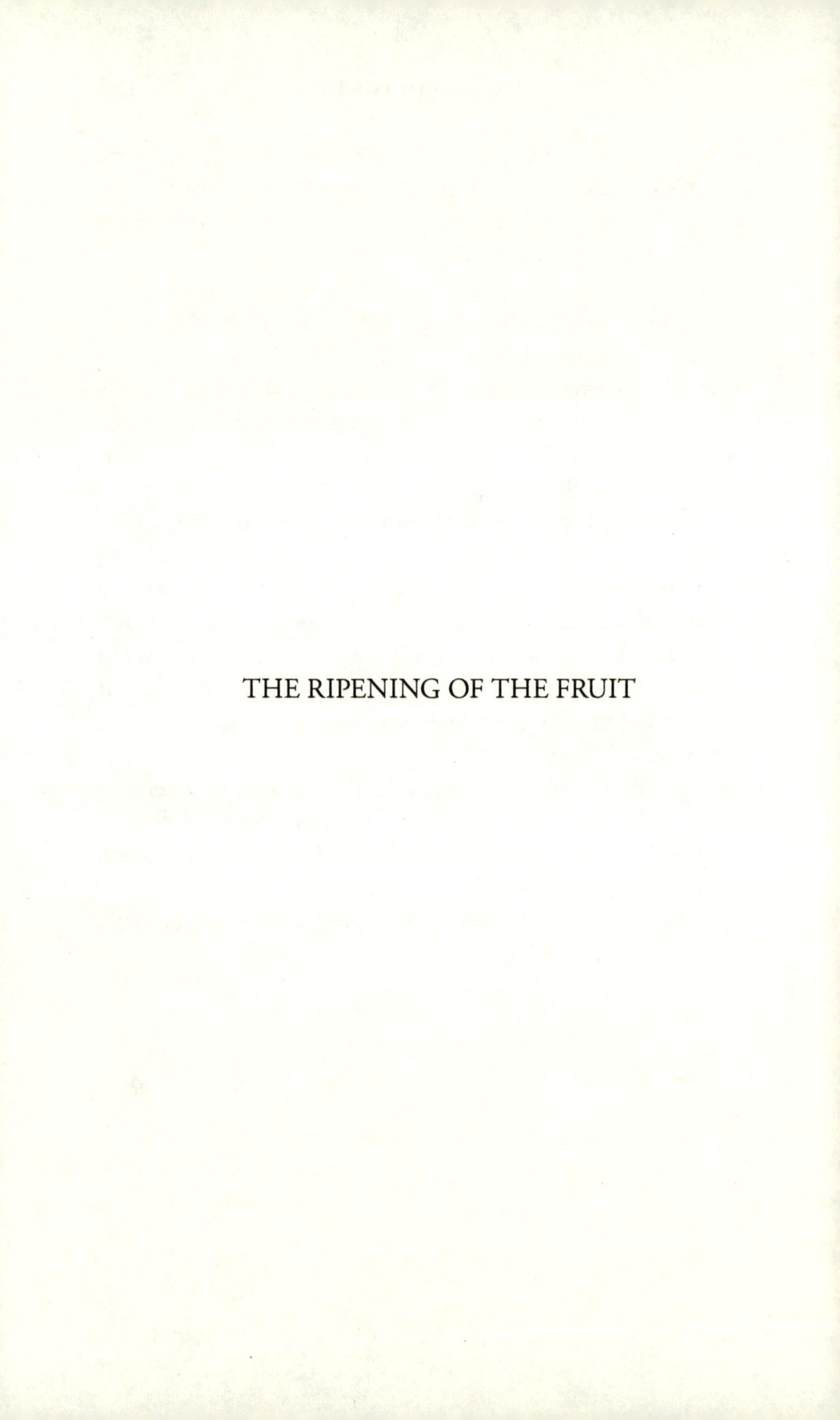

THE RIPENING OF THE FRUIT

CHAPTER XXI

In the grounds at an exceedingly quaint old manor-house in Buckinghamshire a tennis party was in full swing. A local band was playing a waltz under a beech-tree near the river that ran through the grounds and was stocked with trout. A fanciful white bridge crossed it, and led to the hothouses and another tennis-court. One could see the white flannels of the men, and the blue of a woman's gown through a dump of pollard willows. Men and maids brought round champagne-cup, and fruit, and little silver baskets of sweets; tea was served in the center hall of the old house. Mrs. Straker-Ellis's monthly garden parties were very pleasant. People from town, fagged at the end of the season, were glad to escape from the dust and heat for an afternoon in the shade. They afforded the county people of limited means glimpses of town and fashion, in the shape of minor celebrities of the world of literature or art.

A slight woman in black stepped out through one of the French windows, and opening a white silk parasol sauntered on between the gorgeous mass of blooms that lined the garden paths. Her gown was made of some thin material over silk, and had the "chic" of a French gown, made to fit the individuality of its wearer. The pointed toe of a patent-leather shoe and the glint of a jet buckle showed as she moved. Two women sitting in the shade of a tree were talking scandal and eating fruit. "That is the woman I asked you about," said one of them, as she passed; "she is slaying down here. Who is she? Looks French or American. Her sister is here, quite a different type — stout, with auburn hair; dressed in heliotrope silk, with a ridiculously overdressed child in white. These grapes are delicious."

"Yes; Carrie manages things well; she always did at home, though how was a puzzle. *She* is a Mrs. D'Arcy, a widow — oh no, not so young when her face is in repose; certainly thirty. She wasn't married quite two years. She's rather odd. Jack says the husband was a peculiar man, much older, an awful roué, a regular freebooter; fought for the Carlists, smuggled arms to the Soudanese, went in for all sorts of extraordinary undertakings—"

"Did she go with him?"

"Oh, dear, no! — before her time. I don't know who she was — Irish, I fancy. The sister's married to a Californian and is awfully rich. Carrie was up dining with them at the Langham, so I suppose they are all right — doesn't matter much nowadays. She seems to have been everywhere. Jack says, what she doesn't know isn't worth knowing. Carrie met her in Norway. I wish I could catch that man's eye — I'm so thirsty."

"I'd make a bet Carrie Ellis is tryng to nab her for Cecil,"

"Very likely. I know for a fact that Straker-Ellis declares that he will give him one more chance, and that on condition that he marries and settles down. He paid six hundred pounds for the last practice for him, and he had to give it up — simply *had* to. He'll never be steady; he is weak and he is obstinate. Eddie was just the same. Carrie never rested till she got him out to Ceylon. You can't blame her, if you think of how she has had to manoeuvre to get them all out of the way. Well, I pity the widow if she marries Cess; she'll have a handfull."

"I suppose she has money; she has exquisite rings, and her clothes are made in Paris." She paused as a thin, high-pitched voice behind them called, "Cecil! Cess!" with a note of impatience in it. They turned, settling their faces into conventional smiles. The owner of the voice, a tall, high-nosed, fair woman, with an elaborately embroidered gown, and a frill of lace falling from the brim of her flower hat, throwing her too light eyes into becoming shadow, was waving her hand to a big, fair man in flannels. He came lazily towards her — a well-set-up, long-limbed Englishman, with a small, rather flat head, close-cropped, red-gold hair, and laughing, green-gray, hazel eyes, under heavy lids. His thick mustache hid most of his mouth, but when he spoke one could see a thin, straight, red under lip. His chin was small but well shaped. He raised his cap pleasantly, with a "How do, Sophy?" to the informative one of the two. They beamed. He always disarmed women when he smiled at them.

"Well, Carrie! What's up, old girl?"

"Where's Mary D'Arcy? You have been fooling about with that Han —" She checked herself, for she knew what the quick drawing together of his brows meant; she had so much at stake, it was worth humoring him. She said: "I'm so worried, Cess; George is so impatient. He dropped a lot last week over an African deal, and you know how he is until he makes it up again."

"I know, old girl. It's a confounded nuisance, though, tying a fellow up that way. I've been straight as a die now, haven't I, for six months?"

Her patience almost gave out as she thought of the way she had watched him, how she had foregone her rare hours of rest in the afternoon, when she could get into a tea-gown, with a French novel, and lay aside the mask she wore for every human being. In a way Carrie Ellis was a heroine. The eldest of a large family, with an invalid mother and an impracticable father in a poor living, she had literally schemed the whole family into comparative comfort. Whatever heart she possessed was in the keeping of a big, athletic curate, who would have made as fine a professional cricketer as he made an indifferent parson. She had resolutely crushed it down and married George Straker-Ellis, twenty years her senior, with the name of being one of the luckiest men on 'Change. He had been generous; enabled her to get the younger girls married and the troublesome boys shipped to the Colonies. She, in turn, proved an admirable wife. She liked town, but, finding his irritability increased there, she gave it up. Little Rivingden Manor was some twenty miles from her old home. It had been restored and not much spoiled by the former owner, and was just an hour from town. She worked like a Trojan, and bargained like a contractor to a jerry-builder; got it cheap and made it into a perfect semi-country home. Straker-Ellis was proud of his peaches and grapes, and looked forward to Saturday and Sunday all the week. She had found the district overrun by the brewing family, the Weggs and their offshoots — sandy, freckled, pushful people, with an extra veneer of snobbery to every fresh success. The newer professional people detested them, because they had to submit to patronage in return for their bread and butter; the older, impoverished county people disliked them, because it was impossible to visit any village within a day's drive without regretting the destruction of old inns, with their quaint signs of the Barley Mow or the Cock and Jewel. They had been replaced by ugly, pretentious little red-brick houses, with a swinging board with "Wegg's entire" in scarlet letters. Carrie Straker-Kllis could afford, as an outsider, to ignore all feuds. She returned every call, chose her guests as it pleased her, amalgamated the discordant elements, and placed the Weggs on the same footing as the village doctor. When she asked Mrs. Silas, who was the "great" Mrs. Wegg, to dinner, she always took care to have at least two women present who took precedence of her amongst the guests. Her brothers and sisters were all settled; she felt that she deserved peace and liberty to plan her own boy's future. Cecil was her favorite brother; she had sacrificed much for him while he was studying to obtain his degree as a doctor. He was getting to be a very sharp thorn in her side. They had bought a practice for him; he had sold it, bought another, and lost it. Now Straker-Ellis had put his foot down, and given him six months to get settled. She had met Mary D'Arcy in Norway last year; in fact, the widow had interpreted for her in a difficulty with the landlord who spoke no English. She knew further that she was the daughter of a Major Desmond, and seemed comfortably off, had brains, and was presumably a woman of the world, although she seemed never to have mixed in any London set, or to have seen plays or races, or any of the ordinary society functions. Her sister was exceedingly well off, and mixed in the best American set in London, and — no one better offered. Cess flirted atrociously, and always with the wrong person. She put her hand on his arm: "I've always tried to help you, Cess." His face softened. "I wonder you don't admire her."

"I do, tremendously, only she takes things so seriously one has got to be up to the mark all the time; it's such a bore."

A good many curious glances had followed Mary across the lawn. The quiet elegance of her black gown was noticeable amongst all the light summer dresses, for it was a very hot June. The haggard lines and hollows of the delicate face had been creased out by leisure and gentle living. The old eyes, with their mixture of sadness and humor, and the question that leaped into them whenever a new face or fresh scene presented itself to them, were the same. She made her way to a group of men standing round a fair little woman in an elaborate garden-party frock. Mary knew by the poise of her head that Peggy was telling a story, probably larded with quaint and supposititious Americanisms. How it brought back old times — girl-days, the hard-up Bohemian days, when the whole world was an orchard of golden apple-trees, ripe for the plucking! The men laughed delightedly at the climax. Mary hesitated. Peggy liked to have her men to herself. The little niece saw her, ran forward, and hung on to Mary's arm.

"Take me to see the orchids, Aunty; Mumsy is having a good time, and I do miss Pap."

They turned down the path towards the glasshouses; she was glad to leave the crowd. An odd sense of depression hung over her, not for the first time lately; she awoke with it this morning, and it had grown with the day. She remembered once as a child that she and her companions had gone down to explore some cellars in a ruined mansion. Her candle had gone out, and she had taken a wrong turn; the air got stifling; long, dangling cobwebs flicked her in the face and got in her mouth and eyes, almost smothering her; she had shrieked at the horror of it and lost consciousness. The others, hearing her cries, had come back and found her senseless in an alcove. To-day, in the bright June sunshine, with the strains of waltz music, and the laughter of women's voices, and the hearty bass of the men as they called the score — to-day, when there was a little fresh breeze rustling through the leaves and whispering in the reeds, she was conscious of the same sensation; something numbing, baleful hanging over her — something too elusive for analysis — invisible cobwebs smothering her soul, slowly and surely, in a fateful embrace. She had tried so hard to shake them off, but the old voice that was waking again whispered over her shoulder, "How useless to fight the unseen forces to which one holds no clue!" She gave the child to the care of the head gardener, and sat down on a seat under a great copper beech, and leaned her head against the bark, closing her eyes wearily. So might a solitary little Mother Carey's chicken feel that had drifted into smooth water and longed for companions and storm stress. If she were rich enough to travel, perhaps she could find distraction; but her two hundred a year was only enough to live decently. Besides that, she had six hundred pounds lying in the bank, waiting for her to decide what she would do with it. She had promised Miley fifty; he was going out to Africa, her dear boy! If she had been rich, she would have kept him with her — and yet that, too, might be unfair. Strange, how life molds one! Hers had unfitted her to mix with the leisured middle classes; they bored her, she them. She took no interest in their lives, their small ambitions, their social aspirations, their openly snobbish chase after aristocratic acquaintances. She could not enter into it; they resented it; she felt their disapproval, was conscious of shocking them whenever she ventured on an opinion. She was not impressed by things; had never thought anything in life too good for her; had no reverence for rank in itself; if she said so, it was considered a pose. She had felt quite at home at Lady Aymer's, with all the people she had met there, whatever their rank; it was certain she did not dovetail into the class to which she by right belonged; she lacked, too, the gift of saying nothings — poor Jack had told her so when he was ill, and fretting that he could not leave her more. She remembered how he had said:

"Gold is at a discount in the conversation market; it's a tax to supply the change; plenty of small silver is what you want; it's just what you haven't got. I wonder what will become of you; it bothers me damnably; you will be a round peg in a square hole with that confounded two hundred a year."

He had been good to her in his own way, but it was life at a tension, almost a tobogganing downhill. It was only when he lay dead that she had realized that she had, as it were, been holding her breath and sitting tight all the time in fear of the unexpected.

Why did it all come back today? She remembered how he had rushed her off to get clothes; could hear him say, as he drove down: "They ought to be got in different places — in quiet West End houses of good taste; but there is no time; we must take our chance at one of the monster drapers'; there's one at the Circus."

How she had sat like an automaton, whilst he let an injured-looking young lady bring forward one costume after the other with the repeated assurances: "They are quite the newest style; all the rage; everybody is wearing them." How he had drummed with his stick and tugged at his beard, and finally ordered her to fetch "that elaborate young man, walking about inside a padded coat, with a crest of hair like a cockatoo." She could hear him say with a slow emphasis, as if he were talking to someone dull of hearing: "I want an outfit for this lady — a travelling dress, preferably blue serge, silk-lined; also a thinner woolen one; some white serge, washing silk, and muslin frocks — light things for the tropics — and a dinner dress and theatre gown. That young lady," with a wave of hand, "has been good enough to show me various garments that everybody is wearing. That is not what I want. Everybody's style is nobody's style, or hanged bad style. I want dainty, 'good form' things, suited to this lady and no other. I am in a hurry." The shopwalker rose to the occasion, and ordered the, by this time indignant, young lady to fetch "madame." She remembered the almost hesitating fear of his adroitness, as holding a possible danger, that rose in her as he smiled and talked in idiomatic French, with an atrocious accent, to the little sallow woman with the broché train and the old black eyes. How quickly she had grasped the idea, and how admirably she had managed!

It rained the morning they were married by special license — quiet, sodden, hopeless rain. The registrar was a hunchback, Jack's solicitor's clerk had a cold in his head, and Mrs. Jones, the other witness, wept tears of congratulation; he had given her a cable bracelet. The clerk had mumbled shyly, "I bish you bluck." The voyage was a strange one; she was making excursions into the unknown territory of his nature; they were not all pleasant.

He was well known on board; she was conscious that *she* was a surprise. The captain called him Colonel; she had an idea that it ought to be spelt with a K. The second officer, and the chief engineer, a colossus with a Glasgow accent, alluded to narrow shaves they had in dubious quarters in Rio. It dawned upon her that he was a bully, and that it was for her sake, once or twice, that he escaped when he met his match in one man on board. The nicest men were civil to him, but not cordial; he played monte with the Brazilians; they said he was a good loser. She discovered, too, that he was, in her case at least, jealous. It made her shrink into herself, put on a kind of armor, be other than she really was, for the first time in her life. She used to fancy it was like floating on a lake that had the tradition of being volcanic; one could not help the question, What if it were to boil up? She visited almost every country in Europe in that short twenty months. She used to say that, like the children in the fairy-tale who scattered crumbs behind them, they dropped champagne bottles. She seemed to have lost grip of herself, her old self that was, and to drift aimlessly after his death. She had been glad when Peggy wrote to say that she was coming over, only to experience a fresh disillusion, for Peggy and she had come to where the paths divide; it often comes to two members in a family, and it always hurts one of them. Peggy's husband, her children, her ambitions, her friends, filled her life to the exclusion of all Sympathy; she welcomed Mary cordially, brought her some presents, rattled on about her millionaire friends: petroleum, or silver, or wheat kings. She had hopes of being a millionairess herself some day, for Ezra was gradually buying up all the fruit farms round, and in a few years would most likely be the "canning king" of California. He was over in Prance now, trying to wrest the secrets of preserving from the manufacturers there; he had got round the nuns in Lisbon in the cutest way; their candied fruits are hard to beat, but he had subscribed to all their charities, and seen the whole process. She had invited Mary to go back with her; but as she had also expressed annoyance at Mary's having shown too great a familiarity with the conditions of workingwomen's life in New York to some American acquaintances, who had looked surprised, the latter had declined. No! unless one had leave to be oneself, it was best the paths should divide; but it was lonely. She had grown more dependent than she used to be; she missed him in some subtle way. There was a feeling of security in being with him. Curious, it was possible to feel secure and insecure at the same time; one might feel safer on a lonely road beset with tramps, in the company of a dog, even if one were not sure of the brute's temper. Everybody had their one row to hoe.

CHAPTER XXII

The child came out with Straker-Ellis himself; he had given her a basket of peaches. He had come from town, and stolen in by a side entrance to have a quiet smoke and visit his pines. He was an ugly, cross, unpretentious little man, but he rang true; Mary felt sure she could say exactly what she thought to him. The band had stopped as they came to the bridge; they could see that most of the chairs were empty. Peggy was coming to look for them, piloted by Cecil Marriott. She was in a frantic hurry; must not miss her train; was due at the Savoy to meet the Ponsonby-Anstnithers. Mary must come and see her the moment she came to town. She added:

"You mustn't stay too long, or else I shall have to get a strait-jacket for your Wild West admirer. You wouldn't think so to look at her," she said to Cecil, "but she can be a very obdurate person, this sister of mine. Good-bye, dear."

She flurried off with her host, leaving them together.

Mary was again conscious of that curious sensation of invisible, stifling cobwebs. She was glad when he broke in, with a surprisingly thin but sweet voice for such a big man:

"Haven't seen you all day — fearfully tiring affairs; don't know why Carrie has them. You look done up; come into the library and I'll get you some tea. I haven't had a decent drink myself all day. We'll go round by the shrubbery and escape the farewells."

A high-pitched voice called imperatively,

"Mr. Marriott!"

"By Jove!" he cried, "that's Mrs. Silas; she's bearing straight down, — I know, she's lost the poodle, and wants me to find it. Can you run? She knows the short cut. We'll have to fly round those rhododendrons."

He darted down a path, laughing like a schoolboy. Mary gathered up her dress and followed, gliding in and out through the shrubs, until she arrived breathless at the long window of the smoking-room. He put out his hand and drew her in, and they both stood and laughed at one another. "It was awfully mean of me to hurry you like that — I'm so sorry; only I can't stand Mrs. Silas. By Jove! you can run; you're not vexed, are you?" Mary shook her head — she was panting; but the heavy feeling that had oppressed her all day had vanished with the coming of laughter. She took off her hat, and lay back in a big chair near the window. He put a cushion at her back and found a stool for her feet. She had often noticed he did such things deftly; after all, it was pleasant to be taken care of by anyone. Some women have a knack of drawing it forth. Jack said she had not, but that the man who did care for her would never trouble a rap about any other problem in petticoats. She could hear him mutter, "You haven't found your Messiah yet." How the ghost danced in moments, bringing ribald and wise and tender sayings of his with them! The rattle of a tray made her look up. Cecil was wheeling in a little table laden with tea and decanters; he stopped at the door. "Ah, now you've got the dreadfully serious look again; it always frightens me. No, I am not joking, it does. It makes you look like a sibyl. I fed as if you are analyzing a fellow, looking right through him, probing for the weak spots. You looked quite different, jolly pretty, when you ran up all laughter; I felt quite indebted to Mrs. Silas. There! now you are smiling, you haven't an idea how it changes you. I know you take sugar, you may have one of these little frothy things, no more; you mustn't spoil your supper; always have a cold spread on these occasions. How's the tea, all right?"

There was something alive, warm about him — a healthy animal quality, akin to the earth itself; a crispness in his hair, — it was clipped short, — but just about his ears there was a little twist in it, and it glinted red-gold where the light caught it. His skin was clear, and the blood mantled under the tan; his forehead was very white. He talked gaily; she had never heard him talk much before, and she found herself laughing as he hit off the peculiarities of the local people. By and by, when her hostess came to look for her, with the pretense of not knowing where she had hidden herself, she was surprised to find that she was experiencing once more the odd feeling of suspensive excitement, that she had not felt since she was a girl. It lasted all the evening, and she went to bed and fell asleep soundly for the first time for weeks. She woke towards morning, when the birds were twittering tentatively in the ivy round her window; smiled as she recalled a story, and turned over drowsily, pleased that it was not later. She fell asleep and had a dream. She was walking along a dusty, bare road, and when she had gone what seemed an endless way, and her limbs were weary and her throat parched, she came to a wood. She heard laughter — strange, luring laughter — and turned off the road to look for it; it drew her farther into the wood, and then all at once she saw him peering from behind a tree, with laughing eyes and quick, flashing smiles, a vine-crowned, joyous Dionysus-headed youth. And she had run to him, and he had caught her by the waist and lifted her up like a child — then she awoke. It was so vivid that for a second after awakening she could feel the pressure where his grip had been. It made her conscious in a curious way; caused her color to fluctuate, and her look to be less direct; helped the forging of her fate, if she had but known it. It broke down the diffidence he had always felt with her, and he found that she was really exceedingly easy to get on with, when one knew her; easily interested and amused, with an almost childlike simplicity. The absolute direct sincerity of her nature was only another mesh in the net that was closing round her. As a child she had known many men, as a woman none — the law student and the man whose wife she had been for so breathless a space were of too unusual a type to supply her with data to go on. Any girl of twenty, with a summer's flirtations and a season's dances, would have laughed at her naiveness. She was ridiculously young at heart in spite of her knowledge of the shadier sides of existence. She never knew how it came about, but she found herself engaged to Cecil Marriott. She had not meant to be, yet when she realized that it was so, she almost found it a relief to have all thought of, and all plans for, the future decided for her. His attentions were pleasant; she found him a delicately reticent lover; *that* had its charms for her. As a matter of fact, she never appealed to his senses in the least; she mistook indifference for tender consideration. Afterwards she could see how easy an instrument she had been for the clever fingers of Carrie Ellis to play upon. Straker-Ellis had kissed her on the forehead and patted her hand, then entered at once into the matter of buying a practice. Cecil had heard of one in a town in Buckinghamshire, had gone to see it, and finally arranged to take it over. He had never spoken to her of money matters. Carrie had incidentally said, that with a nice home to encourage him to work, "Dear Cess appreciated comfort so much! he could easily make four or five hundred a year; you have —" she had paused with a delicate note of interrogation that touched Mary, so that she had replied:

"Oh, I have two hundred a year." Something in the look her sister-in-law cast at the silver toilet things on her table, and the tea-gown on the bed, made her add, she scarcely knew why:

"Of course we lived at the rate of so many thousand, when Mr. D'Arcy was alive. He gave me the furs and jewelry and handsome things which I have, but there was not much money when he died."

"Men are so abominably selfish in that way," the other had replied, but something in the rise of Mary's head had caused her to turn the conversation into a different channel without asking any further questions, merely saying:

"Well, you can live very nicely in the country on seven hundred a year." Mary had felt a kind of disloyalty in the other's criticism of him. She did not feel called upon to explain how poor she had been at the time he married her; it had never struck her that he had left her badly off, although it had troubled him when he was dying. He had broken down on the eve of a great adventure; it had failed, he swore, because the others lacked his colossal faith in forcing the situation at the right moment — for him.

CHAPTER XXIII

She and Cess were to be married in July. As Peggy was going to a French watering-place with some friends, Mary was to stay with her until then; it was to be a very quiet wedding. She sent the Major and Miley a liberal cheque, and it was not until she saw them, in the little hotel in the Strand where they had put up, that a doubt as to the wisdom of the step she was taking rose in her. She put her head on the Major's breast — he had grown old and gray — and burst into tears. He patted her head, and called her a dozen pet names, with a skill in the coining of endearing terms that is unknown to the purebred Saxon. His little girl, who had always been so sure of herself, too sure; this tremulous, emotional woman frightened him.

"What is it, heart o' gold? to be breaking down like this; sure ye were always the heart o' the rowl. Don't marry him, if ye don't want it; I'll settle him in a jiffy."

She dried her eyes, and laughed, and hugged Miley; big, bonny, warm-eyed Miley, with the humorous, tender, reckless face, that no woman could pass without feeling the woman in her. They dined together and went to a theatre, and she felt as if all her old self that had been asleep somewhere, under the newer crust of herself, woke up to greet them. They laughed and told stories, and used all the old terms that were their very own, that no one else knew — laughed because they remembered them, and used them.

"Look at that waiter's head," Miley had said, how it goes up in a 'pook' at the back."

And Mary had whispered, shaking with laughter, as at an unsurpassable joke:

"Yes, and look at the gold 'curee-caries' running up and down that girl's bodice; no, the one you have been staring at with admiring eyes. Funny how the old words strike warm to one! I wonder did anyone else ever say 'haw' on glass when they meant to dim it with their breath? Oh, I am so glad to have you both with me! I wish I were rich, and we three would stick together and have such glorious fun, behave like 'perfect fools,' as Peg would say."

"Faith, the world's badly divided," sighed the Major, "when the grandson of old Dinny Dinnis, who kept a porter shop you couldn't whip a cat in, could come over with a flunkey as big as a dragoon carrying his sable rug. He's always mighty civil to me, though, and I wouldn't exchange heads for his banking account."

She slipped them a five-pound note each, saying "good-night" to them at three o'clock in the morning. She knelt down by the arm-chair in her room, put her head on the seat and wept — the sobbing, abandoned weeping of a woman to whom tears come seldom. They were her very own. God, how warm they stuck to her! How she loved the modeling of their faces, the oddities of their expression, the curious interchange of soul-play; the feeling of being able to get nearer to them than to ordinary mortals. To creep in and play on their heartstrings, sure of response to the tune she was evoking. She just loved the way Miley misused his shall and will, just loved every bit of him. On and off, all her life, she had felt it, in there, when she thought of them; fierce, and strong, and tender; faults, follies, sins, or crimes, none mattered, with them against the world. It gripped her at times, so that she felt she could go to the scaffold, to death, to hell, for the sake of her own. Yet they always quarrelled when together, their hot hearts and sharp tongues clashing like rapiers. Every fiber of her was touched by them to a burst of melody that must have been keyed first in their mother's womb, or before it, perhaps through all their mothers, a melody that was the very soul of themselves, sounding in no outsider. The words of the Irish clan cry, round the Major's crest, rang in her — "The hills forever!" There was a thrill in it, scores of them tearing down, with the song of the one blood surging in their hearts, the strength of the one bone carrying them on. Was it a Celtic trait?

She felt it in a more limited degree for all Irish people, only they kept her back on account of her breach with the old faith; yet they touched her as no outsiders. English people were different. In some ways she felt nearer even to the colored people, with their clannishness, loyalty, and superstitions. The thought of the man she was about to marry, and a realization of the gulf between them grew upon her. God! a racial difference might even mean a tragedy of nonunderstanding between a husband and wife. She felt she would never speak to him of the superstitions, the dreams that are the birthright of every Celt — he would not understand. She paced up and down, trying to think a way out of the *impasse* she had gone into so blindly. She must have been asleep, or numbed, or what in the name of Heaven was it? What side of her did he appeal to? Not her brain, nor her heart, nor even the pity and tenderness of it that any mongrel or loathsome leper could arouse in her. No, to the desire for love, that was her weakness and her curse. How could she draw back? The practice was bought; he had a fresh start in life, and she would destroy all his chances! Why? She could give no adequate explanation. That demon voice kept whispering: What will you do with yourself? Where will you go? Where will you find a better check for the emotion in you that leads you astray? How will you satisfy the craving for love, to love something, anything, that is so potent in you?

She lay down in her clothes, and woke with a nervous headache, that deprived her of any power of thought. He called in the forenoon, felt her pulse, went out and came back with a draught, and smoothed her forehead and petted her, and was tenderly kind; for ever since he was a tiny, naughty boy, in his first breeches, he had simulated affection for the purpose of cajoling women — nurse, mother, and sisters; years of practice had brought it to a fine art. The Major, Miley, and the Philosopher and his wife came to lunch. She was not to stir, so she lay in the next room and listened to them. The Major had cocked his piercing old eye on his future son-in-law, and was more silent than usual; Miley had tried to draw him out, and then devoted himself to Peggy. The Philosopher's wife and he talked commonplaces; she satisfied his eye and let him eat his lunch. They looked sometimes a little puzzled at the four others, who were going over old ground for Peggy's benefit, telling old stories, reviving old jokes. They were all very tender with her as they said good-bye, and trooped out on a suddenly planned "scamander." She felt out of it, as if she were dead, someway. He remarked that her sister-in-law was very good form, said nothing of the others, for which she felt glad. Later on they went for a drive; she felt intuitively that he wanted to say something to her; she was learning to read his face, although it said little, except when he laughed. When they returned, at tea she went behind his chair, and touched her lips to his forehead; petting things was such a pleasure to her.

"What is it. Cess? You are worrying over something, aren't you?"

He did not reply, but she coaxed him to tell her.

"It was such a nuisance, Ellis was such a close beggar! Of course he had paid for the practice, and he was going to pay in a hundred to go on with, and he had agreed to pay for the furniture; but he wouldn't pay for a trap; talked a lot about earning it — could use a bike. Fancy starting in a good practice without a trap! He had wanted to arrange with the furniture people to pay them off by degrees; then he could buy a horse. A friend of his had a ripper that he wished to get rid of, and just the trap he 'd like to have. Things always went wrong; his friend couldn't wait, and the head of the beastly firm was away; wouldn't be back for some days."

Mary said nothing for a moment, it seemed an underhand thing to do. She went back, and poured herself out some tea, in order to think it over.

"I don't quite like the idea," she said; "it doesn't seem straight to your brother-in-law."

"Oh, he be hanged! he smells of money, and he thinks more of a fiver than I do of a pony."

She lay back and closed her eyes wearily; the same dull feeling stole over her; why did she always think of cobwebs when it came?

"Head bad again? I'm a brute to bother you; lift it, now lay it back; that's better; what a bag of nerves you are!" He was kneeling next her chair; she looked at him. How absurdly clear his eyes were, green-gray pools, with such china whites; it was good to look at something so fresh and sound. He reminded her of a hazel-nut, when the sheath is still green-brown.

"How much would do?"

He sheathed his eyes to hide the gleam in them. "Oh, six — a hundred would do it well."

He saw the slightly surprised look in the eyes that made him so uncomfortable at times, and added:

"I should have to get some forage, and send them down there, you know."

"Well, I will give you a hundred for a wedding present." He thanked her warmly, but with a certain awkwardness. It came back later, and then she knew that it was because he had expected it, calculated upon it, and therefore found it difficult to act a delighted surprise; and — perhaps he regretted he had not made it more.

She fetched her cheque-book and came back. He was looking out through the window, whistling gaily. He stopped when she came in. "Do you keep a banking account, old girl?" he asked with an air of bantering inquiry.

"Only a current account for convenience. They collect my draft for me when it comes. I had a little lying there."

She could not explain why, but the whole thing displeased her in some way. She handed him the cheque; he looked keenly at her as she turned away, flung it on the table, and caught her. "You are the best little woman in the world, bar none! I don't think I ought to take it, you know. I can't give you any jewelry or any present. I had made up my mind to wait until the first year's money came in, and buy you something then."

He said many nice things; there was a curious sadness in his terms of endearment. It often struck her humorously, and she used to think the word she knew would come in its turn. After all, poor Jack D'Arcy may have made her fastidious; he had rather a genius for erotic nomenclature. Cecil pleaded an appointment and left; she fancied there was an air of relief about his back as he went out. She went over the terms, went over them and laughed at them; knew perfectly well that she was only fooling herself into a belief in order to stifle the doubts nagging at her. No use, not a bit; she knew herself too well; knew she had drifted, literally drifted, into this marriage, and yet she could not quite tell how. She took up the cheque-book and looked over the blocks. She had written to her little trustee in Hamburg, her devoted Blumenberg — though anything more unlike a flower-mountain than the little bald, rotund, dry solicitor it was difficult to imagine. Jack and he had been good friends; he was bound to Jack by some service the latter had done him, and so she was left in his charge. What fun she had with him! She would never sign any papers without French bonbons. She used to make him leave everything and take her to lunch, or dinner, or supper to the wonderful *Keller* where Jack declared you could get everything as good, and some things better, than in any other restaurant in the world. Coming to think of it, perhaps he and the law student had treated her more *en princesse* — fairytale princess — than anyone else ever would. The dear, quaint little man! She had written to him and asked him for two hundred pounds. He had taken a week to answer, and then it had been an odd letter — a letter of cautious, good advice. He always told her she let money steeplechase from her. She had forty pounds lying in the bank when the draft came; she had so many frocks she had only bought a new grey travelling gown and a few trifles. One hundred was a big item. She sat down to the table. Something impelled her to secure the money for Miley. She would have fifty coming with quarter-day. Yes, she would draw it out to-morrow. Her curly pate! She wrote a cheque for seventy to "self," and tore it out, but when she went to fill in the block (she kept her accounts on the blocks: "self," a pound; ten shillings for slippers; five, note-paper, beggars, etc.) she hesitated, why she scarcely knew. She dog-eared and wrote "cancelled" across the block, as she always did when she spoiled a cheque, as sometimes happened when she forgot the month, or date, or did something wrong.

They all came back to supper, except the Philosopher's wife. Mary sat on the Major's knee, and laid her head on his shoulder and was very quiet. As she said good-night to Miley she whispered:

"I shall leave the fifty I promised you, old boy, with someone who will give it to you if anything should happen. It will be all right in every case."

Someone said: "I wonder shall we ever be altogether to ourselves again?"

A sudden silence fell over them, until Peggy broke it by making them all come back and drink another bottle of champagne "to our next meeting."

Next day Mary cashed the cheque, put fifty pounds in an envelope, bought a gold watch for ten of it at Altenborough's, and put them into a package addressed to "Miles Fitzgerald Desmond." Then she climbed to a fourth story in Lincoln's Inn Fields, and gave very explicit directions to the little man there. It was to be locked in a safe; she knew the number of the note, and there was ten pounds in addition. Of that, five was to be sent to the Major on the fourteenth of October — his birthday — and the other at Christmas.

It was a very quiet wedding. Her people were out of spirits and the gaiety was forced. The only comment made on it was when the Major, passing the Irish House in the Strand on his way to look up an acquaintance in the Freeman's Journal office, took Miley by the shoulder and said:

"In, you rascal! I want a stiff, a damn stiff whisky. I'm hanged if I can stomach a second-rate Sassenach."

CHAPTER XXIV

It was market night, the week before Easter, in a rising Buckinghamshire town, in the third year of Mary's second marriage.

A traveller in search of a country holiday would have found pleasure or disgust in measure as fortune might lead him to turn to the right or left of the street at the foot of the station hill. Indeed, if he were a cynic, he might reflect that it would not be the first time that a turn to the right road led him to a consideration of the serious facts of life and respectable ugliness, with salvation in the form of mundane solvency thrown in — a long, straight road, with many factories, aggressive buildings, dedicated to various forms of dissent, gas-works, and drainage, with rows of tiny villas, sacred to vulgarity and gentility. A turn to the left would have led him on to a broad road, of irregular pleasantness, on the way to ruin. The old church, with its cobble-stoned pathway winding through moss-grown graves, and its wondrous yew hedge, had an air of aloofness, as if it had grown gray with the old time, and failed to dovetail with the rush of the new — preferring to hide its head amongst the trees and escape the rant of the preachers in the market-place, or the rattle of the tambourines as the "army" passed. There, too, was the plashing river, where the ducks quacked, and the squire's domain; quaint old houses nestling in selfish seclusion on unreasonably large (so the new-town radicals maintained) ground-space; picturesque cottages, with latticed windows fastened by curious iron hasps, with damp green moss clinging to their walls, and the sun-dew in clumps upon their tiled roofs. Lovers' Lane wound to the beech-wood, with a kissing gate at one end and nightingale corner at the other, past the ancient almshouses, where the hollyhocks, blobs of bobbing sweetness, chatted to the larkspur, and the gold of creeping-Jenny and the white of money-on-the-mountain gave an old-time air to their garden patches, and the red-brown pears lent color to wall and roof. The very beer-houses, "licensed by the squire to brew their own ale," had a somnolent air, and when one looked through their open doors, past the hollowed oak benches and low counters with the ancient pewter measures, one got glimpses of cool, lush green gardens, with sunflowers as big as brazen warming-pans, and straw skeps for the bees.

So much any intelligent stranger might have observed without possessing any intuitive faculty; but the town was really remarkable in a way that could only be learned by living there. It was divided into the Old and the New. The old town had its traditions, superstitions, and observances, and woe to the outsider seeking to disturb them! Roughly speaking, it consisted of the inhabitants, professional or in trade, and such of the county residents as lived near, who had been rooted there before the coming of the railway. They had their horses and traps, and could drive very well to the station ten miles away. They resented its coming, as a means of introducing discordant elements — second-rate people, and factories; and worse than all besides, it spoiled the market — as railways have a trick of doing. The farmers' wives sent their eggs, and ducks, and fat fowl, even their separated milk, to London, and became independent of patronage. The old mill was turned into a noisy tannery; factories for boots and rushes, with their crowds of workers, sprang up at the ugly end of the town. A flaring international store, which undersold the staid old grocery establishment, where the prices were as good as the commodities, was followed by a butcher, who sold frozen meat on market days.

A branch bank, with newer ideas as to accommodation, where there was a prospect of fresh business, a young solicitor, and an architect, opened offices, whilst Baptist chapels, and a corrugated iron building with "Ebenezer" in letters of luminous paint, seemed to spring up like toadstools in a night. The hotels deteriorated with the growth of the town. The White Hart was noted before the railway for the liberality of its farmers' "ordinary" and the quality of its wines; but the markets had shifted to the county town. Cherry Fair, and Onion Fair, once of agricultural importance, with round-about and gipsy-horse capers and marvelous shows, became mere half-holidays for horse-play on the part of the factory hands. The commercial gentlemen, who used to come by coach and stay a night, playing whist and drinking good port, came now by a morning train, did their business, and left in the afternoon. So the fine old hostelry degenerated into a bar, and derived its revenue from the billiard-table, around which the wilder spirits of the new town drank or betted. The glory of the George and Dragon became mythical. The Square, once an *impasse* of vehicles, was a waste place, crossed by an odd farmer's cart going to meet the train, or a team of bicyclists scorching to the Cycling Tavern, where one could get tea, watercress, and a snack for nine pence.

The old town threw up its head, banked in the old bank, employed the old firm of solicitors, and ignored the new town completely. It became a point of honor with the new town to fly in the face of the older inhabitants and prove that they could do without them. They fought over rights-of-way, and the young solicitor crowed like a cockerel, to the discomfiture of the older, staider bird.

The children's Sunday-school treat attained to the importance of a tournament between the old order and the new. The squire threw open his park to the church children, gave prizes for flowers, prizes for sewing and potato boiling, hired the town band, and had fireworks in the evening. The old-towners had tea or wine in the great hall, whilst the new town paid three pence entrance and kept to themselves; but then the chapel people threw all differences overboard and held a united *fête* in a meadow, gave their tea free, welcomed everybody, had prizes for skipping and sack running, with liberal games in the afternoon, and a pyrotechnic display from London. Many little church children became dissenters in embryo at sight of the *fête* that was all music and brotherly love without the necessity, of a bob-curtsey to members of the ancient order.

Cecil Marriott had bought the practice left vacant by the death of "the old doctor." Taking the peculiarities of the town into consideration, he could scarcely have done a more foolish thing.

His predecessor was a character born and bred amongst the old people, one of themselves, with his finger on the pulse of all their prejudices. He had known by his dominant, shrewd personality how to reconcile all differences. He treated the ladies of the new town with the same brusque chivalry with which he prescribed for the old Miss Sykes of Ivy Manor; but Cecil Marriott was not of the stuff to tread along the lines he had marked out. Nor, perhaps, was Mary the best helpmeet for him in his position.

She returned every call. The ladies of the old town liked her, but scarcely thought her manner deferential enough for the wife of a mere practitioner; it was unconsciously frank. They felt that she was capable of criticizing the quality of their Madeira, and besides, she did not, as far as they could gather, go to any place of worship. She was pleasant, well-mannered, but from one or two things she had let drop, and which they discussed at their weekly whist parties, exceedingly modern. At heart Mary leaned to them. The delightful seclusion of their homes, their quaint silver and Chippendale furniture, embroidered pictures and old prints pleased her sense of beauty. It cost her not a little to accept the prodigal hospitality of the banker's wife and to submit to the superior gentility of a newly married junior solicitor's. The blatant vulgarity of the manufacturers' ladies was even a shade easier to digest. The one amusement of the genteeler circles of the new town was what they called "musical evenings" varied by card parties for the men. Mary felt boundlessly grateful that she was able to give a truthful negation to the question, "Do you perform on any instrument?" and thus escape being "assisted to the piano." The banker was a little man; his wife was an expansive woman mortgaged to maternity, and the frankness of her obstetric experience was such that it became the object of the other married ladies' lives at tennis, tea, or supper to suppress her gently. This was not easy, as she not alone outweighed them physically, but had money of her own and the expansiveness of temperament that goes so often with genial good-nature. Mary liked her; she found that her plain-speaking tempered their genteelness. One of the things they objected to in Mary was her use of the terms men and women; it almost amounted to coarseness. The men played "nap" on such occasions and the "ladies" were supposed to gossip pleasantly for an hour over their babies, *couchant* or expectant, and the delinquencies of their domestics. Then the cashier, and one or two others who sang, would come in for music. The banker used to bellow patriotic songs of the doings of the British soldier as if he were producing a combination of fog-horn and blanket by some marvelous sleight-of-hand from behind the bobbing apple of his throat. It had a horrible fascination for Mary; she used to watch it, unconscious of how much amused irony was expressed in her face. The architect used to request them to clear a space in the middle of the room and, with an entire absence of humor, and the seriousness of a session of elders meeting to censure an erring member, give them imitations of "Dan Leno" or the "White-Eyed Kaffir;" and when he forgot a line he began all over again.

"It's such a pity you don't like music," said the cashier's wife, who sang the soprano solos of Gilbert and Sullivan's operas; and Mary, forgetting, said laughingly: "Oh, but I do! I never miss any of the really good concerts; only they must be good."

They tried her on books; they were all devoted to the popular favorites, and doubted her sanity when she confessed a difficulty sometimes in reading them.

The poor people liked her; she used to listen to their ailments.

CHAPTER XXV

ON THIS NIGHT MARY Marriott was sitting on a stool before the fire with her head against the arm of a big chair. She looked pale, wretchedly thin, and her mouth had a weary droop at the comers. Sometimes it trembled a little, as if she were about to cry. She had come back the day before from a ten days' stay at Hastings; she had gone there after the little baby, that had lived three days, had been buried. A pile of receipts and bills — alas! the former small in comparison to the latter — lay on the table with some ledgers; she had been trying to add up accounts. Cecil had gone to town; Hall was in the surgery; the bell kept ringing, and a child wailed — she could hear his voice now and then; it was a deep voice for such a little man. People liked Hall; he would have a good practice. She looked back, and the two years and a half of her married life in Chissom came in fleeting pictures. It had been agreeable enough at first, although she had realized quickly how little there was in common between them, how curiously at variance they were from every point of view; but he was kind in his indifferent way. She had thought then it was his way with all women; now she knew that she herself had a numbing effect on his none-too-expansive temperament. She had lived in the day — tried to interest herself in the house and garden. It was pleasant in those early autumn days, when the beech woods were changing hue, to drive with him to some outlying call, have tea at some old-world inn; perhaps pick up a bit of Worcester or quaintly flowered Spode in some cottage visit. There was no great happiness, not one flash of great love; but there had been a grateful restfulness in the first home of her own she had ever had, and he was not an uxorious husband. Lately Mary had thought he almost disliked her. She used to shake off the idea as morbid; yet it had a way of thrusting itself upon her. She looked round the room. It was cozy, with the warm red-and-blue of the carpet, and the glow in the mahogany, and the books behind the glass: and now it was to belong to Hall. Curious how it all had come about, and yet how inevitably: that was her only comfort, the absolute tragic inevitability of the whole affair. Sitting there, calling up thoughts of every kind rather than let her heart dwell for one second on the tiny form that had never been really warm and smelt of cod-liver oil (for they had wrapped it in wool soaked in that), she went over every step of her married life and tried to see where she had failed; tried to imagine what would have been the result if she had been a hard, imperative woman, and she could not see that it would have made the slightest difference. Cecil was bound to drift, bound to sink, bound to be a wastrel of life and its chances through physique, temperament, and inclination. To be true to himself, even, meant inevitable misery. She had tried every way:

tenderness bored him; appeals to his honor or principles were fruitless — his conception of either was elementary. Once she had tried sharp, incisive speech. He had rolled a cigarette and listened in silence, and when her quick passion had exhausted itself he asked: "Finished? Then I'm off."

At first he had attended to the patients, pleased the women by his manner and good looks; but gradually people sat and waited in the surgery whilst she sent for him to the "White Hart." He made acquaintances of all the undesirable men of the district, played billiards wherever he found a table, and finally took to going to Allersham. Allersham had preserved the drinking habits of a past generation, in common with its quaint almshouses and curious market-place. Mary's maid, Jane, was a girl from that district. She had started with two maids, and a man who was coachman and gardener in one. After a year she had kept Jane on to open the door, and helped in the house herself. Expenses mounted in an extraordinary way. Cecil used to invite men to supper and do the catering himself; he had a running account at two wine merchants'. The money that dribbled in during the visiting hours seemed to vanish as soon as it came. She realized early in the first year that it was useless to expect any true statement as to money matters. He had "a bit on" every race meeting, and she learned accidentally that he was proverbially unlucky. At first she had taken the housekeeping books to him weekly and asked for a cheque and the man's wages; she paid all the small current expenses herself. It struck her that he used to avoid her when she set about collecting the little red and black books. At the end of three months he told her that there had been a heavy bill for drugs and surgical instruments. No Desmond was ever mean in money matters: she wished to pay her share; but there had been many things wanted for the house, and a rug for the trap, and lamps. Cecil ordered things recklessly, and she had paid for them. Gradually it came about that she settled the housekeeping bills and paid the servants' wages. She spent nothing on herself, and had grown to look anxiously forward to quarter-day. Miley had left in April. Cecil had grumbled because she went to Southampton to see him off. She can recall the scene so well; can see him standing in the surgery. He was whistling softly as she went in; the light caught his hair and found the gold in it: he always made her think of woods and vine leaves. She can recall the furtive way he had glanced at her through half-closed lids; it always annoyed her to feel that anything was afraid of her; he always gave her that impression — morally afraid.

"Miley is sailing on Saturday, Cess. I think I shall run up this afternoon and have a day with him, and see him off — poor old boy!"

He had not replied. Of all the many tricks of his that annoyed her, his habit of keeping silent tried her most. She would sooner a thousand times submit to the voluble stream of inconsequent reasoning, *pro* and *contra* of her own folk for the most trivial occurrence. She can see her own back, the hesitating poise of her head. What in the name of Heaven had come to independent Mary Desmond? It was curious, she always thought of herself in her old name. She remembers the intense sense of irritation that had risen in her, the curious, uncontrollable feeling of repulsion. At such moments she hated him; was conscious that if something had happened to mar the beauty of his face, it would, for a moment at least, have pleased her. There was no use trying to fight against it. Such moments made her realize how evil a thing marriage could be. She can see herself waiting obstinately for him to speak. She knew quite well that he could be meanly careful where her expenses were concerned. He had grumbled at half a sovereign she had paid for an old silver buckle. There was a satisfaction in making him declare himself. He said at last: "I don't see what you want to go down to the boat for — seems a waste of money."

She can hear herself reply, can trace the irony in her tone: "I am glad you are beginning to think of money; but it's such a long time since I have wasted anything on myself, that I feel I can afford it."

Curious thing, those premonitions! She had gone upstairs with a triumphant feeling of elation at the thought of the watch and the fifty pounds in the safe in Lincoln's Inn Fields. How glad, too, she had been in town! She always felt when she was away from him as if a great, wet sponge soaked in ether was lifted off her face, as though the very soul of her was stretching its arms in exultant relief as if freshly loosed from bondage. She was conscious of a sensation of actual physical weariness when with him. Her dear curly-headed, warm-eyed boy; she had stood on the wharf and watched until his face had melted into all the other faces. A Johannisburg "bookie" who had been home on a "spree" kept calling maudlin greetings to some daughters of Israel and the "variety" stage; and her own heart kept calling Miley.

It was in the first Easter holidays that Jane had said: "A gentleman wants to see you, ma'am; he was here when you was away."

A stout, short, hook-nosed man presented her with a card — the card of the furniture people. She had begged him to be seated, and asked his business: did he wish to see Dr. Marriott? How she had resented the smile that was in itself an insolent comment on the man to whom she was married, though it only came and went in a flash round the flabby mouth.

"We have written so often to the doctor, madam, — I have seen him twice, — that we thought it better to see you before taking any steps that might be unpleasant. Sorry to trouble a lady, you know, but business is business and times is bad. The account has been standing a long time now; the doctor promised to pay the end of first quarter, then at Christmas; now it is Easter."

"Have you the bill?"

"Yes, madam, seventy-five pounds with the interest."

She took it mechanically, asked him would he have anything to eat after his journey, ordered cold meat and beer for him, and took the bill out into the garden. She sat down on the old stone bench, about which the variegated ivy climbed so fearlessly. The purple and yellow crocuses were coming up in clumps, and a thrush was calling across the garden wall. The twitter of the sparrows hurt her head as if every chirp was a tack that some malicious imp was driving in. There was some mistake. She had given Cecil a hundred pounds to buy the trap and horse, so that the furniture might be paid for. Yet there were the entries. He had only paid part of it. What had he done with the money? It was only last week he had asked her to pay her quarter's money into his account in order to keep a balance, and she had declined. He had not spoken to her since, and she had only refused because she had needed it for the tradespeople. Well, it must be settled. Poor Dad had not been so well, and wanted her to run over and visit him. She had intended to get a cheap little gown; had planned a "gallivant." Good-bye to that. She must write to her little Blumenberg and ask him for another hundred. There would soon be very little left. She determined to ask him to invest the balance. She felt it would dribble away, and she had no heart to fight for it.

She went back to the little flabby man with the sharp eyes and told him that in a week's time she would call on the firm and settle the matter finally. Yes, she would state it in writing. She recalls the impulse she had to swear as she signed her name, "Mary Patricia Marriott." Cess had come in later with a man she loathed — a vulgar manufacturer — a man with a coarse voice and impertinent eyes, who paid her fulsome compliments. They were going out again for a drive, and there was a case in town that might need him. She told him to wait, she wished to speak to him on a matter that must be settled before the post. She can see him light his cigarette and wait.

"Harris & Longarm's man has been here." She gave him the bill. He threw it on the table.

"I know; I met him going to the station."

"Where are you going with that man?"

"To Allersham."

"Mrs. Danby may send any moment."

"Damn Mrs. Danby and the whole pack of worrying old fowl! I'm sick of dancing attendance on them. I'll get an assistant."

"You'll find it difficult to pay him; you owe bills in every direction. I have only two hundred a year, and I can't keep house and servants going on that — not as you will have it. Nobody asked me to? No, perhaps not; but unless I pay them, they don't get paid. Up to this, you have simply not met your own expenses. I have promised these people that I would pay this, but I shall write at the same time to Hamburg and invest what little there is left. You have lost some of your old patients; you are going the right way to lose more."

Dr. Nolan, a connexion of the great Weggs, had taken to coming over to treat most of the ladies of the old town, who objected to be told that there was nothing the matter with them when they were quite willing to pay for sympathy whether their ailments were fanciful or not. The banker had sent the "missus" away for the coming of number seven, and Mrs. Atkins had gone home to her mother. Marriott was good company, but he was not steady enough to attend ladies so delicately situated. Jane was a pessimistic chronicle of outside rumors. Mary listened to gossip that she would otherwise have checked, because there was so much at stake. He went to many race meetings and, she feared, lost heavily. Matthew spent half his time going to look for him in Allersham, or the little back parlor of the surveyor's house, which Jane declared was "a bar an' worse," when urgent calls came in.

Hall had come last March. She was ill when he came. She had not felt drawn to him at first. He was a sallow little man, with keen, cold eyes, and a sensitive mouth. Cess had been his fag at school. He was clever; had been with an expedition which an enthusiastic naturalist of large private means had sent to India. There was something repellent about him, and he was painfully ill at ease with her.

It was not until one evening when touching casually on occultism that they had found a common ground of interest. Mary had developed her faculty of pinning fleeting psychical experiences down for examination, and she had the gift of expressing them. Cecil used to listen sometimes, and declare laughingly that they were both mad. There had been no arrangement made. Hall was undecided as to his future, and was in no hurry. Mary felt too ill to interfere or care. As the warmer days came she used to lie out in a hammock near the lilac-trees and watch the birds build. They got to know her loose red gown; even the blackbirds fed their little ones, undisturbed by her presence, and the master wren used to flutter down and call to her, with a voice entirely out of proportion to his size, to protect his home and family from the inroads of the surgery cat. Hall used to bring her out a magazine or a wrap if it got chilly. Once she had said to him: "I wonder if there is anything in it? I once heard an old woman say, 'If you stay out in the free and listen to the birds sing, you will make a musician of the baby.'"

"Who knows?" he had answered, with a red flush that made his skin more unpleasant than its own dingy yellow.

Cecil was in good humor in those days and told her not to worry; things were going on all right. She had been glad to live in her own world, stitching her dreams into elf-like garments. Her irritation towards him had vanished, and given place to an odd, impersonal tenderness. Was he not the father of the little being which was fighting its way so slowly to light and life? It was a kind of doze in which sunshine and birdsong, and fluttering leaves and ripening fruit, and a pain that was all a joy, and a whisper that no other human being could hear, all melted together into a great human symphony. Winter drew near. Cecil went fox-hunting. Talking was of no avail; he declared she was a dog-in-the-manger to object, when Hobbs the farmer offered him a mount on "young uns" he wished to sell; besides, Hall got on splendidly with the cases. And then Christmas, and with it the fearsome expectancy of her coming time. Her thoughts flew back to childhood and the making of the crib. Four weeks before Christmas they used to prepare it: one day, Obedience — that was the cave; the next day. Charity — that was the straw, and so on all through the virtues; each day's practice making an addition to the wonder-work. There was so much to be made, — from St. Joseph to the ass, not to speak of Mary and the Star, and the little, pink Wonder-Babe. Tears of mingled laughter and pain came to her eyes as she thought of how she had absolutely failed to supply any swaddling-clothes — for patience had been the virtue necessary to their making — and all that day things had gone wrong. First of all, her bootlace had broken; then she had been blamed for upsetting an ink-pot and could not explain without telling tales; and her tooth had ached; and as a climax to deprive her of a last shred of hope she had smacked the O'Connor girl's face. How she had cried and begged of "Little Jesus" to forgive her, and practiced all sorts of self-denials to provide others. Now she was to have a little Christ-kind of her own. Then Hall had come to her with a wire in his hand, and told her he must go to Edinburgh; his mother was ill.

"There is nothing very important except Mrs. Danby. I am afraid her case is serious. Don't let him go out of calling reach. I hate leaving you now. I wouldn't go, but that the Mater is dangerously ill, and she has been so good to me."

There was a break in his voice, and Mary hurried him off and got his things together with a very tender thought of the other mother waiting to see him. She felt a strange, fateful heaviness steal over her as he left — the same curious tightening of chest, the sick foreboding that never came without reason. The morning post brought her a quarterly; he must have bought it at the station and posted it there. Strange she could not like him; yet, looking back, how smoothly things had gone for her all those months since he had been there!

Cecil stayed in and saw the people who came, and went on his rounds. Three days passed, and still she could not shake off her dread. She dreamed all night she was running through muddy streets with a wailing child in her arms, and when she got as she thought into safety she found she was in a *cul de sac*, and had to turn and flee again; her skirt tripped her, and when she stooped to lift it the child wailed and her shawl slipped, and it shivered in miserable nakedness. She awoke bathed in cold sweat, with her cheeks wet, as tired as if she had really spent the night struggling to escape pursuit. It was a horrid dream, and always meant trouble.

"You do look bad, ma'am," said Jane, coming in with the tea.

"I feel bad, Jane; I had a hateful dream. What does dreaming of a crying baby mean? I was going about with one all night."

Jane shook her head ominously.

"It ain't no good, ma'am. People says as how there's nothin' in dreams! but I know there is. Matthew sent word he can't come, his cold is that bad; and the boy says Mrs. Danby is took again. Master has gone down there. Danby is put out at Dr. Hall being away."

The rain lashed the windows, and the loose bits of ivy and creeper thrashed the panes, and rapped like knuckles on the glass, whilst the wind howled weirdly. She dressed with difficulty; even the little blue and white basket with its ivory powderbox and tiny things laid ready only made her lips tremble. She went downstairs. Cecil came in and swore at the weather, and things in general.

"It's an infernal nuisance Hall's going away like that! Matthew, too, looks like double pneumonia. Things are as cussed as they can be — enough to make a fellow cut his throat. I wish to God I'd never come to the bally place."

He grumbled and sat at the fire reading a sporting paper until some cronies came in. They went into the surgery, had brandies-and-sodas, and stayed for an hour. Mary fancied she heard the surveyor say, as he left: "Nonsense, old chap, we'll expect you all the same." He was attentive at lunch, and tried to talk to her; then he lay down and slept — he could sleep always. Jane brought in the light, and the hands of the clock were veering round to four when he awoke and yawned.

"Have you any physic to make up?" she asked.

"Oh, hang it; I forgot! I suppose I must. You might paste the labels." She followed him into the surgery. She used to help him before Hall came, but she had not been in there for months. There were a great many new things, and a large case of books. She pasted a label: on each bottle as he gave it to her, saying at the last one:

"Jane can get a boy to go with them."

He looked at the clock and fidgeted.

"How is Mrs. Danby?" she asked.

"Oh, she's no worse. He is always in an infernal funk about her."

"Well, Cess! she's got five children, and Hall thought it was serious."

"Oh, Hall knows which way his bread is buttered! He plays up to them."

"I don't think he does; I never noticed it. He is much blunter with them than you are, but he is very conscientious; they all rely on him."

"That's a good thing."

"You are not going out?"

"Just up to the White Hart to have a game with Rigby. Have you got half a sov about you? Don't be cross, old girl!"

She gave it to him and followed him out to the hall as he put on his coat, laid her hand on his arm, saying pleadingly:

"Don't stay long, Cess!"

Jane put on her cloak, and took the basket to find a messenger. Mary could not settle to read or work. She wandered heavily from room to room, and finally sat down before the kitchen fire; she often went out there, in hours of loneliness, to escape from Hall. When she felt ill and worried, it was hateful to have this man's presence thrust upon her. She was conscious he watched her every movement, and even if it was only to anticipate her wants, it got on her nerves. Sometimes she almost felt as if his arms were about her; even though, on looking up, his eyes were always on his book, she felt convinced his mind, his senses, were in some way occupied with her — too near to her. At such moments a fierce resentment against her husband rose in her; her condition made her shy of men.

Jane had just come back and closed the door when the surgery bell rang sharply. Mary could hear the rain rushing through the gutter in the street outside, as Jane opened the door. The girl came in.

"Mr. Danby wants the master, ma'am; he don't like the way she is at all."

Mary clutched her breast.

"He is at the White Hart."

The door slammed. Jane pushed the wicker chair nearer to the fire. "Sit down, ma'am; you're all of a shake. It's fair unlucky

Dr. Hall being away and Matthew ill at the same time."

"I'm sorry I had to tell him to go to the White Hart."

Half an hour passed; the bell rang anew with a jerk.

"Mr. Danby would like to see you, ma'am!"

Mary went out. The man's great, light eyes looked at her — she fancied reproachfully — out of his wet, white face. There were drops on his beard, and on the tangled gray curls on the collar of his coat.

"I have been to the White Hart and to every other public-house in the town, Mrs. Marriott, and I can't find your husband. Can you tell me where I *am* likely to find him? Dr. Hall told me to watch for certain symptoms, as they might mean a coming hemorrhage, and I am afraid. I've got five children, some tiny; not having any yourself, you—" Something in her face checked him. His voice changed and broke to a sob.

"I don't like to do anything harsh. There's a strong feeling against the Doctor now. But I must send for someone else if he don't come."

"I know, Mr. Danby. You are very kind. Go home to your wife; I'll send to look for him." The man left.

"Put on your things, Jane, — I am sorry it is so wet, — and try to find out from some of the ostlers, without going to the bar, if they saw him go anywhere."

Her hands were so cold, and her heart throbbed painfully. Danby's words had only confirmed the suspicions she had. She had felt for some time that Cecil's position as Doctor in Chissom was getting untenable, and she dreaded the breaking up. Twenty minutes passed. She looked at the little American clock every few seconds. The bell pealed again. She went to the door; the wind blew the rain in under the porch. A tall stripling with great, light eyes peered at her anxiously.

"Father says, has the Doctor come back?"

"I have sent to look for him; leave your umbrella in the porch, and come into the kitchen. What an awful night!"

She gave the boy a chair, and walked up and down the passage. It seemed ages, and she started at every step in the street.

When the gate did click she jumped up as if someone had fired off a revolver dose to her ear. She opened the door. Jane came in with compressed lips. Mary put her finger to her lip, and pointed to the kitchen, whispering, "Danby's boy."

"He's out at Rigby, on the common. Went in Whitley's trap. Miller says there are some chaps from London, and a couple of hussies as well."

"Well, he has got to be fetched, Jane. It is unfortunate about Matthew, but if I send any of the men from the White Hart or any place it will be all over the town to-morrow. Get the lantern."

She went into the kitchen and said to the boy: "Will you put in the mare for me? My girl will show you the stable. Don't draw out the trap; back the mare in. Get the waterproof apron and rugs. Hold the lantern for him, Jane, and show him where the things are. You can change afterwards."

She went upstairs and found gaiters and boots. She put on a thick coat over her gown, wound a muffler round her neck, and pinned a cap of his onto her hair. She was talking softly all the time; a listener might have thought to someone else. She could hear the stamping of the mare on the stones in the yard between the gusts of rain, and the boy's cry of "W'o, w'o back, w'o!"

Jane met her in the back entry, with a scared face and a protesting cry: "Oh, don't ye go, ma'am; it'll kill ye. It's a four-mile drive, an' a night like this — it'll kill ye —"

She dropped her voice as the boy came in, shaking the wet off his cap.

The door-bell rang again. "She has five, Jane," she whispered, "and it would be the master's fault! Come, hold the light up and the umbrella! You can say I have gone for the Doctor!"

She said to the boy, "The mare will stand; get up on the other side and help me up!" She got up with great difficulty, and almost a sob, and fastened the rug. Jane went round and gave the boy the umbrella, to hold it over her. She had opened the gate already. Mary left the mare very much to herself. She had never driven her, but she had heard them say that she was cute as a pet fox. The wheel jolted over the curb as they turned into the street. She cried, "Oh dear, God!" under her breath. A wave of resentment for this man to whom she was tied surged up in her. Often afterwards she felt that was the only moment of the drive that she remembered clearly, and that it had filtered through every fiber of her being, and became a part of herself.

"What is your name?" she asked the boy as they tore along. The mare was fresh.

"Jim."

"Well, Jim, I am risking my life for your mother to-night, and I am going to ask you not to say anything about this drive."

"I won't; I won't indeed." As they passed the boy's home someone hobbled from the front gate to the steps, and the blind of a window dropped.

"Mother must be bad," said the boy. "That was Jenny; she's lame; never walks, scarcely."

"Zk, zk, zk," said Mary to the mare.

They turned sharply to the right. The wind and rain blew against them with a shriek and hiss, so that the boy had to struggle to lower the umbrella. He tried to shelter her by sitting high, but the rain soaked through her cap, and plastered her hair to her cheeks, and ran down her wrists. It came in gusts, and seemed to penetrate everything.

"We must turn here again," said the boy. "I'd go slow, ma'am; it's a nasty bit of road. The house is on the left; there are lights in it."

Mary wondered how the boy knew their destination. Jane would never have told him. The mare stopped of her own accord. The boy got down.

"Tell him to come out at once!" she cried.

The tinkle of a piano — she could distinguish the air — sounded as the door opened. A boy opened it. He slammed it to, and left the other lad on the steps. He looked towards her; she beckoned. She thought of the lame girl at the gate.

"Knock until he comes again, and send whoever opens it to me."

The boy kept up a continuous knock, until the knocker fell with a thud. As the door was wrenched open, and the surveyor appeared in the doorway, the red of a woman's gown gleamed farther back in the hall. She saw him start and look towards the trap, then rush in. The boy came out and climbed up the back. A minute dragged; then Cecil appeared, getting into his coat as he came out. He took the reins without a word. Her wrists ached, and her hands were numb. They turned.

"Where's the whip?"

She heard; but the words only seemed to strike on her ear, as the hissing spit of the rain; it did not occur to her to answer. She merely felt inclined to sing a strong, wild song to fit the rush of the rain, and the shriek of the wind, and the drone of the rising pain in herself, that was a strange pain, unlike any other she had ever felt; a pain in the bone and muscle and fiber of her; an elemental pain, that had none of the weakness of disease in its throes. And she, and the rain, and the darkness above and around, and the wind that had lulled a little, and the beat of the mare's feet, and the bobbing lights of the town, seemed to fuse into one. They pulled up with a jerk at the Danbys' door and he sprang down. She sat there, so blessedly, stupidly drowsy, listening to the drone that seemed now to be dying away in herself. Someone came out and stood like an idiot on the pavement and looked up; afterwards she learned it was Danby himself. She had nodded her head sagely at him, and said, "How stupid you look." He climbed up, told the boy to turn and hold her from behind, and drove her home. She had a dim recollection of Jane undressing her; of being rubbed with towels before the kitchen fire, and of sitting with her feet on a hassock, drinking something — but all that merged into the firelight dancing on the ceiling of her own room, and Hall and a strange woman who smelt of aniseed. Once she remembered distinctly hearing Hall's voice; it came from a long distance, up in the top of the chimney, where the starlings made mock of the other fowl in the air. That tiresome phrase about "fowl in the air" kept repeating itself all the day.

"You are a brute, and if you weren't such an infernal fool, I'd give you a damned good thrashing." No, it must have been the starlings; Hall could never have said that. It was a nightmare, all of it; a nightmare of agony, in which they had given her over to the elaborate ingenuity of a Chinese torturer. That was it. And she had two distinct sorts of pain. That was the funny thing — natural and unnatural pain. It was not nonsense. She knew she was right. She appealed to Hall: "Am I not right? One's natural, isn't it? Inevitable, healthy pain — it goes with a drone; and the other is unnatural, a disease, organic, oughtn't to be?" And he had soothed her, and agreed with her. She had heard him quite plainly say, "As a matter of fact, she's quite right!" He used to put his hand on her eyes and down over her face, and wipe out the words that bothered her, and stop both pains; lay her in a cave that revolved to the right, whirling slower and slower, until she forgot everything; and then, when she woke again, it spun to the left, faster and faster, until it sent her into consciousness, with a jerk; as if she were a bit of chewed paper, shot out of a pop-gun — but there was such a lot of writing on the paper. Then one night she woke up and had no pain, not one bit; she was dead. She could feel how heavy she was. It would take eight men to carry her coffin. Then something cried — such a funny little wailing cry. Then the aniseed woman appeared, and put an anatomy in flannel in the curl of her arm, and Hall bent over her and smiled. He was orange-color, with a thick, blue scrub on his chin, and black all round his eyes. She had laughed in his face; she was really too tired to think what kind of ape he resembled. He had lifted her head, and fed her with a spoon, and she had gone to sleep. Funny, how tired the food made her! She woke up when the morning light was stealing in, and Jane had bent over her. She thought it was morning tea, and she asked her to hand it to her, and Jane had cried. Extraordinary person, to weep when one asked her for tea! The whole world was singularly topsy-turvy. Hall never seemed to go to bed — was like a Jack-in-the-box — a remarkably hideous Jack-in-the-box! She couldn't even ask for tea without his popping up and giving her some —, out of a spoon — it was too funny! And the anatomy in flannel lay with its lips to her breast, and she heard the aniseed woman say it was too weak to nurse. So Hall fed it, too, out of a glass thing. She was in such pain; red-hot snakes coiling and crawling about in her breast. Then she roused one day to an absolutely dear understanding of everything and asked for her baby. Jane had laid it down next her, with tears streaming down her red cheeks, and she had kissed it, and held it dose. It was like a frostbitten snowdrop, a very tiny bud of a snowdrop, that had not the strength to bloom. She went to sleep with it over her heart. Then she woke one night again and watched the shadows of the flames creeping up the wall. They were chasing one another, as the waves do when they run up the sand on a still, warm day in summer. Memory came in successive flashes, until she knew everything, as if she were reading the events of the past month ticked off a tape. Her little baby had died in its sleep as it lay on her breast. Fancy! she had not even known it at the time. She began to cry softly. Someone stirred in the big chair, and Hall came and looked at her, and stroked her hands and looked quite pleased; after that she had lain quite quiet, and got better. When it occurred to her at last to ask for Cecil, they told her that she had refused to let him enter the room — grew delirious if she saw him. She bade them tell him to come. He kissed her; she felt sorry for him. She didn't say anything about the little one, for it just struck her she didn't know if it were a little daughter or a son. She asked the nurse, who replied:

"A girl, ma'am. The Doctor got it baptized. Ee thought as 'ow you 'd like it, an' ee called it Inyess! w'ich was a queer name; not as it made any difference to the poor lamb. Ye 'ad an 'ospital nurse then. She went away after it was bom. She 'ad a case, an' ye were out of danger an' as I 'ave twenty years' experience, she weren't needed."

"Inez? It was my mother's name; that was kind of him."

"You was terrible bad, ma'am, for a month afore it came, an' it was born with its blessed lungs bad."

Privately, Nurse Brown thought she was a heartless and faithless wife, who wouldn't have her own handsome husband in the room, and let that Dr. Hall handle her like an infant. As to what she thought of her as a mother, "Wild 'osses wouldn't drag it from me," she told Jane.

"Nor they hadn't better; nor anything else, such as hot unsweetened," was Jane's reply, "if you want Dr. Hall to let you work in the parish. He says you are a first-rate monthly; but that won't help you if you say a word about my missus."

They had made a *fête* of her coming down. Everyone came to see her, or sent her fruit or flowers. She never knew that her drive to save Mrs. Danby had got about, —but it was not Jim who had told, — that it was for that reason Cecil found it pleasanter to stay at home. She found Hall had kept the Major informed of her improvement, and he sent her snipe and a woodcock. Down in Hastings the problem of her existence rose up and clamored to be heard in measure as she got stronger.

Cecil had written that Hall was prepared to buy the practice. He would only give a song for it; but as he had heard that there was a movement afoot amongst the townspeople to petition Hall to stay, and that they were prepared to build a house for him, there was no use expecting more from anyone else. He abused Hall roundly. Mary knew that it would be impossible to make him see that he was to blame himself for all that happened. "He had heard of a practice in London. Could she sell out and advance the money to buy it? There would not be much when the debts were paid."

Mary had written back that she could not dispose of any capital. Mr. D'Arcy had willed it that way — in case of her dying childless it would go to two illegitimate children of his. The only thing at her disposal was the hundred and fifty pounds which she had told Blumenberg to invest for her; that she was prepared to advance.

Cecil had met her at the station. She felt sorry for him, although she had received a letter from him the same morning, saying that the practice he wanted was now entirely out of the question, as the ridiculous arrangement as to her money made it impossible to realize any of it. She had flushed angrily as she read the letter; she had not spent twenty pounds on herself in all her married life. They drove home, and she asked him what he intended to do. He had seen Ellis's solicitor and found that he could get a loan of two hundred pounds if she would guarantee to pay it in two years. It would come to the same thing; she would have to pay half of her quarter to him, that was all. Mary doubted, but consented. The books had mounted up during the last months of her illness, and bills of which she had never dreamed came in. She discovered that he had been paying for riding Hobbs's "young uns," besides bait and lunch bills from various hotels round the country. It would take every penny that Hall gave to clear off the liabilities in Chissom. Bit by bit she had solved the puzzle; he had dropped over two hundred pounds by betting in the last year, and there were promissory notes out for thirty more.

Straker-Ellis was in Monte Carlo, ailing; must not be worried with affairs. She felt inclined to give him half of what she had, and go away to work again. She was happier in the old days, when she had to earn her supper. A great longing for the Major came over her. Scenes from her childhood in which he played a part came back; she had forgotten all his faults and only remembered his virtues. It was stupid to think of Time as a bony old sage with a scythe. She would always think of him as a quick-eyed youth, with sensitive features and a Botticelli head. She had seen him once, down in Italy, in the chapel of a neglected castle which the Austrians had partially destroyed; he was singing a tender, consoling little air as he worked. Some vandals had plastered over the walls, and he was chipping it away with deft and tender fingers, and as he worked the colors and forms of the frescoes underneath became visible. One forgot the hideousness of the plaster and only remembered the beauties underneath. That was Time; an expert restorer of old values, deft and tender-fingered, with a note of consolation in his voice. Life was not easy, that was sure.

She could not say she was sorry, not very sorry, for the little one; the responsibility was too great.

She wondered what the place would be like. Brixton! she had never been there, scarcely knew how to locate it. Cecil had written it was an infernal hole, but had a good dispensary practice, and the only thing going at the price he was prepared to give. The widow wanted to get rid of it at once. There was furniture enough of a sort; they need not buy any. Worked up, he might dispose of it and buy a better. Hall had kept silent when she asked him about it; he wasn't in favor of doing things in a hurry. She could not explain, and perhaps he understood well enough, but if they were to wait up in town to find a better opening, the purchase-money would dribble away, as money had a knack of doing, through Cecil's hands. There was Hall probably coming to talk to her.

"Had your medicine?"

"Oh, I forgot it!" penitently.

"Of course you did; if it were anyone else's physic, you would be running all over the place with bottle and spoon. It's nasty!"

He dropped a box of French sweets in her lap:

"I wish you weren't going up quite so soon. Marriott is in a fever to get away, but you'll fag yourself to death getting things straight. I'm glad Jane is going with you."

"Do you know the place?" she asked.

"Yes," after a pause; "you'll hate it. I am going to send an old chum of mine to look after you. He and an Irish chap have a practice in Lambeth. He's Scotch. Yes, I know you are like Lamb; but he is a Highlander, and just as superstitious as you are yourself. He is not the kind of man to introduce to every lady — a rough diamond; but you'll be able to discount him. By the way, I'll send you on the mags; you needn't return them; I won't have much time for reading just yet."

Mary laughed, and he flushed darkly.

"I am afraid that is too transparent; you never do find time to read them. I've always wanted to thank you for getting them for me; only perhaps you had better not go on."

"Nonsense; I give a pal a cigar and a drink whenever I meet him. Why can't I send you a wretched journal or two? There's Marriott, I think; and, by the way, I want to say I would like you to think I shall always be your very good friend."

Eight days after Mary and Jane left Chissom. They had been at the White Hart for some days. Cecil had a row with Hall; she had not discovered the reason. But it was followed by one of his obstinate fits, and he had insisted on their packing and leaving. She had sat wearily in the little hotel room, and had been very uncomfortable. It was all so unnecessary, for he had come with Hall the evening before they left, and taken her back to supper. The room looked strange already; her favorite rocking-chair had gone from its place at the fire, and many of the books and some of the plants.

CHAPTER XXVI

It was a cheerless day. There had been a mizzling rain and a cold wind blowing when Mary and Jane arrived at Baker Street. She took a cab and gave the address at Brixton. Cecil had gone there the day before. They seemed to have gone a long way when the driver turned into the Lambeth Road. Mary looked out; the grimy squalor of the locality, with the sickening smell of gas and the pungent smell of vinegar, depressed her. Pale-faced laundry hands were trooping back in fleering groups to work after their dinner hour; the gas burned dully in the shops and behind the square windows of the factories. They crossed Clapham Road, and as the streets seemed to grow dingier and the houses more uniformly depressing, the cab turned sharply into Landor Road — the name on the card Cecil had given her. It stopped before a small double-fronted brown house at the comer of a side road — every little street was called a road. There was a strip of garden, with two ragged laurel bushes and a granite urn half filled with clay. The house looked dirty, and a broken Venetian blind slanted across the middle of the bay window. Mary walked up the path and pulled the bell; it jingled away in the back. No one came. Jane was standing next the cab with Mary's dressing-bag in her hand and a look of blank dismay on her face. The cabby had swung himself down from the box, and was chewing a straw reflectively; he walked down the side street, came back, and called over the railings, "The dispensary door is this side, ma'am." Mary went round. There was a narrow door and a very wide window, with a wire-screen painted brown and the hours of consultation in ding gold lettering. She rang and knocked. It was too bad of Cecil. She could have sat down on the step and cried. She turned to the man.

"You can bring the things into the porch and I'll pay you."

By this time a group of children had collected at the gate with a couple of errand boys. She paid the man and stood in the porch with the rugs and boxes. Jane walked down the path and shut the gate with an assumption of dignity that made the butcher-boy, who had two chops on his trencher, indulge in a derisive "chyike."

A red-cheeked milkman, calling, "Myolk, myolk," stopped his barrow at the gate. He touched his cap and asked, "Any milk, lady? We serve all the best people about — all the doctors' families. Fresh butter and eggs, special nursery milk. Our card, ma'am."

"You may leave a pint," she assented weariedly.

"Dr. Hall said you was to have your gruel, ma'am" whispered Jane.

"Well, get whatever you want." She leaned against the door.

The man brought the can, hesitated, and asked, "'Ave you tried the window, lady; the side one was open when I come by this morning."

He shook it, and finally jerked it up triumphantly. Jane stepped into the room and came through the hall. Mary felt that if the door were not opened quickly, that if the girl continued to fumble with the chain and key, she would scream, or swear, or do something dreadful. Then her whole surroundings faded from her and she could see herself again as a little girl shrinking from a woman who was screaming filthy words at her for no reason; she had merely passed her coming out of a shop. God knows, now, she could understand how that poor creature must have felt — perhaps it saved her from madness. She followed Jane — she felt inclined to do just whatever Jane told her. The milkman helped to carry in the things, and closed the door behind him, cuffing the small boys at the gate as he went out.

"There's no fire in there," said Jane, pointing to the sitting-room, "an' the grate's a mass of rust; better come to the back, ma'am, an' I'll try light the gas."

They found themselves in the dispensary. It was a big bare room with benches, and an old sofa behind a screen. There was a fire smoldering in the grate, and Cecil's bag was on the floor. Their first impression of the kitchen was chaos and dirt — the dirt of years. There was a roaring fire in the range and cinders and ashes running over the fender. A pail of dirty water and a wet scrubbing-brush were in the middle of the floor. A box of groceries, bottles in straw cases, a cut loaf, and some butter on a paper, littered the table.

A key turned in the side door and Cecil's laugh rang through the house; there was someone with him. Mary stood still and waited. So it was for this she had mortgaged her income. She felt angry, more angry than she had ever felt before. It was a sign of the breach between them that she was beginning to think of her money as separate from his. He came in, and the laugh died away. The pupils of his eyes were unusually large and brilliant. If he had been a woman he would have been accused of a dazzling make-up. Mary had learned to know that effect; it was the only sign that told he had been drinking.

"You here, old girl? Sorry I was out. Went to look for another charwoman and get something to eat. Well, Jane, how are you? All right? Pretty mess, isn't it? Got a charwoman for you. Found the old beast opening a bottle of brandy. Ran her out by the neck. Come into the surgery, Moll, and have a glass of port. Here, Mac,' here's the missus."

Mary found herself bowing to a man whose head seemed far up in the air.

"I had a letter from my friend, Dr. Hall, this morning, Mrs. Marriott; he tells me you were his patient, and has turned you over to me. Sit down here near the fire."

He spoke with the broadest Scotch accent Mary had ever heard, and was such a giant, with odd light-gray eyes, set wide apart under sandy, almost white eyebrows, and such bushy hair, that she felt inclined to laugh.

"Have ye had any lunch yet? No! Well, we'll make up the fire." The bell rang. He went and opened the door. A little woman stepped in.

"Ye got the wire then. Ye haven't been long, woman. Ye can buckle to as soon as ye like."

"That's a decent little body, a countrywoman of my own, Mrs. Marriott; ye'll find her handy," he said, as he came back.

"I found your husband committing manslaughter on a beauty of a woman this morning."

He was making up the fire as he spoke. His head was so broad, and so covered with flaxen hair, that it reminded Mary of a mop made of tow. Cecil brought in a tray. Jane had opened a tin of tongue and cut some bread and butter. "Mac" — so everyone called him — cleared the table.

Jane knocked and came in. Mary could see that she was on the verge of tears; her first experience of London was a disappointment.

"Please, ma'am, there ain't no brushes to speak of, nor house flannels; and we want soap, and soda, and monkey brand, and—"

Very well, Jane, make a list, and I'll go and order them."

"She'll make a list as long as your arm. I ordered in a lot of things this morning," grumbled Cecil. "Yes, I know, I saw them; but she can't clean the place with *pâté de foie gras* and bottled anchovies."

"Well, I don't suppose I can be of any use here, old girl. I want to get a cheque-book, and I met a fellow I knew yesterday. I told him I'd look him up to-night; he's got diggings near Victoria."

"How do I go to get to shops?" she asked.

"Depends where you want to go. Clapham is on the right, Brixton's on the left. Turn up Stockwell Road and go into Atlantic Avenue. Mac will show you. You're not in a hurry, old chap?"

"No; I came down to give a hand. Halpin's all right for a few days, and Green is there. I'll go and wash my hands."

"All right, old man, you know your way. Give me a couple of shillings, Moll, till I cash a cheque."

Mary was putting on her gloves. She handed him half-a-crown, saying:

"We may as well start as we are going to go on, Cess. You have had all my money since I married you, and you have spent all you earned. Not so little either; I

looked at the total when Hall had the books made up. You are beginning the same old thing: ordering recklessly from the tradespeople, making a great show at first, and leaving your bills unpaid in the end. You have started already — whiskey, brandy, port, sherry — grocer's sherry." He flushed at her tone. "I'd as soon drink methylated spirit. If I have got to pay a servant and keep house on a hundred a year — I beg your pardon, that is all I can count on; the other has not come in yet — I prefer to order the things myself. I shall send back some of these and get others we need more. I can't live in the place like this."

He muttered the old grievance as to her money being tied up; he couldn't get better at the price. She interrupted impatiently.

"Perhaps it is as well for me that poor Jack D'Arcy knew my weakness and protected me from myself. You are thoroughly selfish. You can be meanly careful about any expenses when they are for the house or me; I found that out long ago if I never seemed to notice it. You grumbled at the bill for the papers or magazines I took in; they were my one extravagance. I gave them up. Hall continued them."

"Oh! you and Hall?"

"Yes?" There was a menace in her tone and a look that made her face strangely like the Major's. "Yes?"

"Oh, nothing; I didn't mean anything."

"No, you dare not; it's well to keep some element of decency. If you had any delicacy you would have spared me the humiliation of being pitied by Hall. I hate talking like this; it's horrible. I hate mentioning money matters — none of us Desmonds were ever meanly careful — but I have got to, in self-defense. I have tried to hint tilings delicately. Bah! yours is the kind of cotton-wool sensibility that wants cutting or burning to get at. If the little one had lived I couldn't even do as I have done. Perhaps it is well it didn't." She looked at him as she spoke; his eyes were full of tears. The old feeling of fatefulness, of tiny, clinging cobwebs, spun by fate, enveloping her softly, closely, came over her, with a kind of protecting pity for this weak, shiftless, unstable being with the irritating touch of maudlin sentimentality that took the place of all deeper feeling in him. She had seen the tears spring to his eyes at "Abide with Me," played on a harmonium, and known him absolutely callous to some poor woman's agony that was prolonged by his delay to finish a "fifty up" at billiards. Perhaps he could not help it. When all was said and done the flaw must have lain somewhere in the first making. It was difficult for Mary, with her great tenderness for all weak, erring, and helpless things; her tendency to trace back to the seed and root of everything, to keep her resentment. After all, his very weakness, the very poverty of his nature, gave him a mortgage on her strength. She laid her hand on his and patted it, as she might have done to a little child.

"There, old boy, we'll say no more about it. I am nervous and unstrung; perhaps it will pass out somehow, only I am not as plucky as I used to be. I get more easily tired in the struggle." He stooped and kissed her, a flashing smile obliterating every trace of distress, and said cheerfully:

"I'll try, old woman; life is such a badly serious 'biz.' I don't mean to do the wrong thing, but I'm hanged if I can get on to the right one. Can I do anything for you? No? Well, I must be off! Mac," he called at the door, "you'll look after the missus; so long!" He whistled gaily as he brushed his hat.

Mary went out to the kitchen. Jane's face was working. She had taken off her best skirt and put on an apron over her striped petticoat. Mary patted her on the shoulder.

"Cheer up, Jane, we'll get through better than you think. We must have fires upstairs. The things will be here about four, and you must air some linen."

The charwoman came in with a pail.

"Do you know anyone else, Mrs. Ferguson," asked Mary, "who could come in to help? There is so much to be done."

"My niece is a big, strong girl, ma'am; she's stopping with me till she finds a place."

"Well, couldn't she come here for a couple of weeks and help Jane to get straight? She can? Well, let her come to-morrow. There, Jane, the first knot is unraveled. Now let us go through these things. Anchovies in oil, *pâtés de foie gras,* bottled asparagus, truffles and liver, champignons Tiparee jam"; she checked them off the list. "Put those in the basket and give them to the boy when he comes. I'll explain."

The big Scotchman had to bend down when he spoke to her.

"How tall are you?" queried Mary, laughingly. "I am the average woman's height, and — oh yes, I am, only I am so slight."

"Six four."

"Heavens! no wonder that woman laughed. What! five of you, all over six feet — reared on porridge? Oh, well, you needn't crow; we raise big men on potatoes in Paddyland."

Very little was lost on the big man; he was shy with women — had been reared in a mountain district, and lived in an attic during his years of study. He marvelled at her tact — "slutherin,'" his partner, Dennis Halpin, would have called it — in making the grocer change the unsuitable items on the list and replace them by those on hers. He followed her like a big mastiff and carried the parcels.

He stopped outside an india-rubber shop and said, with a red flush: "I am going to presume on being your medical adviser — get a pair of goloshes. I never saw such a little paper pair of boots in my life. They look nice, but they're no good for walking."

Mary laughed more gaily than she had laughed for months as she looked down at her feet. They were low-heeled French boots.

"I used not to walk much either when I bought them. I had so many pairs when I married Cess I haven't bought any boots since. I hate goloshes."

"Those aren't so ugly."

He pointed to some half-goloshes with elastic bands to go round the heel. They went in. The shopman remarked, as he brought some pairs,

"These will about fit your good lady; she takes a small size."

Mary felt rather than saw him color — knew how all the little flaxen hairs on his face and neck would show against the red.

"There are some good shops here," she remarked as they came out.

"Yes, but wait until you come and see Atlantic Avenue on Saturday night; there isn't such a sight in London, not to say in Europe.

"Oh no! my practice is in Lambeth. An Irish and Scotch crowd, with an odd gipsy and some ticket-of-leave men — a fearful neighborhood. Sixpenny consultations — you can't ask the poor devils more. Halpin, yes, he's a countryman of yours — Dennis Aloysius Halpin — a real good sort, but a queer chap. We don't keep accounts," with a laugh, "just got shares; we have one tall hat and a frock coat between us to do the genteel calls. No, we get a living, no more; we are not of the stamp to make successes in London. Half the time we doctor for nothing. The married men can't do that. I suppose we are really medical blacklegs, but the poverty is terrible. You've got some rough customers here at both ends of your road; you must keep out of the consulting-room on Saturday nights. Moat Place, at this end, is a very poor part, and there is a rough crowd in Nelson Row and White's Square; both really in Clapham, but they always came here in Nolan's time."

It was almost dark when they got back, and the van of the Chissom carrier was at the door. The man touched his cap and said,

"I am late, ma'am, but I had to be careful; them was Dr. Hall's orders."

There seemed to be a great many things; she had only expected her linen chest, a box of books, and some personal luggage. Jane was beaming.

"Dr. Hall has sent you all the best plants, ma'am, an' the big maiden-hair as stood in the window, and a hamper with some of Mrs. Hobbs's butter. I put them in the consultin'-room."

The familiar plants seemed to come as a welcome-home to Mary; the delicate smell of the fuchsia sweetened the stuffy room. Her own rocker, with the familiar red cushion, and her carved oak footstool stood near the fire. Jane had swept up the hearth, and the room looked friendly. How good of little Hall! that was why she had missed it out of the room. She opened a parcel that had come with the things: all the quarterlies, a new book they had spoken of the night they supped there, and six old colored prints she had admired in the house of a poor patient. Mac watched her face. It had grown curiously soft and young as she bent it over the plants. She had thrown her hat and jacket on the sofa. He had not expected anything dainty from Hall's letter; he had written of her intellect, her interest in out-of-the-way subjects, as if he were discussing a brainy chum. He decided that Hall must be biased by his feelings; there was a warm note in the letter that had roused his interest; he had always thought Hall such a dry stick — one never knew.

Jane and the decent body from Glasgow had done wonders in the meantime. A bright fire burned in the bedroom, a dingy room enough, with awful engravings of biblical subjects. The whole house was indescribably filthy. The sitting-room below was papered in an imitation of stamped velvet, with raised flowers of beetroot and orange hue; a large mirror, framed in dingy gilding, with a corpulent cupid upsetting a cornucopia of roses astride on top, and the suite was mahogany and horsehair. The little room at the back had an old-fashioned table and a good bookcase with some volumes in calf. She decided to make her own of that. Mac — he soon became "Mac" to Mary, though he gave her his full name of Alexander Macpherson smiled at her look of distress when she saw the first room. He could not understand why she said, "What a wicked room! — worse than anything I could have imagined" or what she meant by the impossibility of living with that paper. Her impulsive changes, her way of darting from one subject to another, took his breath away.

"Don't you think, "she asked, "that paper like that is immoral? — the kind of paper that might make a sensitive man murder his mother-in-law if he married into it?"

It reminded him of Halpin; he always said odd, inconsequent things of that kind.

"Ugh! come away," she added; "I don't believe you mind that room a bit."

"Jane," putting her head through the kitchen door, "Tea. I must drown the remembrance of that room in tea. Of course I know you admire the room, Dr. Mac, and I am sorry to disagree, but I can't have tea there, even to gratify you."

She made raids into the kitchen like a schoolgirl, and added to the giant's bewilderment by pertinent questions in between as to a mental case with some peculiar psychical phenomena that was being discussed in a medical quarterly. Then she put on one of Jane's aprons, and set to work to clear the little dispensing-room. All the bottles and shelves had to be washed and the drawers turned out, and as they worked, Jane's voice stole in from the kitchen, aging snatches of a harvesting song as she arranged the crockery on her dresser. And so passed Mary's first evening in the eligible practice disposed of by a doctor's widow in Brixton.

CHAPTER XXVII

New Year's Eve, the second in Landor Road — a frosty New Year's Eve. The house was very quiet. Jane was out at meeting; the consulting-room would not be opened for another hour; one could hear the tick of the little American clock all through the silence. Now and then a troop of boys and girls would pass the house singing the chorus of some music-hall song, generally the street version, with additions that would fail to pass the censor. The fire in Mary's own room had burnt into a clear red heart. She was lying back in the rocker with half-closed eyes, a heap of exercise books (she gave a few German lessons) were piled on the table next her, with some socks and vests which she bad been mending.

It was a cozy little room. The floor was stained and covered by a few rugs, a dado of matting ran round the wall; the firelight danced over the bright covers of the books on the shelves at each side of the fireplace, and flicked the gold lettering and devices on their backs. Some silhouettes in quaint black frames, and a few bits of good old china gave it an air of individuality.

She stirred and looked at the clock. Cecil had gone to Brighton with the Fergusons after an attack of influenza, but Mac would come to see the patients.

Her face had grown sharper, the lines at the corners of her mouth deeper, and stray white hairs gleamed in silvery distinctness in her dark hair.

If Sep or the bow-maker could have seen her they would have found that the greatest difference the years had made lay in the expression of her eyes. The old question that used to flash out and arrest one at a first look with its insistence had given way to one of dreamy introspection when alone, and of a kindly interest or complete indifference when directed to anyone else. It could still flash out at times, startling in its suddenness; but then it was called up by some illuminative sentence, some picture or burst of music, to vanish as soon as it was interpreted or absorbed — it was no longer the dominant note of her individuality. Life had answered it for Mary Desmond, slowly but surely, with disillusion at every stage of the journey. She had accepted it as bravely as she had faced her difficulties, but it had left an underlying shade of sadness in the keen eyes. There was no resignation, but there was a calm acceptance of the facts of life in all their crudeness.

"You have the kindest expression in the whole world," a woman had said to her lately. "You look as if you had tenderness enough to give every scoundrel in creation a share of it, and yet have some to draw on."

"In other words, dear," Mary had said, "you mean that, from a conventional point of view, I have simply grown absolutely unmoral. It is true in a measure. God's wheel has whirled me into such strange corners in His astonishing creation, revolving forwards and backwards, from seed-sowing to gleaning time, from effects to first causes, that I have lost all prejudices, have ceased to be able to judge anyone. The only resentment left in me is roused by cruelty to weak things, the hypocrisies of conventional religions, or the lies necessary to keep the social virtues on their legs. All the sinners have become merely curious or terrible pathological cases in the appallingly interesting hospital of creation. I have ceased to believe in the existence of sin."

She had suffered under the turn of the wheel, but she had come to an inkling of the meaning of her own life and of the inevitability of human isolation with the unexplainable but convincing certainty of a past stage of existence, and the instinctive belief in a future, bringing a realization of the present as a mere phase, only of import in so far as it made a perfect or imperfect link in the whole scheme. One has to climb many mountains and skirt many pitfalls before one reaches the meadows of content.

She went back, as was her habit in quiet hours, over the past two years, calling up the salient points in pictures, each one perfect, with the very color, smell, and atmosphere of it intact. She arrested some of them, dwelt upon them, and questioned their significance.

It was the afternoon of the first August Bank Holiday. The day had been sultry, with a thick sky overhead and mutterings of thunder in the air. All day streams of people had been passing to and fro from the Common; a long unceasing tramp of feet, broken by discordant laughter, the imperative ringing of cyclists' bells, and the crash of the brass instruments of the trade bands going to meetings in Battersea and Hyde Park. In the morning a man had been carried in; he had fainted and fallen from a break, the wheel of another had crushed his arm, and a frightened horse had cut his face. She had helped Cess with him in the surgery; but all day afterwards the smell of fresh blood seemed to cling to her. Now and then a tiny, fitful warm breeze blew towards the house; every time it came it brought a whiff of disinfectant from the smallpox and fever hospital higher up the road. Her peculiarly heightened susceptibility to the electricity in the atmosphere, with the physical disturbance attendant on it that always came before a storm, made her feel restless and unstrung. The surgery bell rang. Cecil had gone out, and Jane had a free day. She went to the door and opened it. A tall woman with golden hair was leaning against the door-post. Her lips moved without making any sound; and as she looked appealingly at Mary, the latter was struck by the singular beauty of her gray eyes; they dominated the whole face. Mary helped her on the sofa, unpinned her hat, and loosened her coat.

"Faint or hurt?" she asked.

"Faint," the woman gasped.

Mary brought her some sal-volatile in a glass. The smell forced its way in again; it made the woman blanch.

"Come out of this into my room; it's horrible," said Mary. "Sit in that chair, put your feet on the stool, and close your eyes for a while; it's cooler here." The woman lay back with a sigh of content with her lids closed; she had an able, ugly face, with a powerful nose and strong jaw. Her hair was lovely — soft, true golden. Mary drew off her gloves, and looked at long, slim white hands. The woman opened her eyes, and muttered, "Oh, thank you so much!" and closed them again. Mary went out to the kitchen, put the kettle on a gas-ring, and laid the tray for tea. She had forgotten to have any. Jane had made her some dainty sandwiches, and covered them with a serviette. She arranged them on a plate, put the watercresses in a glass dish, and cut some cake. It took her a long time; all housewifely matters cost her trouble. She lacked the knack of them. The other sprang to her feet as Mary went in, blushing charmingly.

"I am so sorry; I must apologize. I have been rather overworked lately. It was so hot, too, and I hadn't a sunshade. I don't know what you must think of me."

Mary smiled.

"I think you might sit down, and have some tea with me. It's a charity, you know. If you hadn't come in I should probably have sat by myself, raking up ghosts. Would you like to wash off the dust?"

They went upstairs. The furniture was hideous; yet there was something of Mary herself in the room, with its little white bed, the photogravure of a Botticelli head over the bed, and the few dainty things on the toilet table.

The woman looked round the little room when they went down again. "How do you keep the ferns so green?" she asked. "It's so cool in here; it's such a restful little room."

She was standing with her back to the fireplace, her hands thrust in her jacket pockets.

"Do you always stand?" said Mary.

"Oh, it doesn't fidget me in the least; I like people to do as they please. Only you'd rest more if you sat down."

"May I look at your books? I so want to." She left her cup on the mantel-board as she asked, and ran along the titles, talked enthusiastically of some of them with a sincere note in her quick gushes of enthusiasm. "Oh, there's the new *Contemporary*. I so wanted to see it."

"You can take it out, when you have had your tea and eaten something. Only send it back when you've done with it."

"May I? How good of you! But it's unpardonable of me, an utter stranger. I come and ring at a dispensary door for a draught, and you ask me to tea, and lend me your book, without knowing anything about me."

Her face softened, and her eyes glowed; at such moments she was beautiful.

"Only another form of dispensing," laughed Mary. "Besides, I know what I see of you, and that is as much as anyone knows — of most people. Where does the Celt come in, in you? It breaks out occasionally in expression and voice."

"Oh, both grandmothers, oddly enough. My father was from Norfolk: I am a journalist, I subedit a ladies' paper; it deals with sport for ladies. I came out here to see a nurse at the hospital; I was in there last year; she was very good to me. I had some work to clear off in the office too, so I went there first; the trains are so crowded to-day. No, I don't like it, but I was jolly glad to get it. It's so hard for a woman to get along. I live in a boarding-house. It's rather a Bohemian place, polyglot, you know. I tried the ladies' homes, but I couldn't stand them. Oh, yes, they are greatly improved; but all the same, one has no freedom, don't you know? One is always shocking someone; not really, you know, but they make a pretense of it. I like to smoke when I want to, and play when I feel inclined; I always play all Sunday morning. We have a Hungarian who plays divinely. I work all day, you know, like a machine. Fancy doing that, you know, and then going back to hear a lot of women chattering. Oh, may I really smoke? I think I will. No, I have nothing to do; of course I'll stay gladly."

The bell rang.

"That is Dr. Macpherson. He comes to see the dispensary patients — we have a lot of them — whenever my husband wants to stay out." Mac found a singular-looking woman, with arrestive eyes, smoking in the missus' chair. Mary smiled interrogatively after she had mentioned his name — the other woman named hers laughingly, crying:

"How absurd of me not to have told you!"

They talked books, and music, and women's work. The journalist was full of ideals and illusions; had kept them fresh, in spite of sordid experiences. Mary was laughing as she had not done for many a day. Mac and the journalist were disputing as to the origin of a Scotch air, when Mary interrupted them, saying:

"The Doctor plays the violin; sometimes he plays it for me. It is here now. Suppose you finish your dispute in the other room. The piano is old, but very sweet. No, I will not light the gas; I'll get some candles for the piano. I won't take the responsibility of showing any sensitive human being that paper by gaslight. There are diabolical possibilities of suggestion about it. You will see for yourself, Miss Ingleton; secretly Dr. Mac admires it."

The giant laughed, as if well pleased to be the butt for any pleasantry of hers. The moment the woman put her fingers on the keys she was transformed. She played with her head pensively on one side, and her cigarette between her teeth; scraps from Wagner, mad Hungarian dances, songs of Grieg, studies of Cherkovsky. And when Mary and Mac went to the surgery to attend to women with ailing babies, and men who took advantage of the holiday to come about neglected ailments, she wandered from one thing to another, until he laid the ghosts in the quiet house, and coaxed back forgotten curves to Mary's lips. They all got supper together, and Mac said ruefully:

"Your music has done the little missus more good than all my tonics. Next Sunday Mrs. Marriott is coming to see my partner, Halpin, and me for the first time. Will you come too, Miss Ingleton?"

And as they went out to the station later on he said gravely:

"I hope you'll come again. She lives a very lonely life, and does not care for any of the women she meets."

"I know," was the reply; "I never met any one so kind; to an utter stranger too. I might have been the worst character."

He laughed. "That would have made no difference."

"She has done *me* good, I know," said the woman, musingly; "but I should scarcely have thought that anyone could affect her much. I haven't found the key to her face yet, it is so sad. I wanted to be good to her, and yet I daren't. I had a feeling that I wanted her more than she needed me."

"Only a woman could have found all that out at once," he remarked. "She has the head of a whole good fellow, so that sometimes one forgets that she is a woman at all; then suddenly she is all woman, with the heart of a rebellious little child. One wants, as you say, to be good to her, but there is something in her that tells one that no one can help her but herself. Do I know her long? Only this year actually; but I seem to have known her always. When I said you did her good, I only meant that you took her out of herself a little. She needs outlets for her tenderness."

CHAPTER XXVIII

A SORDID, DIRTY STREET in Lambeth, with a pungent smell of vinegar permeating everything. A hansom pulled up at a door just as the journalist was going into it. Cecil Marriott jumped down and helped Mary out. He was well dressed, with a flower in his buttonhole, but he had altered — not for the better. His eyelids seemed heavier, his face more flabby. His eyes travelled over Mary's figure as she went up the steps; it was a coldly critical look, such as he might have given a horse in bad condition. She looked a lady, yet someway she was not smart; no, decidedly, she was not smart. Mary could have told him that her little foulard gown had neither the hang of skirt nor cut of sleeve of the year; that it was only her own personality that made it wearable, Mac saw no flaw in her, and the journalist thought she looked delicately out of place in her surroundings. The hall was bare and the stairs uncarpeted; there were some unpainted deal shelves in the recesses at the side of the fireplace of the sitting-room filled with books; a bust of Abernethy reposed on the top of one, a skull and an old tall hat on the other. A round table, covered with Italian cloth, bound with braid and made to fit; four arm-chairs and a big sofa — an Irish terrier with his leg in a splint was curled up in one corner of it — furnished the room. It was scrupulously clean, thanks to the Glasgow body who came in to look after them. Dr. Dennis Halpin was shorter by an inch than his Scotch colleague; but his enormous girth of chest, and broad, long body made him look a bigger man; his feet and hands were much smaller. He had crisp, black hair, a perpetual blue shade on his chin, and a genial, typically Irish face. His accent was just as marked. It had taken Mary some months to arrive at the inwardness of the partnership between these singularly different men. She had grown to look for Mac's coming, when Dr. Dennis arrived one evening at Brixton in his stead. The body from Glasgow had supplied the clue to it — they simply drank, turn about. When the fit seized Paddy, Sandy took the practice, and vice versa. Dr. Dennis was the better woman's doctor. He had a great reputation with the women of Lambeth; and occasionally a deputation of expectant "ladies," headed by a little red-headed, voluble countrywoman of his own as spokeswoman, would call at the surgery, with the request:

"For the love o' God, Doctor, darlint, just hould on for a few weeks longer; sure we can't hurry ourselves. We have nawthin' to say agin the other gintleman, but it's yerself has 'the lucky hand' entoirely."

Their bouts had the characteristics of their nationality and temperament. Dr. Mac went away quietly, and when he had reached his limit, got into a cab and drove to the Turkish baths, came back to his work, and was more silent than usual for a day or two, and a total abstainer until the next attack. Dr. Dennis went in for a "tearin' spree," divilment and divarshum, amongst the fluctuating colony of Irish medical men who eke out a livelihood as *locum tenens* in the Sassenach stronghold. When he reached *his* limit he got up, dressed, and went to early mass. At first there had been an antagonistic note between Dr. Dennis and Mary. He had a very Irish idea of womanhood, coupled with his reverence for her; he had decided opinions as to her need for a religion, and her position as a subordinate to man — fostered partly by his religion, which has always been antagonistic to women's independence, and unflatteringly outspoken as to her possibilities as a dangerous factor in the community. They had many arguments, but gradually he had grown to recognize the honesty of her attitude, and to like her for herself. She had never seen them together before, for, as Dr. Dennis said:

"The disease is spontaneous and sporadic, and, as luck has it, it's entirely convenient — it never attacks us the wan time;" but the death of a little sister, a holy nun, of the order of Poor Clares, had sobered him whilst the symptoms were premonitory. It was Dr. Dennis who had thrashed the Irish drayman, locally known as "Mat the Slasher," whilst Sergeant Corcoran and another member of the force watched the contest from the shelter of a doorway. Some neighbors had brought the little woman to the dispensary with a broken rib, the marks of a boot on the side of her head, and a mouth full of loose teeth. As one of her escort had said:

"She never will proceed, poor dear! for he's the kindest man in the wurruld when sober — or real drunk."

Dr. Dennis had handed her over to the care of an English refugee, for their house was a haven for Scotch and Irish acquaintances out of a billet, waiting for supplies, or a ship, or the result of a final, or any other reason in the world needing sanctuary. He had gone down to the Dog and Bottle, tapped the colossus on the shoulder, and said:

"See here, Lacy! I told you the next time you knocked your wife about I'd give you a thundering licking. Instead o' that we'll have a fair fight. If I thrash you you'll take an oath never to lay hands on her again; if you lick me — well, we'll see if the other doctor can't take you on at the same terms next time."

The news flew like an ill rumor, and for twenty minutes after that the Dog and Bottle was minus customers, but the back yard of the distillery next door was crammed with a silent, breathless mass of spectators. The potman seconded the Doctor, and a pugilist, retired on asthma, saw to the drayman. It would need the subtle genius of a Meredith or the enthusiasm of a Borrow to do justice to a contest before which even the battle of the immortal tinman pales, but Lambeth remembers it, and is prouder of it than of its episcopal palace. And when Mat the Slasher, heroically defeated after a sublime fight, put out his hand blindly, for both eyes were scientifically closed, to his badly damaged victor, there was a sob of applause and a wild hurroo, that had a lasting moral effect on the youthful members of the audience, for the oath of the vanquished drayman was Dantesque and horrible in its inventiveness. The Doctor lost some nonconformist patrons of higher grade, and had to let the refugee visit the genteeler patients for a fortnight, although the sight of his face almost recalled the other Mac to the paths of sobriety. As for the drayman, he lost all taste for his liquor, for the memory of his oath weighed upon him, the honor of Lambeth was at stake, and his pals meant him to guard it. The only one dissatisfied was Mat's little woman. She resented bitterly the interference of the Doctor with what she considered her "man's rights," chafed at the blow to the Slasher's prestige as a terror, and sorrowed in secret for the wild bursts of tenderness that came with a realization of what he had done to her in his cups, and were the supreme moments of her existence.

The Glasgow body brought in a tray, and a clean cloth with a hole in it, for, indeed, as she explained, Dr. Dennis had laid his pipe on it. She spread a Gargantuan tea — shrimps, watercress, ham, and cakes. Mac surveyed it ruefully; someway it was not the kind of tea he wanted to have for her, but the puir body did not know how to arrange it better.

"It's only a bachelor's establishment," he said apologetically. Cecil was helping himself to a whisky and soda at a side table. He turned with a gleeful laugh — Mary had not heard him laugh for a long time — and said:

"Get Halpin, Moll, to tell you about his matrimonial venture."

"Indeed, then, you might let that drop. I never could see where the fun of it came in," said the Irishman.

"You must know our friend Halpin went to Ireland for a holiday, and fell desperately in love with a dark-eyed colleen in Cork, bedad, with a fortune in pigs and praties."

Marriott's imitation of a brogue always irritated Halpin. He broke in impatiently: "Nothing of the kind! I'll tell you myself, Mrs. Marriott, though it isn't funny at all. She was just a fine slip of a girl. Her eyes were blue, by the same token, and her hair was the ooloar of Taddy's mjrrtle grove! Faith, I don't see what there is to laugh at! She was beautifully educated, for she was five years in Rathfarnum Convent, and the best piano-player in it. She could play Irish melodies on the harp, and sing in Italian, and paint watercolors. Ye wouldn't find a girl of her class in England to match her anyway."

Mary's and the journalist's eyes met with answering gleams. They knew the type so well.

"I went over for me brother's wedding, and I met her. I saw a lot of her after that. She had a cousin, who's settled in Manchester. She was over too, and she brought a cousin of her husband's, an attorney, with her. He was a Protestant, and paying the girl great attention. Her mother and Father Ryan, a cousin of me own, didn't like it at all, and so they wanted to make a match between us. She had a nice little fortune, and I thought I might as well. She was a nice, innocent girl! Drink your whisky, Marriott, and stop your laughing. Mac, here's only grinning because you are. If there was any joke he wouldn't see it till to-morrow. Well, anyway, she wouldn't make up her mind. She was going to Killarney with the cousin, and then coming over to see London, and she would tell me then. We hadn't been long here. Your husband was staying with us at the time. We had no furniture; were just living in the dispensary. So when I got a wire saying they were coming to tea the next day, ye may think I was in a fix. I ran round to Cohen. He's a very decent little Jew. He has a furniture place round the corner, and I told him he'd have to fix up the hall and stairs, and furnish a drawing-room in the morning. He could take the things away if I didn't keep them. I had a bad operation coming off, so I couldn't see to it. I had to leave it to him."

Cecil interrupted gleefully:

"Let me finish it, old man; I know better than you do. You were so taken up with your colleen, you never saw half the beauties of Cohen's little arrangements. First there was a carpet," — Mac grinned, and Halpin shook his fist at him, — "it was velvet pile, a rich crimson with a blue border, and three big Prince of Wales feathers, bright orange with masonic emblems and a motto in the same color underneath. It was ordered by some lodge and sold with damaged goods after a warehouse fire. Cohen picked it up. Then there was a gorgeous mirror, right up to the ceiling, with a frame of cut-glass over tinfoil, and candelabras branching out with crystal drops. A gilt dock with cupids. Cohen smelt a rat! Alabaster nymphs and Japanese jars on each side. The suite was green plush — a delicate allusion to her nationality. You know it was, man! There was a black center table, held up by gilded virgins, and a sideboard —" He threw back his head, and the room echoed to his laughter; even Halpin himself was smiling. "Ob, that sideboard! Little Cohen was lavish. There was an electro-plated trophy in the middle, claret jugs, tea-pots, biscuit boxes — the whole pawnshop out on loan. As to the details, the fringe round the mantelpiece, or the blue satin chair with gold legs, — to match her hair and eyes, you know! and the flowing white lace curtains and the tea set, I am not up to describing them. You should have seen Mac's awe at the grandeur. He never saw anything like that in the Highlands. Gardiner was here at the time; we had locked him in upstairs. He was hammering the door and singing profane ditties. They were to arrive at four. Dennis came in at a quarter to. Cohen was rubbing his hands with delight, crying, 'Something like class, eh, Doctor?' Mac had to go and sit on Gardiner, whilst Halpin and I had just time to take down the Royal Family in a plush frame, and get rid of the albums and illustrated Bible, when the cousin, the colleen, and a tremendous Johnny arrived."

"Poor Dr. Halpin!" cried Mary, "she must have been obdurate to resist that room!"

"She was a nice little girl, just spoilt by attentions," replied the Doctor. "What was the matter with the room? Only too much furniture in it. Sure, any reasonable girl might have been happy in it! Yes, she's married to the attorney. No, Marriott, you are not going to hurry the missus away. Miss Ingleton is going to play for us. We have Molly Sheridan's piano in the other room. A little patient of ours, Mrs. Marriott. She's going to be a great performer, some day. She's one of a very unfortunate Irish family, and the brokers were coming in, so they sent round the child's piano to us: she comes and practices when she likes."

"Stay as long as you like, old girl!" said Marriott. "I asked Ferguson and a couple of fellows to come and have a game of nap. Oh! you needn't bother about supper; I ordered some oysters. Jane can manage all right. I hear there's a great Irish horse coming on, Halpin; we must look out for it. Good-bye, Miss Ingleton; you must come and look up the wife, you know. So long, old man. See you to-morrow, Mac."

It was curious how his going seemed to lift a restraint from them. Mary was always conscious of waiting for it; with a sense of pain when it came. She was too sensitive not to feel that the others shared it. Mac's feelings were not easy to gauge, but Cess chafed Halpin always; yet both of them went out of their way to serve him. There was something taking in his physical vitality, and a certain moral weakness that appealed to stronger natures. They took the chairs into the other room. An Irish lad with beautiful eyes joined them; the journalist played her best and Mac bent his great sandy head lovingly to his violin, — played rousing Jacobite calls to arms, wandered from weird Gaelic death laments to the consoling air of "Lumps o' Puddin'" caused a wordy warfare in which the Irish lad backed Dennis Halpin as to the nationality of Johnnie's Gray Breeks.

"I tell ye it's Irish; ye stole it. Play it a bit quicker, and if it's not 'The Weaver an' his Shuttle O,' I'll eat me hat! Ye maraudin' lot o' cattle-lifters, ye can't even leave us our music." Mary sat and watched them, growing strangely young as she laughed. In some way they made her feel she was the center of the entertainment. The journalist made coffee for them, as Mac wasn't drinking any spirits, and it was past ten when they broke up.

"How do I get home?" said the journalist in reply to the Irish boy. "Tram, 'bus, and 'bus again. I know all the short-cuts and the cheapest routes of this most ill-managed little village of ours. Getting about in London is more expensive and more difficult than in any other city in the world. But a woman is not qualified to earn her living in London until she can jump on and off a 'bus without stopping it. Thanks, so much, for such a pleasant evening."

Mary went in through the dispensary door. She could hear Ferguson's laugh as she went upstairs. He was a licensed victualler, with a handsome, horsey wife. His sister was an invalid. Cess seemed to spend most of his time with them. Mrs. Ferguson had called on Mary, driving a showy chestnut with a great deal of action. She had honest, handsome eyes and a good color. Her tailor-made gown was well cut; she wore a fox's head with diamond eyes in her cravat, and a scarlet waistcoat with gilt buttons. She looked a prosperous, vulgar, goodhearted woman. She expressed frank admiration for Dr. Marriott's looks, and said her husband had taken a great fancy to him. But, as Cess said, they had not "hit it off." Mary went to supper with them one Sunday evening to please him. He thought they might get him patients; he asked her to dress well for it. The quiet gown, a little out of date, of exquisite French cut, and the old jeweled brooch at the lace in her neck, had an air of elegant, almost aggressive simplicity, and the women disliked her for it. They resented her manner too, which was too natural, they thought, to be good; they fancied that she would not take the trouble to have a manner — for them. The host was a loud-voiced, successful man, with a sneaking reverence for family and a profound respect for money. He was a "Tory and an Englishman," as he used to say pompously. His second stock boast was that everything on his table was as far as possible of English growth. He took Mary in to supper, saying: "Prime-fed English beef, York ham, Surrey fowl; none of your nasty foreign truck for me."

He pressed Mary to eat, telling her she looked as if she wanted feeding up; got noisily patronizing; called Cecil "Marriott, my boy," and rallied him on the lack of his usual spirits, adding: "We'll be putting it down to the presence of your good lady. He is generally the life of the party, Mrs. M. — I assure you he is."

They always had from ten to twenty people to supper on Sunday night, and Cecil seldom missed an evening. They renewed the invitation to Mary from time to time, and were relieved that she made excuses.

CHAPTER XXIX

It was an afternoon in June of this last year.

She was trying to read, but she had been restless and wakeful all the night before, and could not fix her attention on her book. She had fallen asleep at three and had a dream, and in the dream a vision — a vision so terrible in its intense truthfulness that she awoke with a cry, sat up, and stretched out her hands, sobbing; stretched them out imploringly, and whispered coaxingly, tenderly, to Miley to come to her, to listen to her, to forgive her for not having written to him lately, to say that he understood. She thought that she was long asleep and he had come to her, her boy, her dear boy! He was changed; his eyes were intensely sad, and they had looked into hers with a gaze that had made her heart ache so. She wanted to dose them with a kiss. He had grown a mustache, and it changed his face; his skin was tanned, he wore no hat, and his forehead was white near his hair — his thick, curly hair. He stroked her hands as he used to do, and put one finger up under her sleeve and rubbed it to and fro round her arm, his old trick; no one else had ever done it; and all the time the blood was trickling down from his temple; it had dried on his collar, and there was a great dark patch on the left breast of his gray tunic, and it had run over his cartridge belt. And she knew in some strange way in her sleep that it was a vision in a dream — that he had come to her at the last. Was he not her own boy, her heart's own boy? Cecil had heard her cry, and came from his room and lit a light. He half laughed when she told him of her fear, of her absolute conviction of a fatality, got her some whisky, and told her to go to sleep and forget all about it. She had turned away to avoid looking at his half-amused, sleepy eyes. But she had lain awake all night, and in the morning she had made a red cross against the date on the almanac in her room below. Mac came in during the morning and Cecil told him with a laugh of the "missus' nightmare." The big Scotchman took it seriously, and when some days later he heard the newsboys shrieking, "Slaughter of whites in Mashonaland!" he put on his hat and hurried off to Brixton. She was sitting with the paper on her lap. There were not many particulars; the wire came from Johannesburg: a Matabele raid, a relief party surprised, two troopers and a settler killed and twenty Matabele; a note of interrogation after two names, trooper Esmond and the settler. She held it out and pointed to the name and the date of the skirmish and to the cross on the almanac. The big man said nothing, only gave her as strong a sleeping-draught as he dared, and covered her up on the sofa. Jane brought a wire for her; he opened it. It was from the Major; he, too, was anxious. He went out and answered it. Later on, when Cecil came in, the latter thought that they were making a ridiculous fuss, with nothing to go on. But the missus was so devilish queer about some things, though he would not say so; better let her have her sleep out where she was. It was past one; the Fergusons had a bit of a dance.

"You'd better turn in on the surgery sofa, Mac. I'll get you some blankets. Did Jane get you any coffee? That's right."

He brought down an armful of blankets and rugs. The milkmen were calling when Mary awoke. She put the paper in her desk and kissed the boy's photograph on her table and went out to the kitchen for some tea.

"Dr. Mac is asleep in there, ma'am; I didn't sweep the hall, "said Jane. She took him in some tea; he was lying with his hands clasped up over his head. It hurt her, and she gave a little sobbing moan, for her poor boy used to lie like that. How often she had taken them down! old nurse used to say, "It is bad for the heart, honey, to sleep like that."

The big man woke, and a strange look of gladness sprang to the great gray eyes dark with sleep, to change rapidly to one of distress as he saw her. She smiled bravely, saying:

"Here's your tea, Mac. Don't look so concerned, big man. I shall get over it; it's just at first. I reproach myself for not having written to him lately. I have been so miserable; there have been so many wretched money worries. It is the first year, too, I haven't sent anything for his birthday. One gets absorbed in one's own miserable troubles and becomes selfish. Ah, yes, I too, Mac, only it's hard to see one's way sometimes when one is so alone."

That was the only conscious reproach anyone ever heard Mary Marriott make in speaking of her husband. Unconsciously, sometimes she threw a light on her feelings. Once, talking to Mac and the journalist, she said: "It's so hard in life to judge anyone or anything, the issues are so entangled, or to see even that the good is always best. For instance, a fine-fibered, good woman, chaste in her desires, with a leaning to sacrifice, is not always the best wife for a man. Indeed, I can conceive a case in which she could be downright harmful, and where a physically attractive animal woman, with hard common sense and a sound, material bedrock of egotism, might work his salvation. My first husband used to tell me not to marry unless I found a Messiah."

"A wire came for you; I opened it," he said; "I knew you wouldn't mind." He gave it to her. "I wired back; he'll get the answer this morning. I asked him to come over and stay with us a while. Halpin and I will be glad to have him. Oh, don't ye; for God's sake, bairn, don't. I am only glad to be able to do a trifle for ye."

The Major came over, broken and white, and the Philosopher rushed down from the North to know if they had heard anything; she never knew before how dearly she loved him. The Foreign Office confirmed the news for them, and the papers added the omitted D to the name. Cecil told the Fergusons about her dream, and they agreed with him that it was most extraordinary and most unpleasant — a nasty medium sort of thing. They felt almost as sorry for him as he did for himself. He had experienced some awkwardness in condoling with her, had broken in upon her first grief and soreness of reproach to broach a troublesome money matter, fearing that she might be foolish with the Major. She had guessed at the reason, and had turned on him, crying:

"For God's sake, let me be! If it were not for you, I should not have neglected my poor boy. I never missed a year, not since he was so high," lifting her hand to her knee; "but I hadn't even a jewel left I could raise on. Go, for heaven's sake, go, or I'll say something I'll regret."

She and the Major used to take long walks — meet out somewhere. He seldom came to her house, for he found her so changed that he disliked meeting Marriott. It was hard to recognize his cynical, independent, high-spirited girl in this softened, all-seeing woman in the shabby clothes. The two partners used to mix him punch whilst she told stories of her childhood. He always ended by saying, "She's a great woman, a great little woman, but she's a damn lonely one."

The journalist adopted him, as she put it. Marriott was betting heavily, had bought a bicycle, and was out a great deal. Mary depended largely on the dispensary practice, as her hundred a year went no way, with rent, and taxes, and housekeeping, for Cecil pocketed the visiting fees of the better-class patients whenever he could. The two men were putting even longer intervals between their bouts (Halpin said Mac didn't play fair), and it got to be a regular thing for one of them to go up every evening. And so it came to pass that one evening, in the gorgeous saloon of the Railway Tavern in Atlantic Avenue, a well-known "booky" christened it "the Rose, Thistle, and Shamrock Show."

"I have been there several times," he said, "and I never know whether I am to be treated to a 'Haw, haw, English, don't ye know?' (with an imitation of the sporting Doctor that met with instantaneous recognition), or a real Scotch or Irish 'Who makes the book anyhow?'"

The two partners stood by her loyally. Then one day Peggy came down upon them, a vision of tears and ravishing French mourning just bought in Paris. She had heard of it in New York. Ezra had to be in France for a month yet, so she had just come along — she felt she must, but she had to start for California almost immediately. She had crossed by the Ligne Transatlantique; there was no use wiring. She wanted the Major to go back with her right away. When she looked at Mary's face the tears filled her still pretty eyes, but when she looked at her clothes she walked straight out of the room. As she told the Major afterwards, she could not bottle up her feelings any longer. Thank God, she had married an American man! She was glad she had not wired to Mary to come to the Savoy; her own maid was more up-to-date. She did Mary good — roused her out of her dreams, acted as a tonic. Peggy's ideals were delightfully materialistic; it pleased her to dress Mary. She made her do her hair in a new way, to suit a charming hat. "It's absurd, you know," she insisted; "you must change the fashion of your hair, unless you mean always to wear the one kind of hat! I shouldn't think anyone ever wanted to. You look another woman, quite young and awfully distinguished. I think you're wasted, Mary, absolutely wasted."

Mary and the Major used to exchange humorously sad glances of understanding, for they had travelled in diverse paths to complete accord in their philosophy of life, which, they laughingly said, was their religion. Peggy lost patience occasionally with their philosophy. She said her prayers regularly, she declared; went to her religious duties, and made everyone in the house do the same, but she failed to see any merit in a religion that led to social annihilation in Brixton. Mary and the Major used to wander through picture galleries, dine in odd restaurants, pick up the journalist, and go to the pit of some theatre. Their sorrow for poor Miley was not to be eased by adherence to conventional forms; it was too deep-set. It ached through the play as it never ached in quiet hours, for every touch of comedy called up his mirthful eyes and quaint twist of features, and Mary found her lips tremble when they ought to have been curling to laughter.

"Cheer her up a bit, an' the Lord love ye," the Major had pleaded to the journalist after his farewell supper at the Doctor's.

"I will. I am going to take John Morton to see her. She's a great friend of mine; stood by me in my darkest time, when I nearly fell into the depths."

"The author?" asked the Major; adding, "Faith, she writes extraordinary books for a woman. I've come to the conclusion, my dear, at the end of a life of varied experience, that I know no more about women than I did when I was supping milk out of my first pap-boat. I wonder what the divil became of it? It was an exquisite bit of old silver."

"Well, perhaps she does, and maybe the critics are right when they say they're not artistic; but they're human, and she gets at the heart of vagabond women like myself. I love them. She'll like Mrs. Marriott. Why, of course I'll kiss you and write to you too."

The Doctors turned up at the station, with new top hats, to see the Major off. Cecil had sent his good wishes and a silver-mounted flask. Mary and the Major never spoke a word, but she broke down when he got into the carriage. The receding train and her own tears blurred his face, until there was nothing to be seen but the white smoke of the engine dispersing slowly, like cobwebs floating on a summer breeze. The two big men took her in a cab to Gatti's. They met a humorous Irish acquaintance as they went in through the door. A few words gave him the key to the situation, and Mary found herself coaxed to laughter, and appealed to arbitrate m disputes in which her own "especial" Mac was getting worsted by his Irish opponents.

Cecil seemed in bad spirits —was silent; the old gay look was transient. He sat and smoked, or lay brooding with his eyes closed. She had not repaid all the two hundred yet, because she had been forced to ask for time once or twice and keep back a quarter's payment. She had given up remonstrances, realizing that it was useless to try and give this invertebrate man a backbone.

"Is anything special the matter?" she asked one day, laying her hand on his head; caressing came so naturally to her, that she forgot it irritated him. He jerked his head aside.

"Everything's the matter. I am sick of the whole show. It's beastly, never having any money, dragging on from day to day in this Godforsaken hole, without a change even. The confounded weather, too, is so hot. The Fergusons are going to Scotland; they asked us both to join them. I don't suppose you'd care to go in any case. His brother has some good fishing."

The sun slanted in, and touched his hair to red-gold. Funny how things came back after months, ay, years, although at the time one could not remember having noticed them even she could see quite distinctly a bit of a round little head, showing through an embroidered flannel covering; it had a quaint, erect little tuft of red-gold hair sticking up. After all, the helplessness of that little morsel of humanity was, when all was said and done, only relatively smaller than that of this man, into whose keeping she had so carelessly given her future. She said gently:

"I can stand you ten pounds, Cess" (Peggy had given her a cheque), "if you like to go; only I don't think you can expect Mac or Halpin to do all your work for you. There is a regular epidemic of diphtheria in Lambeth."

"You are a good sort, old girl," he exclaimed, eagerly. "I wouldn't take it, only I feel so beastly seedy. Brown isn't doing anything, — awfully hard up too. He'll be glad to get his board and lodging. Can't think why anyone ever becomes a doctor — beastly fagging way of getting a living."

"When will you go? Oh! so soon as that?"

She could hear him whistling cheerfully, as she sorted out his things upstairs, looked out fishing stockings and flannel shirts. Debts, promissory notes (there were two shortly due), every trouble was forgotten in the prospect of the change. He sprang up the stairs, three steps at a time; his eyes had lost their dead look, his lips looked red, his skin clear; she could not help contrasting the grayness of her own face, as she caught a glimpse of it in the wardrobe glass. Perhaps he noticed it, for he said:

"I wish you were coming too; you need a change."

"We'll talk about that later on," she replied quietly.

He went off the next day in brilliant spirits, coming back in the hansom with a lot of magazines and some roses to cheer her up. The bill for the magazines came in due course, and Mary paid it — smiling humorously at this queer, irresponsible mixture of a man.

It dragged on to the middle of August. She spent a good deal of her time in the consulting-room, for she had become known to all the regular people. She knew the "chronics" and their fads, and they asked for "the Doctor's lady" when Brown failed to please them. She heard from the Major — he was enjoying his trip; and she had a line from a pal of her poor boy's, enclosing an old photograph of herself and a prayer-book with her name in it. She sat and looked into the eyes that stared back at her so questioningly out of the younger presentment of herself. It was so strange to look at it, and think that once she had really appeared like that — an absurdly glad girl, with a smile lurking in eyes and mouth — so ready for everything! Ay, the old faith in the golden apples had been starved to death. After all, one was such a little atom in the great scheme! Someone, perhaps it was poor D'Arcy, had said to her once:

"I have often thought, when I have galloped over an ant-heap, and scattered millions of the tiny, crawling mites, and crushed thousands of others, that any one of us must mean less in the working out of the great scheme than any one of these little crawling creatures."

And she had replied:

"Ay, but perhaps to the ant the whole scheme is but a trifle, compared to the importance of its own existence."

August dragged on — a glaring month, making London gasp under dust and heat. The smell of the disinfectant, and with it, she sometimes fancied, the smell of the disease, seemed to penetrate everywhere; even her own little room was like an oven. She used to lie up in the bedroom, with the blind down, listening to the flies buzzing up the window, the rattle of the milk-cans, cries of the street venders, organs, and children — there was no rest any hour of the day. She was haunted by the mirage of a green nook in a dark, quiet wood — a cool, moss-grown glade, where the sun only stole in through a screen of foliage, to make an exquisite green-gold haze. Jane gave Dr. Brown his meals, so she avoided meeting him. Dr. Dennis had gone to Ireland, so Mac was tied to work, of which there was plenty. The journalist was busy, for some of the staff had holidays, and she had an engagement to play through all the Sundays in August for a Jewish family. So Mary saw no one.

CHAPTER XXX

ONE AFTERNOON IN MID-SEPTEMBER she was writing in her own little room; whenever steps echoed up the street she raised her head and listened, for the journalist was bringing John Morton to tea. She was a little curious to see her, for nothing she had read in the papers gave her any real idea of this woman, who seemed to make such stanch friends or bitter enemies. The bell rang.

"Here we are! How are you? My friend Mrs. Marriott, John Morton," cried the journalist as they came in. Mary looked down on a bit of a woman, with singular eyes and an odd face, that ought to have been beautiful, yet missed it somehow — a face with expressions chasing one another so quickly across it, that it never had time to acquire an expression; and a complexion that changed from clear to muddy in a few hours under stress of an unpleasing emotion. So it came to pass that some swore she was beautiful, others found her plain; yet both were right. She laid a lot of papers on the table as she came in.

"You're like a bit of thistle-down, you wonderful little creature," said Mary, amazed.

"Ah! perhaps that's more apt than you meant." Though her voice was soft, her enunciation was crisp and clear. "Did you ever look at a bit of thistle-down in autumn? It floats away on a chance breeze, with a good grip of a sturdy brown seed; it drops somewhere, and the seed burrows a place, fights for its bit of ground, and sends up a hardy thistle with lots of prickles and hard to root out. If you were a critic, you might push the simile farther and say, 'A nuisance of a plant, but the donkeys like it!' No, there isn't much of me really. So you're Mary Marriott?" looking up probingly into the other's eyes — "the woman I was supposed to cheer up. It is the other way about, I think; you don't need me. Where did you get the tenderness and the quiet in your eyes? I am going to kiss you. Yes, thanks, I'll take off my things. I never go anywhere, where I have to keep them on; I hate conventional teas." She looked at an old photograph of Mary's on the mantelpiece as she spoke.

"You were more hard there, eh? What do you do with yourself in Brixton? What kind of an atmosphere has it? London is only an aggregate of parishes; they each have a distinct atmosphere. I don't think I was ever out here before. I know you have a Bon Marché and a new theatre."

"Oh, it has its peculiarities. It is a stronghold of the rank and file of the 'profession,' as they call it- sorts of queer branches of it too. We have a contortionist, a family of knockabouts and the Reilly sisters, serio-comics, on the books. They've just come back from an engagement in the Copenhagen Tivoli, and brought me some Danish gloves. A younger sister is learning to walk on razors with her bare feet; two brothers are trapezists, and the third is a dandy coon. We treated the Mexican Amazon for indigestion, and a Japanese sword-eater for lumbago. He spoke beautiful French. Fancy we get more than our share, as I can generally interpret, unless it is some out-of-the-way language. They are odd, extravagant, and a very good-natured set of people. They come to see me when they return from their tours, and I hear a great many extraordinary tales from the women. I never forget a face. A beautiful little woman came in this morning with her baby; I spoke to her, and couldn't think where I'd seen her; then I remembered in a flash. It was in the '(circus in Christiania; she was dancing on a wire rope, with a Japanese parasol; old Pastor Strauss, one of the Roman Catholic Mission, a big, brown-bearded Luxemburger, applauding vigorously from a *loge* in the grand circle — having baptized, confessed, confirmed, and married a large number of the troupe that morning."

She told them many humorous and terrible tales of the consulting-room.

"You could write if you liked," said the little woman.

"I don't want to. I had ambitions long ago — was eager to tilt at all the windmills, fight the dragons, and seize the golden apples locked in the Ogre's casket. Sometimes I think one misses one's way by wanting to do things instead of waiting. I am only fit now to sit down and give anyone who wants it a bit of myself.

Half the world is starving for love. I have such a lot of it to spare, 'quietly,' and it's the only thing I can do well."

There was a pause in the room; the little woman wiped her glasses and said: "It's possible to have a genius that way. I met a woman once who had. She and the husband were vagabonds; lived everywhere — for three months. He used to say she was a repository for the storage of other human beings' woes. They simply dumped them into her keeping, and went on their way lightened. I met her at an hotel, at a time when I was in great trouble. She looked ill and worn — always gave too much of her vitality away, in fact, to any outcast who wanted it. I never can explain how it came about. I found myself confiding in her. She didn't say much. It was odd. I have often thought of it since. She was sitting on a chair in the veranda, and the lap, lap of the sea below came in between her voice. She sat absolutely still, but I felt as if something came from her to me — something warm and soothing, as if she were a skillful masseuse, stroking all the aches away with tender touch. He used to try to protect her, when he thought that selfish people were trespassing on her good-nature — used to come in and ask, 'Have you seen my blue pencil, dear?' No doubt she is still going about, scattering largesse, and he is still asking for the pencil. Perhaps your mission lies that way; Lai here says so. By the way, I did that volatile sweater who owns your magazine an ill turn on your account. I heard she wanted to know the Irving-Kers, so I told them how much she gave you a week to do the work of three men. They won't know her. Sorry? Of course you are, but I'm not. I never give quarter to a woman who grinds another. It's curious, but a woman in power is nearly always a tyrant. I can be a vindictive spitfire of a woman when I see unfairness."

"Don't mind her, Mrs. Marriott; she's the best in the world, in spite of her tongue."

Amongst the papers she had brought there was a German weekly, with a review of her latest book. It had an article, too, on the distress in a Bohemian mining district. An epidemic of a choleraic nature was raging. The people were dying like flies in cold weather in spite of the heroic labors of a German socialist. He had been working amongst the people for a year, teaching the children, reading to the adults; he had organized relief parties, nursed them, buried them, and finally succumbed to the disease himself. His death would be a blow to the particular body of socialists of whom he was the most ardent propagandist. The closing scene of his life was not without a touch of romance. A woman — she was believed to be an English member — had come in response to a wire, and was married to him some hours before he died. The marriage was not without significance, as his wife intended to finish and publish an important book upon which he had been engaged for years. At present she was carrying out his work by caring for the children. The photograph was taken by the correspondent.

"He had a singularly handsome head," she remarked, handing it to Mary to look at. Mary turned from it to the photograph of the burial. Haggard, hollow-eyed peasant men and women kneeling round the grave; the officiating priest, a man in uniform, and a woman were standing next the coffin. Mary looked closely at the latter's face, gave a cry of astonishment, fetched a magnifying glass and held it over the face:

"I know the woman," she cried; "at least I did, long ago."

She told them the story of the bow-maker; she was quite stirred out of the apathy that had been stealing over her in the last years.

"Let me look again," said the little woman.

"Strange, after all these years. There is a woman who knew what she wanted in life; saw her way clear, and was perhaps happy in her renunciation. One can't help feeling glad she was with him in the end. The most striking feature in our time is the gulf between man and woman; for either she is a doll whom he must dress and humor, or an opponent clamoring for suffrage, and canvassing for votes in the lobby. It never can become merely a question of politics and labor. The one question for each man and woman will always be: 'Is this the other half I am seeking to complete my nature, the one I desire for my happiness?' So you were a worker once! You would find things changed now."

"I do; I remember when, all the way from St. Paul's to Charing Cross, there was no choice between the coffee-room of an hotel, a few too expensive confectioners', or Lockhart's. The A B C's and all the other tea-shops have risen since my time."

As she was going she said to Mary:

"You mustn't stay too much in this little room of yours, you dear thing! You'll get the cobwebs round your brain and heart; better have them in the corners of the room. Come with Lal to a lecture next week; L'Etrienne is going to give it at the Lady Sappers' Club."

CHAPTER XXXI

A FEW EVENINGS LATER they were driving to the Club.

"It seems funny," said the journalist, "to have you coming to the Sappers'. I knew she would rouse you. She is like orange bitters; she gives you an appetite."

The big room, crowded with every type of woman, and a good sprinkling of men, was a revelation to Mary; things had gone with leaps and bounds ever since her time. The journalist pointed her out many celebrities. She had read that the lecturer was a wordmonger and an amorist. It struck her he was a humorist, poking fun at the Sappers in his witty address.

"The debate is always killing," said the journalist.

A stout, humorous-looking little woman, with a snub nose, turned-down lace frill, and woolen tam-o'-shanter was sitting on Mary's left. The lecturer had accused women of a lack of humor. A lady rose to dispute this statement with portentous gravity,

"You'll see," whispered the little woman; "she'll quote Mrs. Poyser. There! I knew she would; they always do."

The debate fizzled out. The lecturer was borne off to the refreshment-table by a bevy of women, whilst animated discussions were carried on by the guests. The journalist threaded her way to where John Morton was standing in the midst of a circle of women. She caught Mary's hand as they came near enough, and pushed her into a chair next her. She was replying to a tall, vigorous-looking girl, with short hair, tailor-made dress, shirt, and waistcoat.

"But, my dear lady, you will never convince me, unless, of course, you are speaking individually — then I will defer to your opinion — that woman as a whole is not entirely handicapped by her best qualities. She may as well be honest, face the music, and recognize her disability. She cares more about being loved than she does for all the triumphs of science, or legislation, or morals; at heart, you know, "smiling wickedly," she isn't much of a moralist."

There was a protesting chorus. Mary met the journalist's laughing eyes.

"Love, love, love," continued the little woman, "is just what she craves from her cradle to her coffin; the need of it is the pivot of her whole existence; she never gets enough of it — from the right man. The tragedy comes when she happens to be a monogamic woman — oh, there are plenty of polygamic ones knocking round — and she won't realize that no whole, natural man is congenitally built that way. Cultivate it? Why should he? The bane of our age is the mixture — spoilt daddy and spoilt mammy! A fleeting dimple, a swing of hip, is more potent than the best-stocked cranium in Europe. Unadulterated femininity is a deadly weapon, if wisely directed, against the male. I am going to lecture some day on 'the subjection of man to the furbelow' — its puritanical value, you know —"

There was a mingled chorus of laughter and reproaches.

"But I thought you were advanced, from your books. Do you want woman to retrograde — to lose all she has fought for?"

A shower of questions rained down on the little woman. It reminded Mary of the patter of hail upon glass.

"Not a bit of it" she replied; "only I want her to get on the right track. Let her develop herself to the uttermost as a woman, not as an atrophied animal, with degenerate leanings to hybridism. Your way leads to three sexes — man, half-man, and what is left over."

"Oh, do make her keep it up," whispered the tam-o'-shanter woman to Mary; "it's such fun."

"I don't think there's any need," answered Mary laughingly, for an irate woman three times the size of John Morton had joined the fray with a fierce:

"You deny, then, that woman is equal to man, or even superior?"

"No. I think, if she has a head at all, she's likely to have a much clearer grip of the concrete things of life; trained, she is more practical, less hampered by imagination, poetry, or even religion—"

An indignant chorus drowned her voice in a moment.

"She is much more likely to shine, in the time you are making for, as a county councilor than, let us say, as a poet laureate. When once that is recognized she will, no doubt, in the future, form the bulk of all municipal bodies, comptrollers of works, inspectors of buildings and nuisances, factories, and weights and measures; whilst man will continue to supply the world with art and good cooking, as he has done hitherto."

"It's just horrid of you!" cried a sweet, thin, little American with a *mêrode* coiffure and a lingering stress on each vowel. "You have dashed all my illusions. You were one of the vurry first people I wanted to meet when I crossed over from America, and I so loved and admired your works, too!"

"So sorry! I'll give you one bit of comfort. There's one thing no man can do —" Her face was curling in a humorous way as she bent her mouth to whisper where the girl's little ear ought to have been visible.

The latter laughed joyously, crying, "You're just real wicked."

Then John Morton escaped, taking Mary, the journalist, and another woman to supper.

"It's a sign of the times," she said. "When women want to meet now, they lunch, or dine, or supper one another, and are getting to know what wines to order."

But Mary had an idea that the gist of the evening for her lay in a remark the little woman made, as they drove to Victoria:

"It does you good to see what other women are doing now and then; clears off the cobwebs, helps you to see the possibilities in your own corner."

The autumn had glided uneventfully into the winter; she was again at the eve of another year. Jane's laugh, and Mac's and the journalist's voices sounded through the house. She must have been absorbed in her visions, for she had not heard the door-bell ring. She sprang up to meet them.

"All alone?" said the journalist. "We met in the tram, all coming to wish you a Happy New Year! John Morton sent you these, with love and greeting." She laid a basket of lilies-of-the-valley and violets and a new book on the table.

"Halpin is interviewing Jane," cried Mac. Gardiner turned up, and a bone-setter, so we thought we'd come and watch the old year out with you. Yes, I brought the fiddle, and some cigars for Marriott. Have you heard from him?"

"Yes; he says he's getting on splendidly. I'm so glad you've come. There is a whole turkey to be eaten; I only had a mite of the breast to-day. You are going to stay the night, Lai, of course; take off your things."

The big man was watching her with kindly, puzzled eyes; there was something wistful in his look as she caught it that made her sorry for him. She asked gently: "Well! what is it, big man?"

"That is just what I don't know, little missus. You look as if you had been listening to music, fairy music, that none of us can hear."

"Perhaps, big man, I have been getting into tune with myself. We often think the world is out of gear when, really, we only need to apply the tuning-fork to our own souls to find 'the hole in the ballad,' as they say in Ireland."

They had a pleasant, quiet evening. Mac lost himself in melody.

Dr. Dennis had brought some old wine, and brewed it with spice. Neither he nor Mac were drinking whisky. And when the bells began to peal from all the churches, they opened the door to let the old year out, and stood listening to the different metallic voices. From across the Common a little tinkling chapel bell came to them, "like a precocious child," as Mary said, interrupting its elders.

"So much for this year with its measure of sad and glad!" said the journalist.

"The divil fly away with you!" cried Dr. Dennis, waving his hat as the last stroke of twelve pealed. "Come in now, and not be catching your death of cold!" And Mary gave the big man her hand, and said:

"'Thank you for last year,' Mac, as they say up in Norway."

CHAPTER XXXII

THE BALANCE OF THE year's accounts were all on the wrong side, and the sporting Doctor had lost most of his better-class patients; for a rival had set up in Stockwell Road, with a hired brougham and a man in livery. Cecil put the practice up for sale, advertised it, and put it in the agent's books. The rival doctor made inquiries; his own house was poky. Mary needed all her patience, for Cecil was irritable, drinking more than he used to do. She was never out of the surgery in consulting hours, and watched the dispensing anxiously. He was being dunned by creditors, and the "booky" came and made a row. Sometimes he had maudlin fits of remorse; he wanted to go away somewhere, out of this beastly country; he would be all right anywhere else. Mary listened patiently; she knew too well every place would be alike. He had taken an unreasonable dislike to the rival doctor, and made ridiculous and damaging statements about him. It was fruitless to try and convince him that the man owed his ever-increasing practice to his own hard work. He had a row with Halpin, and ordered him out of the house.

The spring broke early and tried Mary sorely; not since the year in New York had it told so upon her. It called and lured with insistent voicing, making her eyes fill and her heart weak. She used to watch the children playing; one little girl used to kiss hands to her, and make her yearn for the little atom buried in Chissom. She had put a little stone over it, and Jane told her that Dr. Hall kept it covered with flowers.

Derby Day. Cess was keenly interested in the second favorite; he had talked of nothing else for weeks. He was going with the Fergusons; she was to drive. For days before he was like a schoolboy. He came into Mary's room in the morning, laughing as in old days, as he asked her to sew on a button. She had gone down in her dressing-gown and poured out his coffee; and when he was going out through the door she had called him back, and put up her mouth to kiss him. She had not done so for a long time, and she wished him luck and a pleasant day. She stood at the door and watched him; he looked back from the turn of the road and waved his hat as he saw her standing there. The spring seemed to creep in and sing a gay little song of its own, with a hint of summer in its lilt. She wrote a letter to the Major, and went up to the little red library on the Common, sure of finding it empty, and skimmed through the magazines. The boys were crying "Extra, speshul: winners!" all across the Common as she came out; there was an air of *fête* the quivering expression of a common interest in most of the faces. The 'bus conductors hailed the boys for papers, and the driver even of a rival 'bus called down to know results.

A pink May-tree in full bloom was shedding its petals on the asphalt footwalk. All the trees in the garden of Mistress Gwinne's quaint old house were shooting and budding and blossoming. Birds piped and sang in the old gardens, and the flower-venders in the High Street offered fragrant heaps of primroses and daffydowndillies with golden trumpet-hearts for sale. What a glorious Derby Day! No one could be miserable in such weather. She hoped Cess had won; thought of him without any bitterness, radiant-headed, as she had seen him in the morning; wished she had money to make him happy. She hummed a little air as she turned down Landor Road — a little air that was born of the May, and the sun, and the flowers, and the quivering human interest everywhere. Jane had made her some scones for tea; her room looked pleasant; it was good to be in one's own bit of a home anyway, and perhaps the fresh start might mend matters. She talked cheerfully to Jane over plans she had formed, and went upstairs; looked at herself in the glass, thought what a hateful thing is age. She recalled how she used to look at faces, and question in her heart if ever she could grow old as they had done. It was like death. One knew it was the only thing for which one had absolute grounds for belief, and yet somewhere down in one's consciousness (she wondered if other people had it too) one often felt a kind of doubt, a stupid query: Might not the miracle happen to make one the one exception to the universal rule? Of course one laughed at oneself — but the question was there all the same.

She opened some drawers and pulled out flowers and feathers and ribbons of former hats. She had noticed a pretty one on a woman sitting in a landau as she went into the library. She could remodel one of hers to look like it. She sat on the chintz-covered couch in her bedroom and twisted the flowers, and tried the effect, humming snatches of melody as she worked — inconsequently happy for the moment, without a care in the whole world.

How long the evenings were getting! The traffic was increasing: breaks full of drunken people, costermongers in donkey-shays singing music-hall songs, the tramp of feet, and the sound of voices; streams of people going up to the Common to see the race-goers coming back. She tried on the hat; it made her look younger. The oddly-tinted flowers in her hair were becoming. Jane came up and talked as she always did — friendlily, but not familiarly. The surgery bell rang; the girl went down again. She could hear Mac's voice. Surely Jane gave a half-suppressed cry! Mac was coming up two steps at a time; he shook the house — great elephant! She smiled at the thought of his shock head. She would say something outrageous, something really Irish to him; she knew how he would bend to peer at her. It was such fun to puzzle him. She opened the door: the smile about her lips stiffened as she saw his face.

"I come — Ferguson sent down for one of us to come —"

"Yes, Mac?"

"There has been an accident and, poor little missus, ye must —" Mac's accent was very marked, as it always was under stress of emotion.

"Is it Cess?"

He nodded his head, patting her hand awkwardly.

"Go down, and I'll follow you," she said, quietly.

She went back into the bedroom and lit the gas. The room seemed to have grown very dark since she had gone to the door; the flowers in the hat made a splotch of color on the bed; it hurt in some way, as if she had struck her eyeballs. She took out a black felt hat and a dark coat and put them on. She could not get the sleeves of her blouse in; she swore at them — simply swore at them. She did not know why the unusual words passing through her lips seemed to break the curious sensation of paralysis that had seized her, and she became conscious that her heart was thumping painfully. Jane met her with wide-open, frightened eyes, in a white face. She had never noticed before how strangely like a skull the girl's hollow-eyed, cock-nosed face was.

"I am ready, Mac. Yes; perhaps I'd better have some whisky. Do you know how it happened?"

He told her all he knew as they drove along; it was not much. A waggonette full of tipsy men and women, driven by a drunken driver, had run into them; the horses had got frightened, and swerved sharply. Mrs. Ferguson lost her head, and in trying to right matters she had run into a wall. No one knew exactly how — probably in trying to reach over to seize the reins which she had let slip — Marriott was thrown off, and one of the plunging horses had kicked him in the head. He was dead when they carried him into the next inn.

They had a long, silent drive in the midst of turmoil. They were met by vehicle after vehicle of boisterous spirits, coach-horns, plunging horses, concertinas, comic songs, the laughter of women, and men's voices raised in blasphemy or quarrels; passed a patch of common, stretches of shops with dimly lighted windows, a piano-organ outside a tavern, with four girls in white aprons dancing a *pas de quatre*; more common, then an inn. Upstairs, with a sheet over his face, and huddled on the floor next him a big woman, in a tan racing-coat, sobbing as if her heart would break, or was broken, was all that was left of feckless, selfish, laughter-loving Cecil Marriott.

CHAPTER XXXIII

A LATE SEPTEMBER EVENING, mild, warm, with a little western breeze ruffling the gorgeous leafage of the woods. A path wound up from a valley, in which three workmen's cottages stood in a row at the foot of a meadow near a tiny village in Hertfordshire. The path led to a wood, and if one looked down from the Stile at the entrance to it, one could see the village, and farther back a town, and gently rising hills in the distance. The mustard-broker who had bought the woods had tried to monopolize it for his pheasants. He had wired off all the sweet little glades, that looked as if the fairies had carpeted them for midnight revels: the kissing copse, the nut glen, and the lovers' way were marked by a board with "Trespassers will be Prosecuted." But the path was free, for the people had risen, demolished his barriers, and established their right of way. It led through a Wonder-world of shifting color to another stile, which looked down over the railway cutting and the little station of Chalfont Road.

The train from town glided in. One passenger, a slight woman in black, stepped out. She climbed up the path to the wood. It was quiet and cool in there; vitally quiet, not dead. A rabbit darted across her path; a squirrel ran up a tree; a belated blackcap was singing deliciously from the crown of another. She loitered a little. She had been up to town to see the last of the big Doctors; had put up her mouth and kissed them both with tears in her eyes — a poor thank-you for loyal service. Lambeth would know them no more; they were going to British Columbia. Dr. Dennis had a brother there, and Mac was of the opinion "that a practice in London, in certain circumstances, might be as fatal to a white man as a lengthened sojourn in a Pacific island."

She reached the stile at the end of the wood, and leaned over it, gazing down to the valley. The smoke was curling up in little rifts, the sky was stained warmly: in those three cottages John Morton, the journalist, and two other women were awaiting her coming. Standing there the mood of the evening — the autumn mood with its resignation, that is not death but the promise of life to come — crept in, to find echo in herself. Forgotten scenes grew vivid: scenes out of questioning childhood, ardent girlhood, womanhood with its disillusions. Each seemed in some strange way to dovetail into a realisation of herself, that came to her there as she stood, enabling her to grasp, as it were for the first time, the very kernel of her being in the palm of her hand; and the tears came to her eyes as she thought of this yearning, ardent soul of hers, that had been straying like a little beggar-child on the wayside of life, asking for love, love, love! Why had no passer-by paused to lay it in her outstretched palm? Some had left a kiss or a flower, or bartered a stone for her company for a while, but no one had given her what her soul craved. Was the fault in herself or in the time; or was the truth to be found in the words of John Morton? — "The men we women of to-day need, or who need us, are not of our time — it lies in the mothers to rear them for the women who follow us." As she stood there, thinking, the valley seemed to stretch out to an illimitable plain, filled with myriads of women. Each one looked up towards her, and there was a demand in every eye: child-girls, maidens, virgins, and harlots, good women and criminals, wise and foolish; woman in her prime and in her dotage. One pleaded for a smile, the other for a tear; for words of help or sympathy, of praise or understanding; all units, even as she, chained to the solitary cell of their mysterious woman's nature, to which the Creator alone holds the key. Her heart streamed out with a rush of infinite tenderness, of love and sorrow, to all these asking souls; and the tears that filled her eyes washed out every rest of bitterness, every trace of self-seeking, and a great peace gathered in her soul, and the question of her childhood, and maidenhood, and womanhood, seemed to be answered, and she stepped into the inheritance of her self. Her eyes shone through her tears, as the eyes of a woman who has been weeping the slaying of her man-child, and looks up to find him unharmed at her feet. A slender, crescent moon cut a scoop out of the sky, and threw her figure into relief against the white stile; a breeze whispered in the trees, and the lights gleamed out of the cottage windows below. A golden bar was thrown across the road, a suddenly opened door, and shadowy forms came up the path and stood at the gate below, and called up to where she stood alone on the height, "Mary, Mary, Mary!" with tender, eager seeking in their voices, that seemed but as the mouthpiece of hundreds of other voices, calling to her from the valleys where the shadows gather. And her heart seemed to grow hot within her, and to bum out the last atom of self; and she hastened down the slope with eager steps to where the women were calling in the gloom.

THE END

Suggested Further Reading

A Leaf from the Yellow Book Terence de Vere White
Keynotes George Egerton
Rosa Amorosa: The Love-Letters of a Woman George Egerton
Madame Bovary Gustave Flaubert
Hunger Knut Hamsun
Jude the Obscure Thomas Hardy
Daisy Miller Henry James
A Portrait of the Artist as a Young Man James Joyce
English Poems Richard Le Gallienne
Dracula Bram Stoker
The Picture of Dorian Gray Oscar Wilde

www.ingramcontent.com/pod-product-compliance
Lightning Source LLC
LaVergne TN
LVHW091127080826
845145LV00008B/2070

* 9 7 8 1 9 4 3 1 1 5 0 9 9 *